THE WORLD BEYOND THE WILD

The stranger opened his crack-lipped mouth and spoke. Alldera did not register the words; she had been without the sound of another human voice for a very long time.

"Don't be afraid," he said again slowly. "Don't be scared of me."

The stranger caught up her hand and pressed it against "his" body. Under the slick-surfaced tunic Alldera felt the unmistakable soft shape of a female breast . . .

MOTHERLINES
Suzy McKee Charnas

"For too long science fiction has been dominated by masculine/sexist writing, but in recent years a group of women writers has been bringing new life and maturity into the field. These women are explicit and committed feminists. We're proud to be among them."

—JOANNA RUSS

—SUZY McKEE CHARNAS

Berkley Books by Suzy McKee Charnas

MOTHERLINES
WALK TO THE END OF THE WORLD

SUZY McKEE CHARNAS
MOTHERLINES

A BERKLEY BOOK
published by
BERKLEY PUBLISHING CORPORATION

This Berkley book contains the complete
text of the original hardcover edition.
It has been completely reset in a type face
designed for easy reading, and was printed
from new film.

MOTHERLINES

A Berkley Book / published by arrangement with
the author

PRINTING HISTORY
Berkley-Putnam edition published July 1978
Berkley edition / October 1979

ISBN: 0-425-04157-3

A BERKLEY BOOK® TM 757,375
PRINTED IN THE UNITED STATES OF AMERICA

This book is for J. R.,
who reminded me that new
stories have to be told
in new ways; and for the
many others who helped me
to find the right way for
this story and stick to it.

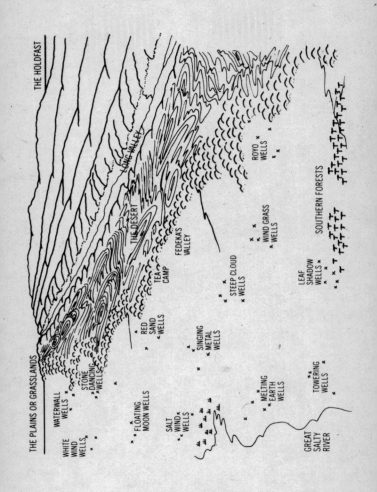

THE HOLDFAST

THE PLAINS OR GRASSLANDS

LONG VALLEY

THE DESERT

WHITE WIND WELLS

WATERWALL WELLS

STONE DANCING WELLS

RED SAND WELLS

FLOATING MOON WELLS

SALT WIND WELLS

SINGING METAL WELLS

TEA CAMP

FEDEKA'S VALLEY

STEEP CLOUD WELLS

ROYO WELLS

WIND GRASS WELLS

MELTING EARTH WELLS

LEAF SHADOW WELLS

SOUTHERN FORESTS

TOWERING WELLS

GREAT SALTY RIVER

I
Prologue

1

Alldera crouched tensely by the river, staring at tracks in the soft mud. The water was shallow here, and something had crossed to the far side; no, two things—two strings of tracks separated and came together again.

She had not seen a living being in the months since her escape from her homeland, nor had she expected to—other than perhaps the monsters with which legend peopled the wild country, but she had not really believed in them. She looked fearfully back over her shoulder.

There rose the valley wall and then the mountains, beyond which lay the strip of coastal plain men called the Holdfast—her country. In the bloody confusion of fighting there—men killing other men and their femmish slaves, over food—she had made her lone escape. It seemed she was alone no longer.

No man of the Holdfast, no fem fleeing as she fled, had made this spoor. Trembling, she traced the shape of the deep prints with her finger. Something heavy walked on those round, blunted feet. The marks were crescent-shaped and as big as her fist, with a sharp angle sign in the middle of each. Monsters' tracks.

Weakened by months wandering as a scavenger in the Wild, she squatted there, fighting back her terror with its tinge of eagerness for contact with life, any kind of life. She tried to consider her situation clearly, turning her inner gaze back over the course of her flight.

At first she had had some faint hopes of finding other
runaways, the "free fems" of stories, whom she could
join. That hope and the first fierce exhilaration at being
free had soon faded into anxiety. Choosing to cross the
borders of the Holdfast into the Wild, she had chosen
new dangers.

The Holdfast river, which she followed back into the
mountains in search of the ruins of an Ancient shelter,
unraveled into several streams. Not knowing which
branch to follow, she missed the Refuge and its hoped-
for stores of supplies and wandered deep into a maze of
rock walls and slopes set between thorn-choked gullies.

The roads of the Ancients, dissected and smashed by
landslides and floods, were now only fragmented rem-
nants of the broad, smooth, legendary ways and
sketched connections between mere patches of rubble.
She avoided the jagged shards of old walls standing in
their fields of broken glass; there was nothing to eat
there, nothing alive.

Her food pack soon flapped empty, her stolen
clothing exposed as much of her as it covered and clung
in strips to her skin when there was rain. She began to
realize, in bitter despair, that she was pregnant.

In her mind she cursed the fetus for a rape-cub, un-
wanted seed of the masters whom she had escaped.
Hunger made her bold, she tasted everything she could
strip from standing plants or dig out of the earth, but it
was never enough; how could she make milk for a
newborn cub? Doomed from the outset, the cub
nonetheless functioned as a hardy and efficient little
parasite, stealing from her the nourishment of whatever
she could find to eat. Her bowels were in a continual
state of bloat and cramp. Sometimes she chewed on
roots or leaves that made her sick for days, and she
hoped that one of these painful episodes would kill the
cub so that she could expel it and better her own chances
of survival.

But the cub seemed as tough as she was herself and
would not die. She felt its heartbeat and its growing,
living weight dragging at her body as she traveled. There

were moments of intense pleasure at the thought that this cub, at least, the men would never have. Most often she thought, this cub will kill me, it is a weapon of the men planted in me to ruin my escape.

At length the mountains smoothed to rolling waves of earth, and a day came when she looked down not into another brambly groin in the hills but across a wide valley, a soothing sweep of green and open country with a sparkle of water down the heart of it. This was not some new stretch of the Holdfast river flowing east to the sea but a broad, sunny water rambling north to southwest. The valley was richly embroidered with dark trees along its waterways, and it seemed endlessly long under a warm, quiet sky.

Here was refuge of a kind. On the lower banks of the creeks feeding the river she found plants with sweet stems, and large-leafed vines yielding a pulpy fruit. The shining river smelled bad, though; close up she saw skeins of bright slime drifting in it and in the streams on the other side.

Water was important to her. Pregnancy did not afflict her with nausea and moods, but it did make her sweat constantly and heavily. She was thirsty all the time. Staying on the clean side of the valley so that she could drink safely, she ranged farther southward searching out food plants that she recognized and trying to stay ahead of the full bite of the coming winter. No cold weather came but the rains stopped and food grew scarcer. Sometimes, resting from her endless foraging along the banks of a stream, she would bend to stare hopefully into the empty water; according to legend edible creatures had once inhabited the waters of the world.

The water still only showed her—on this day, the day of the monster tracks—her own broad, bony face framed in a mat of dull, tangled brown hair. She glanced down at herself. The only rounded line to be seen was that of her belly. Her hands, feet and joints looked coarse and swollen, surrounding muscle having melted away. Her skin healed slowly or not at all where it was scratched or bruised. Her gums were tender. She could not pretend to be some proud free fem out of a song; the fems' tales of running off to make a life in the Wild were dreams.

What was real was the monsters. Here was their excrement heaped on the gound like pungent dumplings—even shit reminded her of food, and rightly: without provisions she would die this winter.

There was no choice but to follow and try to find the monsters, persuade them to help her. One way or another, it would end in food: they would either feed her or eat her.

She spent a day following their tracks. She lost their trail, cast in circles for it, terrified of simply walking into them around some roll of the land. She kept stopping to catch her breath and to peer ahead as the day waned. She had to cross the river after them at the shallow place where they had crossed.

Something red caught her eye. In surroundings which provided little now but greens, browns and the black of shadows, it was stunning, not some sly earth tone passing for red but a brash flare of scarlet.

She crept closer. The red was a rag knotted around the end of some sort of bundle that was wedged into the crotch of a tree. With a stick she poked the bundle down; it was a large bag made of some supple fabric, closed with a drawstring that ran through the stitched and puckered hem. She loosened the drawstring with difficulty.

She was afraid to put her hand inside. Cautiously she raised the heavy end of the bag and eased some of its contents onto the ground: there were dark, hard lumps the size of her hand, a bundle of long, flat dried things strung together, and some smaller bags. One of the latter contained pine nuts like those she had gathered for herself from trees on the middle slopes of the mountains. The sight of the small, smooth shells spilling out onto her palm and the smell of resin on them made the unbelievable real: she had found some sort of food cache.

She sat chewing and crying, fighting to keep from bolting so much that she would vomit it up again. She slept on the spot, hugging the bag with both arms.

The next day, carrying some of the food with her, she continued westward on the monsters' trail. They had followed a faint pathway that led west from the river up the slope of the valley to its rim. Beyond, there lay a desert.

Alldera had seen smaller patches of such desolation back in the Holdfast, where it was said that they had been made by the Ancients' methods of mining or of war. This desert was a seemingly limitless stretch of dark earth, all rucked up into long rows one after the other as if the fingers of a giant hand had been drawn parallel through loose dirt. Lonely hills rose sheer-sided to dilapidated peaks, windtorn, undercut, sometimes topped with a clutch of stunted trees. Swatches of green marked isolated groves. Puffs and veils of dust rising on the breeze were all that moved.

The trail of the monsters led off the rim of the valley and angled down into the first trough of the desert. There the prints were lost in a drift of dust.

Alldera dared not try to follow them. She retreated and made a bed of branches where she had found the supplies. They had left food; they would come back.

The nights grew cold as the moon turned through its cycle. There was no rain, the streams shrank. Her belly was bigger, she could not get around so easily; she was hungry all the time. A sun-warmed rock some distance from her sleeping place became her station; it was easier to withstand the urge to nibble more than her day's ration if she removed herself from the food during the long, idle hours. She watched to the west for signs of the monsters' return. She watched to the east, too, imagining other Holdfast fugitives finding the valley just as she had done.

If others did come, she would have to either fight for her bit of food or run. She was growing too weak to fight, too weak to run. But she did not really believe that anyone would come.

*   *   *

Sheel, scouting ahead of the other two members of the patrol, rode with one of her bows strung in her hand. She trusted only herself to keep fully alert, and besides, she liked riding apart, undistracted by conversation. It bettered her chance to be the first one to sight an enemy and kill him.

She sat forward in her saddle, giving her mount a loose rein so that it could pick its own careful way over this stony, up-and-down country. Sheel's eyes scanned the slopes, eager for a hint of movement, a track in the sandy soil among the thin scattering of trees.

Riding the borderlands with light rations and three full quivers of arrows made her feel alive as nothing else did; here on the vulnerable outskirts of the plains she felt most strongly the rich vitality of the land she was guarding. Her senses were wide open to the sharp scent of pine, the grate of a pebble under her horse's hoof, the long, sunlit lines of the foothills advancing up the lower reaches of the mountains. If men had crossed from the Holdfast, she would know it.

She had killed a total of seven men during a dozen patrols in her lifetime: four from a distance with the bow when she had been sure of her shot, three close up, bursting from cover on horseback to drive home her hunting lance. She hardly minded the chore of concealing the corpse afterward so that no man following could find it and speculate on the manner of his fellow's death. Mystery was demoralizing to such fearful, aggressive creatures as men. They prowled in her mind, clumsy, angular beings, loud-voiced like horses so that you always expected them to be bigger than they were. She had tracked men for miles, listening to their desperately hearty voices, watching, sniffing their fear-rank breeze. They were truly the sons' sons of those world killers, the desert makers of Ancient times; torturers and thieves by nature, wherever they went they left scars. The borderlands were disfigured by the stumps of the trees they cut, the pits they dug and left heaped all around with cast-up earth, the scattered charcoal of the huge and dangerous fires they lit to ease their fears of the dark. They did not even bother to cover their ordure.

Sheel patted her pony's shoulder and reined in at the foot of a slope. Dismounting, she loosened her saddle girth and tied her reins to the branch of a gnarled pine. Then, with a full quiver slung over her shoulder and her bow in her hand, she padded to the top of the ridge and lay down there to scan the wide, rippling country, breathing with pleasure its warm odors. The sun burned on her leather-clad back and legs and on her leather cap. Those rocks down below resembled the rocks in which she had buried her first kill.

She had flayed the dead man's arm to see what made his muscles bulge so unnaturally, and had come away dirty with his blood but no wiser. His sexual organs had seemed a ludicrous, dangling nuisance and hardly capable of the brutalities recounted by escaped femmish slaves. Having everything external and crowded into the groin like that must make walking more uncomfortable for a man than riding at the gallop with unsupported, milk-full breasts would be for a plains woman. A stud horse was better designed: a sheath held whatever penile length was not stored coiled within his body.

What a perversity—a creature that would own her if she let it, yet it had nothing to boast of but a coarse strength that was still less than the power of one worn-out old pack mare. Men's only good feature was that they were a peerlessly clever and dangerous quarry to hunt. Their terror at the end, when you came up and waited a little way off for the dying to be done with, was wild-eyed and bestial.

Movement caught Sheel's eye, there on a hillside she had already passed. It was her two companions, following after her. She did not want them to catch up with her yet.

She ran back down the slope, tugged her girth tight, caught up her reins and mounted to ride on ahead.

Alldera thought about her cub. It took many days'

thinking. Her mind, sluggish from starvation, turned slowly now.

She was not surprised that the cub was still alive in her starved body. The hard lives of Holdfast fems over generations had made tough dams and tough offspring.

She remembered the cold table to which the Hospital men, masked and gowned and stinking with terror of "femmish evil," had strapped her when she had had each of her two cubs—both fems. Each cub had stayed with her till weaning and had then been sent down into the kit pits to live as best it might with its peers, until it was grown enough to be trained by men to work and to serve.

This cub would never live that life. It would never live any life. Alldera's body had swelled with the months, but her breasts stayed slack, emptied by privation or by disease, she had no way of knowing.

Suppose the cub were male? This idea stirred up a mist of rage and fear that stopped all thought, except for the simple knowledge that she could not keep any cub alive after its birth.

She decided that when it grew large enough to be taken hold of, she would try to do the massage that fems knew to detach a fetus from its hold so that it would be aborted. She thought wretchedly of the pain. The creature would not easily be twisted from its life-sustaining hold. It would be no readier to give up and die than she was herself—that thought gave her a pang of grim pride.

One night—in her fifth or sixth month, she could not tell, so starved and bloated was she—she dreamed of the cub: born plump and bloody, it was laid on a fire to cook. Then she ate it, ravenously taking back into her own body the substance of which the cub had been draining her all this time.

The dream woke her. She walked slowly in the valley by the moon's light, hugging herself against the cold. Waking at night was bad; it was too chilly for her to fall asleep again.

On her way back to her camping place just after

sunrise she crossed fresh tracks. The monsters, returning, had paused near her camp and then gone on toward the desert.

It was months since she had first found their footprints. By the time they came again, no matter how strictly she rationed her food, the bag would be empty and she and her cub would both be dead.

She hung the bag over her shoulder and followed them up to the western rim of the valley, glad to be moving and doing, even though she was perhaps only pursuing her own death; that was better than just waiting for it, like a slave.

The desert was just as she had first seen it, a huge washboard that ran beyond sight in all directions. Once more the monsters had simply plunged down the steep slope leaving a dark line of disturbance in the loose soil, but this time their tracks showed fresh and plain in the fine dust of the trough floor.

She adjusted the bag so that it would not flap on her shoulder, and she scrambled awkwardly down.

Water had cut rough gullies across the furrows, making passes in the ridges between the troughs; using these gaps the monsters were bearing westward through the desert. Alldera threaded the maze on their trail but could make no speed. She was too weak, her joints hurt, the cub's weight dragged her down.

There was a stark, dreamlike beauty to the place. The dark soil seemed to soak up sunlight and burn with it. Tufts of grass sprouted here and there in the shadows of rocks. There were even a few spindly trees, or older ones with thick, stunted trunks. Occasional red twists of Ancient machinery protruded from the dirt: thin shells rusted out to nothing, great lumpish cores of which the more delicate and projecting parts had long since fallen away. In the deeper ravines there were reefs of debris trailing out from undercut walls—flood sign. Where water stood it was laced with green slime, and the monsters themselves did not stop to drink it. The filth in the valley's river must come from streams draining this poisoned place.

Once she thought she heard the monsters up ahead crying to each other in high, shivering voices.

When it was too dark for her to see their tracks, she stopped and sat down beside a prow of rock. Chewing very slowly—her teeth hurt, and she had no saliva to moisten the food—she ate one small, hard loaf from the bag. There were four more left.

Sounds woke her at morning. Her trough was still deep in shadow under softly lit ridges above on either hand. As she rubbed the dust out of her eyes and tried to remember what it was that she had heard, sounds came again, high, almost whistling, shaking as if with rage, and then a shout very like a human voice, not far away.

Alldera clawed her way up the side of the nearest ridge, scraping her hands and feet on the rocks and starting a small slide of dirt and rubble behind her. She felt heavy, slow and desperate, thinking of them traveling on while she toiled after them, more slowly today than yesterday, more slowly still tomorrow. Breasting the blunted ridge top, she could see the dust-coated foliage of trees a few furrows over. She stood up on the rounded spine of the ridge.

Not twenty meters off figures moved in one of the rough passes between two furrows; monsters indeed —three of them.

Their bodies were long, slung horizontally on two pairs of legs. Two trunks rose from their backs, one human-shaped with arms, the other smooth and topped with a head like a log of wood stuck on at an angle, and a sweep of hair hung from the back end, like one lock from the top of a shaven scalp.

They were terrible to look at, but they were her only chance to live. Alldera filled her lungs and screamed.

Two of the monsters checked in the pass, bumping each other. The third turned and took great plunging leaps to the top of the ridge they were crossing. It halted and faced Alldera. The humanlike trunk extended something toward her, a stick held out straight up and down at the full length of the arm as if warding off the

sight of her. There was something threatening in the
stillness behind the gesture, the concentration before
delivering a blow.

Alldera waved her strengthless arms and called out
again.

The long head of the monster dipped and murmured.
The human head uttered a cry, excited words and what
sounded like laughter. The stick weapon was lowered,
tucked away somewhere. Incredible, to manage all those
limbs at once—

The monster came apart.

The human torso vaulted into the air and landed on
two human legs beside the creature on which it had been
sitting. With terrible clarity Alldera saw her error: they
were men, nothing but men, who had somehow caught
and tamed true monsters to obedience.

She slid down the steep side of the ridge in a spout of
choking dust and began to run waveringly down the
trough floor. There were shouts and the pounding of
steps behind her; running was hopeless. She knew the
art of kick fighting, but that was beyond her now.
Raging, she bent and groped in some flood wrack for a
rock, a stick, something to take in her hand.

The beast drove toward her in bounds, its fistlike feet
hurling up sprays of earth. The rider had a coil of rope
in his hands. As Alldera cocked her arm, holding a rock
that she knew she hardly had strength to toss, something
swished through the air and slapped her around the
chest and shoulders. She was jerked off her feet as the
beast tore past her and she crashed flat on her back, her
body ringing with shock, unable even to roll onto her
side or her stomach to protect herself.

She heard him dismount, his soft-footed steps approaching, the play of muscle, bone and clothing as he
squatted beside her.

Framed by a long, loose cloth that he wore over his
head and falling down his shoulders, his smiling face
was red and small-eyed, with dirt ground into the
creases around his features. He wore a belted tunic with

big, flap-topped pockets in the skirts over pants of the same weaveless, greasy material, and boots tied snugly under the knee. He stank.

Alldera strained for control of her bruised and exhausted body, promising herself, I will swallow my tongue and die. Before he can raise a hand to me.

The stranger opened his crack-lipped mouth and spoke. There was a peculiar light singsong pattern to his voice. Alldera did not register the words; she had been without the sound of another human voice for a very long time.

The stranger pulled off his headdress, freeing a thick fall of gray-shot hair. "Don't be afraid," he said again slowly, and Alldera understood. "Don't be scared of me."

He caught up her hand and pressed it against his own body. Under the slick-surfaced tunic Alldera felt the unmistakable soft shape of a female breast.

2

Sheel strode into the sweat tent, humming, and pulled off her shirt, savoring the idea of calling a duel on a woman who had spoken persistently against her during the inquiry about this new fem.

Redder in the face than ever, Barvaran came in to join her in cleansing themselves for the judgment of the camp. She had brought in the last of the hot stones on the prongs of a long wooden fork. She placed the stone among the others in the pit in the middle of the floor and stood back, rubbing water from her forehead with the back of her thick, red wrist. She looked sullen and distressed. Sheel regretted not having Shayeen there with them; Shayeen was still too sick to come.

Sheel knelt at the entry to lace the door flaps up tight. She looked over her shoulder. With only the two of them in it the tent looked vast. Ordinarily there would have been a dozen women filling the space. Barvaran seemed a figure of red sandstone glistening with rain across an expanse of earthen floor.

Picking up the water bucket, Sheel joined her by the pit. The whiplike ends of the tent poles were lashed together with special knots well above their heads. There, where the roof was highest, Sheel stood up and tugged off her breast wrap, dropped it by her shirt and pants.

Barvaran took the horsetail sprinkler from the bucket and flicked a spatter of drops onto the hot stones. With a thunderous cracking sound, steam shot up, heat spread in a stifling cloud. Sheel endured it for a moment, breathing the searing air in small sips. Then she sat down; the air was cooler near the ground. She took a hardwood scraper from the tray nearby and turned it in her hands, examining it. She still had a scar from a scraper that somebody had nicked by working on a hide with it.

"They won't be long about it," Barvaran said miserably. "There isn't anything to think over. Shayeen was sick, you used the excuse of her illness to ride past that food cache instead of checking it, and I let you do it. We left that fem there to die."

"We didn't know she was there." Sheel was bored and impatient with the argument. "And it was Shayeen who almost died."

"She says she wasn't so badly off that we couldn't have spared time to go and check the cache, like any other patrol heading home."

Sheel did not answer. Sweat stung her eyes, she could feel her skin cooking over her bones. She thought of the bowl of cold water set outside the entry, but she would not be the first one to reach for it.

Barvaran's expression still accused her.

"I didn't know the fem was there," Sheel repeated for the hundredth time. "It's months since anyone has found man or fem in the borderlands, everyone knows that. I was right to say we should get Shayeen home as fast as we could, and you were right to agree. Look how sick she still is."

Barvaran got up and went to the entry. She reached out beneath the laced flaps and a little sip of cool air came in from outside. She drank, and brought Sheel the bowl. The cool water was a joy on the lips.

"We were wrong," she said mournfully.

Sheel expelled her breath in an exasperated hiss. She began picking over the bits of soaproot laid out on the tray by her knee. To try to lighten the mood and prevent a real quarrel she said, "Did you have a look at this fem

Alldera when they got her cleaned up? I bet she didn't have to escape. I bet the Holdfast men kicked her out so they wouldn't have to look at her any more.''

She grimaced, thinking of the fem: a plate-faced creature, the bridge of her nose flattened so that there was no strong feature to balance her wide, heavy-lipped mouth; eyes a nondescript green-brown, wideset below a broad band of forehead and above the sweep of the cheeks; brown hair too fine to add height to the wide skull. For the rest, she was all bone and belly, with a blunt, square frame. Altogether no prize, yet Sheel knew she would have to suffer on the worthless slave's account.

She muttered fiercely, ''I wish all those fems were dead.''

Through the shimmering, steamy air she saw Barvaran arrested, hands lifted to wring out her thick gray hair. ''No Riding Woman has a right to say that,'' Barvaran exclaimed. ''For all the history of the plains we've rescued any fem that came as far as Long Valley, saved her and healed her and sent her to the free fems—''

Sheel mashed a piece of root with a stone, making sudsing paste. She hit hard, pounding out the sound of Barvaran's rough, anxious voice. Bits of slippery white fiber shot in all directions.

''For all the history of the plains,'' she said, when Barvaran had paused for breath. ''What about the history of the Holdfast? Think of that. Can you tell me we have some duty to help such cowardly weaklings?

''Back in the Wasting, when our lines' first ancestors shaped their own freedom and ours after them, what was the fem's ancestor doing? Trotting after her bosses, following those high government men into hiding from the ruin they themselves had brought about with their dirty ways and their wars and their greedy dealings. And when the men looked out of their Refuge and saw the world outside sinking into wreckage and they turned around and blamed the women, did those women fight?''

"Some of them must have," Barvaran said uncertainly. She rubbed sudsing paste patiently into her hair. "A few."

"Yes, but how many, and how hard did they fight? Their female descendants still came out of the Refuge as slaves when the Wasting was over. They let themselves be turned into the 'fems' who built the men their new country, their miserable Holdfast."

This time Barvaran did not answer. It was too easy to shut her up, to overwhelm her plodding mind. Sheel pressed her, "Are you listening? All all that time our ancestors, women mind you, not fems, were building a life that Holdfast men would destroy if they knew it existed."

"I don't know what any of this has to do with this fem Alldera and her baby."

Sheel began raising a lather in her own hair with stabbing fingers. "She's just like the rest of them, the runaways, the 'free fems'—they crawl all their lives under the whips of Holdfast men, and those that can't take it any longer run away. We find them, make them a place here on the plains, praise them for their courage—courage, to run off and leave the rest of your own kind to rot!" She paused for breath. What a pleasure it was to speak freely against what all the camps agreed was right.

Barvaran leaned to throw more water on the stones. The steam was less, but the heat seemed to build higher and faster than before. Rubbing at an old hunting scar on the hard red calf of her leg, she said in her slow, stubborn way, "That's all over now, Sheel. This fem says they're wiping each other out back there, men and men and men and fems. It had to happen, with their food so scant all those years and the young men half starved under the rule of the old, greedy ones. You're angry at a dead place."

"Not dead, still living—here. We have the runaway fems with us. Weaklings, misfits—what would have become of us women if we were as soft with our own as we are with them.

"And now there's this new one, and her cub besides."

"Her child," Barvaran corrected gently. She took up a scraper and moved so that she could use it on Sheel's skin. The wooden blade rode deftly over the long plane of Sheel's thigh. Barvaran had fine control of those great red hands of hers, even now in her distress. She never hurt where she could caress. Useless to try to make her understand the shame, the insult these fems brought to the clean life of the plains.

"It could be a male child," Sheel growled. "Would you speak up for it so tenderly then?"

"The fem says she's had two other children, both female. And Layall Fowersath has examined her and thinks this one will be female also."

Sheel snorted. "The fem is so weak and confused she doesn't know what she's saying; and as for Layall Fowersath, like all Fowersaths she can usually tell accurately the sex of an unborn foal. But this isn't a horse's offspring we're talking about. This is a man's cub from the men's world. Male or female it's dangerous—like anything from there."

"The free fems have never hurt us."

"Just wait. You'll see some day that I'm right."

"You said all this at the inquiry," Barvaran said. "Nobody agrees with you."

"More do than you think, but they keep it to themselves." Sheel turned her leg more firmly against the scraper's edge. With another such tool she drew down the curve of Barvaran's torso in a neat pattern of overlapping strokes. The heat brought out fresh moisture as soon as the old was swept away.

Barvaran looked at her. "Some women say you can't tell fems from their masters, Sheel. Everyone knows we should kill men because men are dangerous and crazy. They don't even know how to die. But you almost killed a fem this time. Fems are damaged and need our help, but you treat them as if they were men too. Some women say you've killed too many men, Sheel, and the killing has crippled your spirit, and you shouldn't go out on patrol again.''

"Who says so?''

"If I tell you, you'll go feuding with the one who said it. I just think you should know: women say that when you speak of fems, you talk like a woman with no kin.''

Sheel slapped a gob of suds back up out of her own eyes. "We'll have a feud right here between the two of us in a minute,'' she began threateningly, and stopped. Who was this wretched fem to set her against good, dull Barvaran?

The lacing of the entry was suddenly pulled loose, admitting a rush of cool air. Two women entered, stooping, and walked to the center where the others rose to meet them. Even at its highest point the curved tent roof brushed the raincloud hair of Nenisi Conor, who was tall, angular and dark like a woman's shadow on the ground in late afternoon. One of the black-skinned Conor line and imbued with the Conor trait of justice giving, she was a perfect speaker for the camp, unimpeachable. The Conors are the shadows of our consciences, women said.

Nenisi Conor looked at Sheel. "Women think you did wrong to be careless about the lives of the fem Alldera and her child.''

The other woman was of Sheel's own line, a lean replica of Sheel herself, yellow-haired and blade-faced. Her name was Palmelar. She was famous for being poor in horses because she gave away her wealth to needier women. She was well chosen also, someone whom Sheel had to respect.

To her Sheel said harshly, "Does our Motherline agree with this that other women think?''

Palmelar nodded and met her eyes, smiling as if rejoicing in the judgment.

And here I am looking foolish with soap all over my head, Sheel thought furiously. She stared away over their heads. "Well, how many horses am I fined?'' Each horse paid out of her home herd she would replace if it took her the rest of her life.

Nenisi answered, "The fem has no use for your horses. But there is her child. You must forfeit half your home herd to the child of the fem Alldera."

Half. And for a fem!

Barvaran was looking from one of them to the other. "But what good are horses to a fem's child?"

"Our child," Palmelar said happily. "The fem's child is to be one of us."

Sheel could not hold back an ugly bray of laughter. Had they all lost their senses? A fem's child could never be a Riding Woman for a dozen reasons. She said the one thing that summed up everything else: "The child will have no kin!"

"She'll have all the kin she needs," Nenisi said. "Alldera Holdfaster the fem will be bloodmother to her. Barvaran will be one of her sharemothers, to offset negligence of duty on patrol; and Shayeen, who was too sick to be blamed but who was there; and I myself, as spokeswoman for the judgment; and you too, Sheel, so that you can pay for your ill will and the deaths that it almost caused. We'll all be her family, which is an honor; the child from the Holdfast may grow up to found a new Motherline among the camps of the plains.

"Now, is the judgment sound, Sheel Torrinor?"

Sheel could not speak. Barvaran cried, "Yes!" The three of them wept and hugged each other while she stood in their midst, stifled with her own rage.

II
The Women

3

The comfortable doze in which Alldera had floated for so long dissolved at last. She found herself in a warm, dim place walled and roofed with some pale, translucent material. All around her were activity, voices murmuring, laughter. Something soft cushioned her back. She could see sharp blue sky through an opening off to one side.

What's happening, where am I, what dangers threaten?

A contraction twisted her belly. She cried out at the familiar pain. People closed around her, patting her, whispering encouragement, holding her hands firmly. Her feet were gripped and braced against the backs of people seated on the heap of bedding.

Someone at her side said briskly, "Breathe. Remember. You know how to make your breathing work for you."

She did remember, though she could not now tell whether this was knowledge learned in the secret world of Holdfast fems or in her long dreaming here. There was a way to use the rhythm of respiration to mobilize the body so that it worked not against its own strengths but with them. Fear vanished. She felt full of power, as if she could burst the cub out of her body with one great thrust. It surprised her to find that time was needed, and pain.

The voices of the others joined in a throaty singing.

Their song took its rhythm from her breathing and rein-
forced it. She surged over the pain on their music. The
words, which were beyond the tight center of her attention, must have included humor. Rills of laughter
erupted and were carried in the song.

She poured with sweat. After the first huge passage of
the head she felt the cub's shape, limb and shoulder,
work its way out of her. Always before she had been too
frightened to feel anything but pain.

A person with long, shining black hair was crouching
between Alldera's legs. She put out her hands and
something dropped into them. Another leaned in and
carefully pinched the last of the blood down the cord.
Alldera was astonished at the simplicity of what they
did, their calm. The black-haired person bent and
sucked the plugs of mucus from the tiny mouth and
nose of the raw, squirming bundle in her hands.

People came and put their faces against Alldera's
streaming face. Hands massaged her body. In that
lilting ripple of speech that she found she understood
easily now, several said that she had done well.

She could not gather strength to reach out to any of
them or answer in words, but she thought fiercely each
time one of them approached her, I love you forever for
this. At that moment she felt capable of it. If she had
not been a fem, trained for her life's sake to hide
feelings, she would have wept.

The cub, washed and dried, was placed against her in
the crook of her arm. It was a wrinkled, splotchy-
looking female, unfocused in every wandering movement and every shapeless murmur from its wet little
mouth. On its angular head was a crop of moisture-
darkened hair. There was nothing to tell Alldera which
of her masters had sired it. The cub looked very much
like the other two she had borne back in the Holdfast,
but fatter. Holdfast-born cubs were always skinny. This
one was heavy, tiring to hold. She could not imagine
how it had had time to grow. Surely only a few weeks
had passed since these people had taken up dam and cub
in the desert, both of them little but bone.

Odd, this was the creature she had planned to kill. She was glad now not to have done it.

Someone relieved her of the warm, soft, wriggling weight.

"Here it comes," someone else said cheerfully. Alldera thought in alarm, Mother Moon, not another —were there two, and I didn't know? But it was only the afterbirth, and she wanted to laugh.

She woke, her senses sharp and clear. The soothing haze of previous weeks seemed gone for good.

She saw that she lay in a broad tent. Under the taut roof a skirting painted with designs in faded colors encircled a floor covered with tawny sand. It seemed a wide, dim, comfortable sort of place. Chests and boxes, dark with use, squatted along the wall. Near the folded-back flaps of the entryway stood some contraptions of straps and uprights. Bags and bundles were piled around what she took to be the hearth, a blackened metal cage set on a tray. Close beside the cage on a broad platter were heaped little lumps of what must have been fuel.

One by one she identified the sounds outside: voices, footsteps, the breathy calls of horses.

Where was her cub?

Someone came in. "Awake?"

An apparition stood there, a person whose skin was as dark as smoke. From Holdfast songs and chants Alldera knew of the Blacks who had been among the enemies of the mighty Ancients—a lie, no doubt, like most of the men's beliefs. But she could not help shrinking back as the dark person came forward and dropped into an angular crouch beside her, bringing their faces almost level. The stranger's features were rounded and smoothed as if by many rubbings with fine sand. She was barefoot and wore only a twist of tan, soft stuff knotted around her hips. A string of blue stones crossed the base of her neck.

"I'm Nenisi Conor," she said, "one of your family. The others are still showing the baby around and celebrating it. How do you feel?'' Nenisi asked.

In past pregnancies Alldera had suffered strong af-
terpains in her body's effort to get rid of the last clotted
blood. She felt nothing like that now.

"You're better off than I am," Nenisi said, her long,
dark lips pulling down at the corners in self-mockery.
"My teeth are hurting me today—an affliction of my
line, among several other afflictions, so if I complain
women just shrug. I'm taking advantage of you while
you're still new among us and you'll listen to me tell you
about my horse-farting teeth." She exposed the of-
fending teeth. They looked large, sound, and very
white. She leaned closer, regarding Alldera attentively,
seriously. "It must feel very strange to you, all this—"
Her slender hand floated as she indicated the interior of
the tent.

"Beautiful," Alldera said fervently. "It seems
beautiful to me. Where I come from—" Her voice
failed and she turned her face away. Her lips were trembling.

"There are no men at all," the black woman said.
"None. You're safe."

Alldera wept, and was ashamed of her tears. But
Nenisi only waited, watching sympathetically, and
waved away Alldera's attempts to apologize for her out-
burst.

Nenisi took up a bundle that unrolled into a sort of
rug and she settled herself on the sandy floor. Her limbs
looked very long and thin. The flashing pallor of her
palms as she gestured and the pink cave of her mouth
working in her dark face bemused Alldera.

"You've been with us a long time already, though it
probably doesn't seem so to you. You came to us in the
Cool Season, and now the Dusty Season has begun.
We've kept you in a healing sleep, a thing we do for
fems rescued from the borderlands. Most women are
too lively for healing sleep, but we find that a few
months of complete rest are good for fems fresh from
crossing over. You needed time for yourself and your
child to recover tranquilly from a rough trip."

"What magic did you do to save me?" Alldera said wonderingly. "I was dying when your people found me; I felt myself dying."

"Hardly," Nenisi laughed. "You had your own magic with you—your child. Why, I recall once in my fourth month of pregnancy, stones were thrown at my home tent over this very point. My friends—most of them as big-bellied as I was—wanted to get me free of my hovering sharemothers so I could ride with them in a three-day race that had been forbidden me." She sighed. "Everyone knows that any normal female is tougher and healthier in the first half of pregnancy than any other time in her life, and my friends just could not accept the fact that Conor women are exceptions. We lose our babies easily—I never did bring a child of my body to term. There are other lines just as delicate, like the Soolays and the Calpapers, and it's always a struggle to keep their youngsters slowed down so they don't miscarry.

"You, however, are as normal as they come, and you could say that that baby kept you alive out there."

"Funny. I was going to try to kill her," Alldera mused, but then she saw by Nenisi's face that she had said something terrible, and she steered hastily for safer waters: "How did you keep me asleep for so long?"

"Asleep," Nenisi murmured. "Yes, I suppose you're not really wide awake yet, are you? You'll soon find your balance. All we use is medicine made from plants and soothing talk. We were even able to coax you into moving about in your sleep, to keep your body healthy and fit to bear.

"While you were lying here dozing and healing yourself, your senses were taking in a lot of what was going on around you—us, the way we live, the way we talk. Not everything will be completely strange to you."

I love the way you talk, Alldera thought. Nenisi's speech was little different from Holdfastish, but she drew everything out with a singing drawl, nudging in extra syllables, lilting up and down the scale. Alldera did not want to break into that music with the hard-edged, barking speech of the Holdfast. Keep silence, she thought; listen and learn.

"I want you to understand," Nenisi went on, "you're to rest, take your time, not worry. Don't fret about your baby; women are trampling all over each other trying to take the best care of her that any baby of this camp has ever had. You have family here."

Family, kindred; suddenly Alldera was afraid. Perhaps they took her for something other than what she was, to give her such unreserved welcome, warmth in which her bones and sinews seemed to be dissolving. When the mistake was discovered they might turn on her—

"Who are you?" she whispered. "Why do you care?"

"We're the Riding Women, the women of these plains—"

There came the sound of running steps, very light and swift, and a high babble of voices. Then the tent was full of moving figures, small, naked, and filthy, jostling and pressing close to Alldera as they passed her.

They were a skinny, grimy mob. Their matted hair bounced on their shoulders as they spun away in a swirl of shouts and high-pitched laughter, and they flowed back out of the tent. They brushed past an adult figure in the doorway and were gone.

The newcomer, a sharp-featured woman, ducked inside. Alldera thought she knew that predatory face from her tumbled, nightmare memories of the journey through the desert to the plains.

"No wonder the childpack is running away," commented the woman. "That slave is uglier awake than she was asleep."

Nenisi's chin lifted, giving her an armed and guarded look. "The childpack is looking for all the excitement and feasting that surrounds a new baby, as you know very well, Sheel. They didn't find that here, so they left. And Alldera is not a slave. Where there are no masters, no one can be a slave."

The sharp-faced woman moved silently on naked, sinewy feet. She wore trousers and a cloth looped around her neck and crossed over her breasts to tie in the back. She took up a wooden bowl and filled it with white liquid from a bag hanging on a pole.

"Fems are so fitted to slavery that they'll find masters wherever they go. Be careful this one doesn't turn you into her master, Nenisi." She drank.

Nenisi sighed and said to Alldera with exaggerated regret, "This is Sheel Torrinor. Good manners are not among the Torrinor traits. Like me, Sheel is of your family. I hope you can stand her."

"You don't mind being a fem's sharemother," the newcomer said, ignoring the black woman's bantering tone. "I hate it."

Alldera did not dare to say anything. She was relieved when Sheel Torrinor walked out, bowl in hand.

And yet, there had been something bracing about her attitude. Under Sheel's cold dislike, the helpless, melting feeling of being more beholden than any human being could bear had receded and ceased to overwhelm Alldera. Enmity from an icy bitch was something she understood from the Holdfast, where she had known boss fems like that: ruthless but effective overseers, most of them. Sheel's contempt had yanked her roughly back into reality.

She was an escaped fem taken in by a strange, marvelous people, befriended by a black person whose teeth hurt, rejected by another stranger as slim and hard-looking as a knife.

"I'm sorry she's so rude," Nenisi said.

"But she's part of my 'family'?" Alldera ventured cautiously. "What's a 'sharemother'?"

"One who shares the mothering of your child with you. I'm one of your sharemothers. Sheel, unfortunately perhaps, is another."

"But why should she be, if she doesn't want to?"

"Good reasons."

"I'd rather not have her forced to—"

"Don't worry about her. She'll do what's right, however ungracefully," Nenisi said; and she talked of other things.

*   *   *

Four women inhabited "Holdfaster Tent" with Alldera
as her family of sharemothers. When they came in to eat
and talk that evening, they seemed to bring with them
the spirits of a hundred other women whom they had
spoken to or heard about or seen doing this or that
during the day. All of that was laid out in conversation
during the long, hot twilight over pots and pots of the
bitter drink they called tea.

The mounts on which women had ridden home to the
tent were tethered outside for the night. Alldera heard
the horses snuffling at the ground, sighing and groaning
like humans, talking briefly to each other in their
peculiar voices. She shivered at their strangeness; there
had been no animals at all in the Holdfast.

Of all the voices in the tent Nenisi's was the most
supple, a rich and rippling contralto which she seemed
able to turn reedy or plummy by turns, like a musical instrument. She made the others laugh a lot. They did not
keep the small, smelly fire going after sundown, and
when Nenisi's dark skin vanished into the gloom she
became a sort of invisible spirit with a playful voice.

Sheel sat across from Alldera. She had a narrow jaw
and her front teeth projected so that she had to hold her
lips closed over them. The strong muscles around her
mouth gave her face a sculpted, rapacious look.

She did not speak to Alldera.

There was a woman called Shayeen, visible by the
fire's embers as a shining being of smooth, red-brown
metal, black hair that looked oiled, and a gleam of
bright metal at wrist and throat. She spoke rarely, and
then mainly of games and contests, wins and losses, in
the past and to come. Twice she asked Alldera polite
questions without real meaning beyond perhaps the
wish to acknowledge her presence.

The fourth woman of the family sat on Alldera's
other side and nursed the cub. She kept stroking the top
of its fuzzy head with her big, square, chap-knuckled
hands. Her name was Barvaran, and she was squat and
coarse-looking. There was dirt in the creases of her skin,

as there had been when she had first leaned over Alldera
after capturing her back in the desert. The others reeked
of horses and sweaty leather, but Barvaran smelled
strongly of herself.

Alldera wanted to edge away from her. She had
known labor fems as ungainly and unlovely as this back
in the Holdfast. The drudges of that world, they had
been too dull to be anything better and had been saved
from extinction only by the strength of their thick
backs.

Though Barvaran seemed to have no nursing cub of
her own she did have milk, as indeed they all did. The
sharemothers passed the cub around for a suckle at each
one's breast before unrolling their bedding for the
night. Milk, they said, came easily to them, and nursing
was something Alldera would seldom have to do. She
was relieved, for to her it was simply a boring, im-
mobilizing job.

Outside she heard the sounds of horses and
somewhere not far distant the high chatter of the childpack moving closer and farther, closer and farther, and
finally stopping.

She woke with a full bladder and blundered about in
the darkness looking for a pot, or failing that the entryway so that she could step outside to relieve herself.
She was slowed by her weakness after the cub's birth.

One of the women got up, handed off the cub—which
she had kept sleeping with her—to someone else, and
guided Alldera out. It was, Alldera guessed by the scent
and bulk of her, Barvaran, who led her past the edge of
the camp to a sandy gully that she called "the squats."
Alldera crouched, wincing, in the dry watercourse. The
rawness of her vagina made urination an ordeal.

The sky was beginning to pale. As they made their
way back among the closed tents, Barvaran said,
"You'll get used to drinking tea after a while and it
won't wake you so early any more. Camp is nice now,
isn't it—quiet and tidy-looking."

In this thin light and with her clangorous voice toned
down out of mercy for the sleep of others, Barvaran

seemed quite different: warmly sympathetic, manner a
little shy, an honest soul sunk in a crude and odorous
frame.

Alldera almost walked into the childpack. Heaped
together, their skinny limbs asprawl, they lay snoring
and snuffling under the wide fly of one of the tents.
Repelled, she retreated a step, jostling Barvaran.

"You'll get used to them too," Barvaran said. "I
know it's not much like your country here."

The truth was that, like Barvaran herself, the childpack was all too much like something from the Holdfast. The pack reminded Alldera of a batch of very
young fems in one of the wide, deep pits where fem kits
were kept between the time they were weaned and the
time they were taken for training. She thought of her
own life in the pits, bitter with hunger and struggles
against others just as hungry, and of a time she had
spent immobilized in her own filth by illness while her
companions ate up all the scant ration thrown down to
them by the men. . . .

These camp children did not seem hungry, only dirty
and wild, and Barvaran herself seemed not alien and
forbidding but familiar. Alldera said hesitantly, "Barvaran, can I ask you—how do you have children,
without men?"

"Oh," Barvaran said, "we mate with our horses."

Shocked, with embarrassment Alldera felt her own
cheeks heat. Clearly she had asked an improper
question and had been turned with a crude joke about
those monster-like beasts. She would not ask again.

The other question, the necessary question, haunted
her, dammed in by timidity and a feeling that it would
be somehow absurd and insulting to ask it. Finally it
broke clumsily out of her one day when she found herself alone with Nenisi, who was hunched under one of
the tent flies straightening bent arrow shafts over a
small fire. Finding Nenisi by herself was not easy, and
Alldera leaped at the opportunity without thinking.

"Will you help us?" she said.

Nenisi looked up at her.

Alldera rushed on, stammering, "I wasn't just running away, I was sent to find help in the Wild, some hope—I didn't think there really was anyone, and I'd given up and was just trying to save myself, but now—you—the other fems still enslaved back there—"

"There is no help," Nenisi said. She sighted down the arrow in her hand. "It was decided long ago that we women would never risk the free world of our children by invading the Holdfast for the fems' sakes. We all agreed."

"I see." Beneath her numbness Alldera felt feeling stir.

"Besides, it's too late. No one, man or fem, has come out of the east in months; not since we found you, in fact. We think they're all dead—"

"Yes, I understand," Alldera insisted. That was what she had sensed herself, alone in the borderlands. That was what she had wanted to hear. She turned away to hide the horror of her feelings: the dark surge of grief for her lost people was shot through with the joy of being truly free of them at last.

At first she reveled at the sight of female people running their own lives without so much as a scent of men about them; even the several very pregnant women seemed sturdy and capable and utterly unworried by their vulnerable condition.

Her jubilation receded as the hot, dry weeks wore on. She was invaded by weariness, depressed for days at a time by her undeserved survival into freedom and by the conviction that she would never learn to manage all the newness surrounding her. Loneliness assailed her. She longed sometimes to caress Shayeen's glowing skin, and often caught herself staring at the sculpted beauty of Nenisi's long dark face. The conviction of her own unworthiness turned her desires back on herself. She did not dare approach these women, except in her dreams.

The blazing afternoon skies began to fill with clouds each day now, and the women stood outside watching in the heat. Four dry months almost behind them, they said; four rainy months coming, then four cool months after that, making up the year. The Dusty Season was about to end.

One afternoon it rained not at the camp but a distance to the south. Alldera could see the clouds trailing dark sweeps of rain past the horizon.

The camp sprang into motion, shaking her sharply out of her lethargy. In a riot of shouting and laughter the women brought all thirty tents of Stone Dancing Camp down in the middle of the day. Alldera stood aside with the cub slung warm against her back, and she watched Holdfaster Tent reduced swiftly to leather and rope, all stowed away in capacious saddle packs. The tent poles were hitched in bundles alongside the flanks of a brown horse, the butt ends trailing on the ground.

Every tent was similarly transformed into a dozen laden pack ponies. Everywhere were horses, their noise, their smell, their bulky, powerful bodies moving in the dust they raised. One round-bellied animal exploded twice out of the hands of its packer and was rapidly and firmly reloaded each time. Alldera was terrified of being trampled or kicked by a horse that she would not see until too late.

She watched Shayeen, covered in dust, first tugging a cinch strap with both hands, then slugging the pony in the flank with her fist so that it gasped out its deeply held breath and the buckle on the cinch could be closed.

To Alldera's immense relief no one suggested putting her on top of a horse. She half lay, half sat on a sled of heavy leather slung between the tent poles out of reach of the brown horse's heels. Cub in lap, she rode the jouncing progress of the pole-butts. The brown horse, urged on by Nenisi on a spotted mount, led a string of others from the emptying campground. Around Alldera groups of horses plodded in the charge of other mounted figures. She saw the childpack darting among them and heard the children's shrieks of excitement.

The whole crowd of mounted women and pack horses descended from the low ridge on which they had been camped. As they poured down onto the salt flat below, the group shook itself into a crowd of mixed riders and pack animals surrounded by a wide ring of scouts. Within this circle of outriders the childpack ranged freely.

Alldera recalled something Nenisi had told her of another creature of the plains, one Alldera had not yet seen: a low running beast furred in all the colors of the plains. The women hunted these "sharu" and wore their skins and ornaments made of their curved claws and teeth. The sharu ate anything, from grass and seeds to meat. That was why the childpack, which wandered at will all day, slept every night within the perimeter of the camp. She guessed that that was also why they ranged today inside the ring of scouts.

This gave her a very secure feeling. She knew herself to be something of a child herself here, carried along while everyone else rode.

Discomfited by the idea of Sheel seeing her in just that way, she asked where the rest of the family was. Nenisi pointed across the moving crowd at one of the scouts on the far side: "That's Sheel." Then she waved in the direction of the long, low curtain of dust drifting ahead of them well to the left. "The others are helping to move the herds.

"Pass our daughter up here to me—the air is fresher, and the sooner she gets the feel of a horse's back the better."

Despite the miasma of heat and dust surrounding them the women talked and laughed as they traveled toward where they had seen the rain. Nenisi threw her head back once and sang part of a song about how when they got to the new campsite the grass would already be up.

A pack horse up ahead got kicked by another and broke away squealing. The childpack swarmed after, getting in the way of the rider in charge of the pack string. The rider laughed and snapped her rein ends above their heads in mock threat.

Alldera's mouth tasted of earth; yet their exuberance

was catching, and her heart beat fast. "Everyone's in such good spirits," she said, wanting to show that she felt it too, but shy of intruding on a joy that she did not understand.

"Of course," Nenisi answered, "the rain frees us from our wells, you see. Now we can freely travel our country again."

Alldera bent her head; the sense of their freedom had taken her by the throat. They could move where they liked. The physical fact of their liberty as she felt it at that moment, drowning in dust, bumping along at the brown mare's heels, made her weep.

Sometime that night they stopped; the rising sun showed among the rough circle of freshly raised tents a scatter of thin green grass on the damp earth.

After that, Alldera began to fit into the women's life.

4

Daya leaned her back against Kenoma's long-muscled lég and watched the flames. The angry talk drifted over her and into the surrounding night.

The free fem crew was gathered at the tailgate of their wagon where a tall fire burned. They kept their backs turned to the dim shapes of the Marish camp called Windgrass some distance away, dark and silent tents against the stars. They cursed the Mares and everything Marish, as free fems did after a day of trading with them.

Daya stopped listening. She was bored with their sniping and thought ridiculous the rumors of a new fem hidden somewhere in the Mares' camps. She relaxed into the pleasure of being enfolded in the enormous spaces of the sky and the land, for already this crew were on their way back to the tea camp in the foothills. Their trade journey over the plains was nearly ended, and she was sorry.

She loved it out here. She loved to be one of the many points of living warmth that peopled the vast darkness over the Grasslands. She loved the grit of the soil under her thighs and palms, the glimmer of firelight on the yellow stubble beyond the edges of the camp, the evening stir of air as the day's heat drifted starward. She felt her thoughts flowing out over the tableland. She pictured horses dozing or listening with upswung heads for a rustle in the grass; and the wide-flung camps of the

Mares, groups of broad-winged tents herding loosely together in drowsy silence; and the hungry sharu sleeping in their networks of burrows; and of course all the free fems, radiating outward crew by crew across the great expanse from one Marish camp to another. She loved this life at least as much as she loved life in the tea camp in the hills.

Of course there were risks, difficulties, irritations in living anywhere. Daya had been a pet, bred for the pleasure of men's eyes as well as other pleasures. Despite the scars that marred her beauty now, she was still young, small and slender enough to be attractive even when she had no wish to attract. She did not enjoy being fought over by other free fems, so she took pains to acquire a companion like Kenoma whose truculence discouraged ardor in others. But jealousy inclined Kenoma to turn her banked violence on Daya at the smallest provocation.

Right now by the fire Daya could feel the tension in Kenoma's thigh drawing tighter, promising release in a scene, perhaps a thrashing, later on. Kenoma was only safe for a short while longer; the risks of staying at her side were beginning to outweigh the advantages of her companionship.

Daya did not want to worry about that now. She held the sweetness of the brush smoke deep in the chambers of her nostrils. She felt Kenoma stir and tauten, and heard her say harshly, "This is the last fem they've brought out, maybe the last one they ever will bring out. She's ours."

How annoying, how foolish, Daya thought. What does it mean even to say "last"? Time was different here. Life did not rush from crisis to crisis and turn instantly into some new and dangerous course at a master's whim, as it had in the Holdfast. There were different rhythms in the Grasslands, long and slow and repetitive. Nothing came in "firsts" and "lasts" here, but as "another" or "again." The Grasslands was like a great disc of earth revolving endlessly under the great disc of sky and season. They should not talk of a new fem as if she were unique, as if she were capable of making a difference to the wide wheeling patterns of these plains.

Yet this new fem's long stay with the Mares had touched the free fems' imaginations: "Maybe she brings a message the Mares don't want us to have." "Maybe the men are preparing an invasion, and the Mares are keeping her with them to get information out of her." "No, it's the Mares that are preparing an invasion, so they're pumping her all about the Holdfast first."

Daya was handed a bowl of beer to drink and she let her fingers slip along the hand of the giver. Kenoma noticed, slapped the bowl out of her hand, and kicked the other fem so that she nearly fell into the fire. Sandaled feet scattered the coals as fems jumped up, cursing, ready for a fight but amused too; Daya was famous for her amours and the problems they brought her.

She dodged and evaded Kenoma's angry blows, and seeing that the big fem had taken off her sandals earlier to ease her feet, managed to draw her to the scattered fire. Everyone roared with laughter to see Kenoma bellowing and hopping on first one foot and then the other.

"A story," Daya cried, holding up her hands in mock terror as Kenoma, limping, closed in on her. "A story, in exchange for peace! Let me tell how it is that this poor pet fem became marked goods, too ruined to be worth your anger, Kenoma."

Daya was a favorite storyteller among the free fems, and it made no difference that they all knew the story she proposed to tell. This crew had all been labor fems of one sort or another in the Holdfast, regarding pets like Daya as pampered traitors. They loved any tale told and retold of the haughty brought low. Under their urging, Kenoma's fury gave way to sullen acquiescence.

"There I was," Daya began, "fresh from my training in Bayo, up for the bidding on the steps of the Boardmen's Hall in the City." She sprang up, she paraded before them, moving in the sinuous, exaggerated style

of a highly trained pet fem. Languorously she blinked at
them as if they were men come to buy.

She told the drama of the bidding to be her master
and of how a man of the Blues named Kazzaro had
bought her. She imitated her master Kazzaro's high-
shouldered, nervous posture and showed them how he
fretted about his clothing and patted his spreading bald
spot. He had been clean, decent-looking, and relatively
rich, and she had counted herself fortunate. "He had
the eye of a man who sees a fem for her sex, not just her
decorative and useful qualities. I knew I could make
him itch for me no matter how he might hate himself for
it. He was the sort of man who has young men hanging
on him for favors in return for their love, but who
watches the serving fems and then looks away, ashamed
of his interest in mere females. You can tell that I was
young, because it never occurred to me that such a man
would already have a pretty fem or two dancing attendance on him."

She told of his house, the magnificence of the tiled
walls, the floors cushioned in thick carpets of heavy
hemp dyed vibrant blues and greens. Enthralled,
nodding, murmuring, the free fems drank in details of
carved wooden shutters, painted roof beams, rich glazes
and luxurious pillows, sweet scents wafting on the warm
air. The more she embellished, the better they liked it.
She added a tinkling mobile of metal chips, and a
display of Kazzaro's prize collection of small ceramic
figures used in the game of Tail.

"I was young and naive, but not so naive that I
showed him how impressed I was by all his opulence. I
walked like this behind him, as cool as if I had been
raised in such surroundings instead of in the shitty,
stinking straw of the kit pits.

"But how my heart thundered, how I longed to be
alone so that I could touch all those luxurious things!

"He opened the door behind the metal gate to the fem
quarters. There was another pet fem, lying there on a
couch and watching the small fire." Daya let her fingers
crook into claws and curled her lips back from her teeth

in a snarl. "Does the world hold anything more cruel than the jealousy of a pet fem for her place?

"I thought, I can hold my own here. The other fem was not young, and her beauty—clearly wonderful once—had faded."

She told how Kazzaro had taken her over to the couch too, so that at first Daya had thought, he wishes us to do sex together before him. She had been taught how to do this for a master's entertainment, but she could not help being nervous the first time she was called on to actually perform.

She told how slowly, through misunderstanding and confusion, she had come to realize that Kazzaro was captivated by the older fem, Merika; that he was so besotted with her that he kept her shut up for safekeeping. He feared that some older man would see her, want her, and take her from him.

Merika was prey to the suicidal melancholy that often strikes a beauty as age advances. She dreaded the day when her master would realize that she was losing her looks. She needed companionship, that was Kazzaro's reading of her state, and so he had bought her Daya.

Daya and Merika became lovers, being closed in each other's company and finding each other's character congenial.

"I was young, sure of myself, and credulous. Did I realize how it affected the aging pet when our master noted the pleasure of his guests when he lent me to them in Merika's place? On the other hand, it pleased her that I replaced her monthly in the breeding rooms. Kazzaro could not bear to send her there. Did I see the satisfaction on her face when I was swollen with pregnancy? Did I understand why she kept plying me with the richest tidbits of her own food, I who was as slim as a boy and so doubly fetching to our master? He was a man, after all, with a man's natural interest in his own sex and a proper male lover named Charkin. In me he could have male and female beauty both at once, while Merika grew softer and rounder and plumper all the time, for want of exercise and because of her age."

Inevitably, Merika's fear of losing her privileged place overcame her desire for Daya's company.

"You all know," Daya said, making her eyes mournful, "the treachery of pet fems toward each other. Hear now how Merika treated me!"

Meticulously she set the scene of the private appointment of Kazzaro and Charkin at Kazzaro's house: the careful cleaning of the room, its decoration with magnificent hangings, the day-long preparation of special dishes in the kitchens below, Kazzaro's meditations on his wardrobe and what scents to wear.

For Charkin, his own chief lover, he liked to have Merika and his other pets come and serve the food. It was an extravagant use of slaves trained in more rarified arts, and this amused him. He had to be able to show Merika off sometimes to get the full value of owning her. So the two pets had enjoyed the privilege of attending his guest.

The evening had gone ill from the beginning. Charkin was nasty and ambitious by nature even for a man. He argued that Kazzaro could be a greater patron still if he would stop spending all his wealth on pets. Then he would be able to buy a bigger house and support many more young men—and Charkin would of course be the first and highest among them.

The free fems watched eagerly as Daya mimicked first one man's voice and manner, then the other's. She shifted to Merika's stealthy doings down in the serving pantry. Merika had carefully broken the best serving dipper across the bowl and stuck it back together with a thin coat of glue.

Later, when Daya ladled up a portion of hot food for the guest, Merika had only to knock the edge of the stew bowl against the dipper, and the heated glue gave way. The dipper split, slopping blue stew all over Charkin.

"He let out a roar, Merika shrieked and bolted, and I was left standing there too startled to move. Charkin snatched up a broiling spit that he'd just eaten clean. He lunged and drove it through my face from one side to the other! I felt it tear my cheeks and smash two teeth, and my mouth filled up with blood.''

The free fems sighed, half horrified, half satisfied.

The skewer had not been hot enough to make clean wounds. They festered. Kazzaro sent Daya down to work in Blue Company's kitchen where she could learn to handle food utensils more carefully and where, more important, he would not have to look at her. The fems around the wagon savored the part that followed, the tale of a pet fem set down in their sort of world. They nodded and commented while she rounded out the story.

''To my surprise, I liked it in the kitchens. It was always warm, and there wasn't anything like the rivalry I'd seen in the pet quarters. The men overseeing the kitchens were young, and the older men kept them hungry. What we fems did didn't matter as long as we weren't caught stealing food. The overseers themselves stole food all the time, but we were better thieves than they were. I enjoyed learning to cook, too, for it's a great art.

''But have you ever heard of a pet fem without enemies?'' She spoke of how certain kitchen fems had maneuvered to get her into difficulties with their boss fem by making Daya look like a troublemaker. Any time fems fought out their private quarrels, Daya's enemies said her flirting had provoked the fighting. The boss fem could not afford to have a demoted pet fem full of spite making problems in her crew, or all would suffer. So she got Daya slated for transfer to the brickyards. Faced with having to try to fit herself in among yet another set of labor fems there, Daya preferred the risks of the Wild. It was at that point that she had made her run for the border—another story.

She never pointed out that here among the free fems of the Grasslands she found herself once more a pet among labor fems. She kept that joke to herself.

''So she won, this Merika, your rival,'' Kenoma sneered. ''She drove you out.''

Daya raked the scattered coals together with a stick. "You could say so. Once afterward we talked about it briefly, and she told me that she hadn't planned anything so drastic—just a beating for me and demotion to some position less close to Kazzaro."

Kenoma snorted with disbelief. "She said that because she was scared otherwise you'd poison her food in the kitchens."

No one wanted to follow that up. Now that the appetite for drama was sated, their mood drifted into reminiscence. One older fem, who was picking up glowing fragments of the fire in her calloused fingers and tossing them back into the hot center of the flames, shook her head and said softly, "I worked in kitchens all my life there. We knew how to mount a real feast of cooking in those days, none of your sketchy little campfires and pots of stewed greens—no offense to our fine cook!"

Daya nodded graciously.

"Why, I remember, when we set up to feed some high Boardmen," the old fem continued, "in the house of Boardman Kun; we started with sixteen different kinds of waterweeds—"

Daya leaned back against the tall wheel of the wagon, listening, secure for the evening.

5

Alldera sat knotting the dry fibres spread on her knee into a menstrual plug. She could not yet turn out dozens of them during a conversation without looking down at her work, as the women did; but she could make enough for her own needs. There was no water to spare during the dry, dusty weather to wash out a fem-style bleeding rag.

She looked up now and again at Sheel, who nursed the cub and helped Nenisi cook—so strange to see that soft round cub head against Sheel's conical breast.

The two sharemothers talked as women talked whenever there was time: of horses, water, grass and weather, but most often of their kindred. Alldera loved to listen and took pride in being able to follow more and more all the time. Tangled skeins of events were unrolled, like the history which pitted a wealthy cousin of Shayeen in what seemed eternal enmity against someone of the Faller tent. This naturally involved Sheel because of a sister of hers who was a sharemother in that tent. Dozens of women were mixed up in the quarrel, including women of other camps.

Shayeen had her enemies, Nenisi had hers, and Sheel had many. Even Barvaran was entangled in some huge row of years' standing which appeared to turn on horses used in payment of a debt and the different valuations placed on those horses by at least six sides in the dispute.

No one ever asked Alldera about the Holdfast, and

she was glad; that life seemed to her to have been in-
finitely inferior to the women's lives here, and she
would have been embarrassed to speak of it. Besides, as
a slave she had never been free to speak except on command, and she was still shy.

Two riders passed by the open front of the tent,
turned to shout questions. Answers came from other
tents, and the two riders came back again and stopped.
Sheel and Nenisi jumped up and ran out to embrace the
newcomers as they dismounted, talking, patting and
stroking them in the way the women had.

Watching, Alldera thought enviously that they did
not know what it was to be always at the mercy of men's
hands.

One of the visitors was old, brown-skinned, gray-
haired, well-wrinkled. She limped badly. The other
might have been Nenisi, except that Nenisi already
stood there. This visitor was slender, black-skinned,
with the same smooth-featured, mobile face, the same
hands flashing pale palms as she talked.

Alldera was beginning to get used to the way these
people appeared sometimes in identical pairs, trios, or
even more. At first she had thought it a powerful magic,
for in the Holdfast twins were a sign of witchery and
were killed at birth with their dam. Here, Nenisi had
told her patiently many times over, there were whole
strings of blood relations called "Motherlines," women
who looked like older and younger versions of each
other. They were mothers and daughters, sisters and the
daughters of sisters. Nenisi said the look-alikes did not
live together but were scattered through the tents of this
camp and other camps.

The dark woman standing like Nenisi's living shadow
was a Conor from another camp, a woman whose teeth
must also be prone to ache when she was anxious, as
Nenisi's did. Alldera had heard Nenisi grinding her
teeth in her sleep; this woman must grind hers, too.

Nenisi drew her double into the tent by the hand.
"This is the child of my sister, cousin Marisu Conor

from Windgrass Camp; and this is Jesselee Morrowtrow, one of Sheel's mothers.''

The old woman studied Alldera, head to one side, not speaking. Sheel took her by the hands, called her "Heart-mother," and seated her near the fire with her back half-turned to Alldera.

"At the last Gather when I asked where you were," Sheel said to her mother, "they told me that a horse had kicked you while you were doctoring her. I thought it would be healed up by now. Live around horses, you'll limp half your life."

"Don't believe everything you hear," the old woman said. "A crocodile bit me."

"Nenisi, what's a crocodile?" Alldera whispered. She feared for a moment that she had asked the wrong Conor cousin, but then she saw Nenisi's blue necklace and was reassured. She did not often make such errors any more.

"A joke," Nenisi murmured, "though they do say such Ancient creatures still live, far to the south where the plain turns to forest and marsh."

"A crocodile!" Sheel marveled. "Like the one whose skin you showed me once when I was little—only that turned out to be a sheet of bark stripped from a fresh tent pole."

Unperturbed, Jesselee continued, "There I was, prowling the shoreline marshes by the Salty River. I'd dreamed of one of the drowned cities of the Ancients, and I thought that meant that some treasure would be washed up for me. Instead here comes this knobby dark form, floating silently nearer and nearer—"

"And it gobbled you up," said Marisu Conor, snapping her teeth loudly together. They all laughed, Sheel loudest of all.

Imagine, being so easy and happy with a grown woman who had suckled you and with whom your relations stretched back through your entire life! It was wonderful to bask on the edge of the ease the women had with each other, the rich connectedness.

They showed Jesselee the cub, which went into one of its fits of sudden activity and nearly blacked the old woman's eye. She seemed pleased, laughing and commenting that it seemed to have plenty of spirit. She said she would be staying a while.

They talked about Salt Wind Camp where Sheel had grown up, way to the west. The winds which sometimes blew damply off the river had weakened her chest, Sheel said sadly, and had etched the cold into her bones, so that she seldom returned there. She said she could not forget the wind patterns on the water, though, or the whispering reeds along the water's edge. "I used to play, as a child, that I was an invader from over the river or else a gallant defender of our camp. I didn't know in those days who the real intruder would be."

She glared at Alldera, who had passed the point at which Sheel's unkindness could reduce her to tears. Alldera looked at Jesselee and said diffidently, "I'm glad you'll stay with us, Jesselee. I think I know all my sharemothers' tales by now."

Jesselee rubbed at her stiff knee and nodded. "I'm sure I can recall some new ones to tell you. Even someone as close as one's heartchild always has something still to learn—a tale, a skill, some manners."

Sheel bit her lip but said nothing, and Alldera felt filled with victory.

First you made sure that the long Rainy Season dampness had not made the tea moldy. Then you shaved it fine. Alldera had only been given the job of making the midday tea once before, and she had used water that was too hot and had had to sit by and watch the family members gulp down the bitter stuff anyway, because tea was too valuable to be wasted.

She leaned over her work, sat back again to shake the hair out of her eyes. Over the months her hair had grown out long and as healthy as it ever got, and she was always meaning to cut it shoulder length, the women's favorite style, and never getting around to it.

Unintentionally she caught the eye of a woman who

was walking past, one arm slung companionably over
the withers of a spotted mare that ambled beside her like
a friend. The woman smiled. Alldera did not recognize
her, but smiled timidly in return, and bent to her work
again.

Concentrating on the tea making was hard. Behind
her Barvaran and Shayeen were chatting together about
childhood. Shayeen, seeding peppers for the array of
kettles in front of her, complained intermittently about
the stinging of her fingers. She had piles of the fresh-
picked peppers still to cut, for it was Holdfaster Tent's
turn to lay out food for the childpack today.

The children knew it and were gathered nearby,
giggling and fighting around the edges of a huge puddle
on the margins of which their feet slid and splashed.
They pushed each other into it. A few of them squatted
down to imitate the adults over make-believe fires of
piled stones.

Barvaran kept an eye on them, stopping her conversation to shout warnings at them now and then. She
was simmering milk and laying out the squeezed dregs
from the pots in lumps to dry on the tent fly. The
children were notorious thieves of whatever food they
found lying around, perhaps because they were never
punished.

Alldera braced the tea brick on her knee, watching a
shaving curl away from her knife blade. The scent of
cooking milk was making her mouth water. She had
developed an inordinate fondness for the fragile plates
of fresh cream cake that could be lifted from the surface
of a cooled pan of simmered milk. The milking of mares
in foal took much of everyone's time, and the whole
camp lived on fresh milk these days. Alldera could not
pick up the trick of seizing the small, waxy teat way up
under a mare's leg, so she felt guilty about her appetite
for the pale, sweet food.

Now: start with the cold water to moisten the
shavings or it comes out too bitter. Enough cold, she
hoped; then water from the hot kettle, but slowly, not
too much, cold again right away so that not all the

powerful taste would be leached out in the first steeping. That seemed good; the rising scent was mild and minty.

Barvaran was speaking with affectionate humor of a pack game that hinged on guessing whether a child who was "it" had a finger in her nose or not by just listening to her talk in the dark. It was weird even now to think of these women as having once lived the wild life of the childpack and to think of the cub of Holdfaster Tent joining that life. She was growing fast. Alldera remembered how the leather sling had sagged against Nenisi's back this morning when the black woman had ridden out to the milking lines carrying the cub with her.

Barvaran and Shayeen talked of a wild dancing game played with the horses, of sleepy sex games, and—in a subdued manner—about harrying the unfit from the pack. Many died in their first pack year. When the children brought in one of their number who was ill to be tended by the adults, that child was generally discovered to have exceptional qualities.

With a rush of confidence Alldera decided to make the next step; the mixing of flour and water to make noodles, which the women put in their tea along with milk and salt, making it into a meal. She hoped no one would insist on helping.

They were too deep in talk. Shayeen was saying wistfully, "You start to bleed, and the younger ones drive you out, and that's the end of the free life. There's no place to go but to the tents, where you remember women once carried you and nursed you and mopped your bottom. And sure enough, there they are, all waiting to make you into a proper woman with a name and a family."

"Oh, it's a terrible time, I remember," Barvaran agreed. "There I was with blood running down my legs and a new smell of myself, all hateful and sour, in my nostrils. My pack mates had to beat me away. Somebody finally whacked me on the head with a horse bone, I still have the mark, look here. That did it."

"Blood at both ends is a strong argument," Shayeen said. "Did you ever hear of a Maclaster child who ran with her camp's pack for almost seventeen years? Just would not start bleeding.''

''Some funny traits show up in that line sometimes.''

Sitting back, her work completed, Alldera suddenly noticed how cool the morning was once she was not bending over the heat of the tea fire. She tightened her breast wrap—by now she could adjust the knot behind her back by herself—and slipped her long leather shirt on over her head. She put on her headcloth and the rawhide crown that snugged it to her head, and stood up.

The pants that Barvaran had lent her fit fairly well, closing at the waist with a drawstring; but the legs had to be tugged down every once in a while because Alldera did not like to wear the soft boots that helped to anchor them. She had gone barefoot all her life.

She sheathed her knife and buckled on her belt. The women wore the knife sheathed at the small of the back, where the tip could not catch the thigh upraised to mount a horse. Alldera stayed clear of the horses and wore her knife at her hip. The horses' size and strength and impenetrable mixture of cunning and stupidity terrified her, and she still thought of the women's power over them as a kind of magic.

Someone called outside—Nenisi's voice. There she sat on her best bay mare, straight-backed and masterful, having left the cub with someone out at the milking lines. Hastily, Alldera poured out some tea and took it to her.

Nenisi did not drink. ''Look,'' she said, and pointed with her chin, as the women often did.

Out beyond the tents a group approached on foot over the plains, hauling a wagon. The wind was blowing the wrong way. Alldera could barely hear the creaking of the wagon's wheels and only scraps of voices, through the group was at no great distance from Stone Dancing Camp.

She knew them at once for fems. They had a squat, stiff-jointed look about them, none of the suppleness of riders, and the silhouettes of their clothing reminded her

unmistakably of Holdfastish dress. As they came closer
she could make out the broad, shallow hats they wore
and, instead of shirt and pants, smocks with skirts mid-
thigh over bare legs. Some of them carried staffs in their
hands or across their shoulders. Each staff was
tipped with a glinting point.

Fems carrying weapons and traveling unmastered: a
dream of her own people.

Flooded with a great sense of relief, of homecoming,
Alldera dropped the tea pannikin and began to cry. Yet
she did not want to run to greet them.

Barvaran, at her shoulder, said, "Those are free
fems, come to trade from their camp in the eastern hills.
They'll go right to the chief tent; we have to get our
trade goods together. You go ahead." She patted
Alldera awkwardly on the shoulder and joined Shayeen
in rummaging inside the tent.

Reining close, Nenisi leaned toward Alldera. "I have
to ride out again. Alldera—if the free fems say anything
that confuses you, I'll try to explain it later. It would be
best if you didn't mention your child to them."

Something was wrong; Alldera could feel Nenisi's
anxiety, but she could not read its source. Nenisi
galloped off.

Alldera walked slowly toward the chief tent, alone.
She felt dizzy with excitement and apprehension.

Everyone crowded around outside the chief tent,
many women laden with goods—piles of skins and
hides, sacks and pouches of dried food. The fems had
parked their wagon out of the camp. They made a
procession to the chief tent, carrying loads balanced on
their heads. Their heavy sandals scuffed the ground as
they advanced. They had left their spears, but each one
wore a hatchet looped to her belt. To Alldera they
looked coarse and graceless, out of place here. Each of
them chewed a wad in her cheek and spat brown juice.

The smocks they wore were of cloth, patterned with
colors. As they walked the smocks swung, and the
colors appeared to move. Suddenly, jarringly, Alldera
saw how drearily brown the women and their sur-

roundings were. Around her stretched the low plain with its yellowing grasses, under the wide tan sky. The camp itself was earth brown, leather brown, the various red and yellow and black browns of the women's hair and skin, and the colors of animal hides.

Why, the women were like their horses—as there were so many dun horses in the camp's herds, so many blacks, so many stripe-legged bays, so there were this many dark-skinned lines of women like the Conors and the Clarishes over there, so many lines with red hair, so many sallow women like those Tuluns bending over their stacked goods, hair like coal and bodies as narrow and muscular as the necks of horses. Grouped at the chief tent, they were like some woven design in which each broad, clear thread could be traced in the image of each Motherline, repeated from individual to individual and from generation to generation.

She shook her head and blinked, frightened by this vision and the distance it put between herself and the women.

One of the fems came forward and spoke with the Shawden chiefs. Then they all laid out their goods in rows before the tent. The women milled up and down the narrow aisles, picking up bricks of tea and sniffing them, shaking out coils of rope. The fems watched, tight-mouthed, sharp-eyed, and spoke only when they were asked questions.

Alldera was glad she had not run out to meet the wagon. She stayed at the outer edges of the crowd, peering at the newcomers. When they spoke she found their voices grating after the women's liquid speech. Their truculent attitude was evident in their glances, their asides to one another, the way they withdrew slightly to avoid contact with passing women. Their demeanor repelled her. She wanted—what? Certainly not these closed and suspicious faces.

She turned and wandered away among the tents to where the fems' wagon stood, outside the camp. Troubled, she drew nearer. Femmish leaders had designed her escape so that she might bring back a

pledge of aid from free fems. Now here were real free
fems; she felt off balance, flooded with guilt for her
abandoned task.

She walked the length of the wagon, touching the
bleached and weathered wood of its lower walls; it
smelled of dust and tea and sweat. Suddenly it rocked
under her hand. Someone jumped down from inside
and looked around the end wall at her, then leaned back
to speak tensely to a hidden companion. Another face
appeared.

"That's no woman, that's a fem—look at the butt
and legs on her, sprinter's muscle. You know these wild
people never walk if they can ride, let alone run
anywhere."

"Then it's her," said the long-faced one.

"She's young," said the other, shaking back dark
hair, eyes measuring Alldera from head to foot. "Hey,
don't they keep watch on you? Where's your guard?"

"I have no guard." Alldera stood where she was, suddenly wary. The two had a predatory look.

"You mean you're not a prisoner? We came to rescue
you, fem."

It was too late to pretend that they were wrong, that
she was a Riding Woman. "No one's held me prisoner,"
Alldera said. "I live like the others here." She realized
that it would be a mistake to tell them she had not
learned of their existence until today. She could picture
their sneers at that, their knowing glances.

One said, "Don't tell us you've just been living here
contented as one of their stupid horses, ignoring your
own people." Their hatred of the women came off them
like heat.

"Come on, what are you waiting for?" the long-
faced one said. "Get into the wagon, quick, while
nobody sees. We'll go get a few of the others, haul off
as if we were going to make an early camp for the night,
and just keep on going. The rest will catch up. Then let
those Mares come galloping after us and try to take you
back!"

Alldera moved a few steps back toward the tents, alarmed by visions of blood and battle.

"Where are you going?" The black-haired one closed in on her.

Alldera glanced around for help, a witness, anything. She heard the long-faced fem say low-voiced to the other, "Look at that, they must have bewitched her to keep her from us."

Too late, Alldera bolted.

They sprang after her. A spear shaft thrust between her legs brought her down with a racking pain in her shin. She could not help it, she lay and hugged her leg, and they dropped their weapons and took hold of her, lifting her toward the wagon.

"You explain to Elnoa back at the tea camp," the black-haired fem growled. "We want to know why they've kept you from us, and everything you know about them. Nobody's lived among them as long as you have, we need your information."

"You can't take me!" Alldera cried through tears of pain, as if in a nightmare that they meant to take her to their master. "Let me stay—" A hard hand clamped over her mouth, cupped to avoid her teeth.

"Mare lover!" spat one of the fems.

As they wrestled her back against the tail of the wagon, trying to heave her inside, something jarred a cry from the one on her left. The other fem gasped and let go. Alldera twisted free. Sprawled on the ground, she heard the thump of blows, saw the frenetic figures of children leaping up from the tall grass to fling stones at the fems.

She looked up at the black-haired fem's angry face squinting at her from inside the wagon where the two of them had taken shelter. She heard furious words: "Come in here, curse you, while you have the chance! Come on, what is it, you like these horse-fuckers, these dirty, rag-tag savages that bathe in their own sweat, dirty beasts, cock-worshippers—"

The wagon rattled and shook with the impact of the

childpack's missiles. The long-faced fem paused for breath. There was blood on her cheek and a bruise swelling where a stone had hit her.

"Have they gone and mated you to one of their stallions, then?" she cried. "You got fucked by a horse and you like it, is that what's happened?"

Alldera got up and ran. The childpack raced past her, touching, laughing, and vanished.

Curled around her own misery and confusion, she lay in the tall grass on a rise outside the camp, watching from hiding until the free fems had packed up their goods and left. They moved the wagon out, pulling it in the midst of a ring of scouts like women moving camp. The scouts, on foot, did not go any great distance from the wagon, perhaps for fear of losing sight of one another behind a swell of ground.

From the rise Alldera listened to the sounds of evening descending on Stone Dancing Camp. As women lit their tea fires, voices spoke and laughed. Riders came home from settling the horses on night pasture. Each sang a personal song that identified her to the woman who met her with a bowl of food and who took from her the mounts she had brought to be tethered in camp for the night.

Alldera recognized Nenisi's self-song. She saw Nenisi ride in and give something to Barvaran: a bundle in a leather sling. That was what she had gone to do, then: take the child further out of camp while the free fems were there.

Alldera got up and limped down toward camp. Nenisi came out on foot to meet her. They stood beyond the outermost tents in the dusk.

"Where have you been? I've been looking for you," Nenisi said. "They've gone. That's their fire, way over there." A wasteful blaze. "You look upset. What did they say to you?"

"How many are there like them?" Alldera said.

"Maybe half a hundred, all free fems found by us in the borderlands, as you were found."

So many, all this time. "They said I was a prisoner here."

"Sit down with me, let's talk. They themselves are the prisoners—not of us, but of the way things are. They say they wish to return to the Holdfast, invade it, save the fems there. They live in a camp of their own in the foothills and make preparations to go home. When they venture too far toward the Holdfast, our patrols turn them back. This makes them bitter against us.

"But anyone can see that it would be foolish of us to go and show ourselves to the men of the Holdfast or let the fems go back and speak of us there, when we've kept the secret of our existence from men for so long. Even if there are only a few men left—and many of us feel that—we have a right to protect ourselves; don't you think so?"

Alldera realized guiltily that she had accepted that desert, too, as she had accepted that the free fems were a myth. She said, "You took me in among you; why not the free fems too?"

"You have a child here; kindred. The free fems aren't related to anyone."

"Why didn't you tell me about them before?"

"Why would you need to know? We are your family. Anyway, you never asked." A sigh of defeat. "Maybe not telling you was a mistake."

"How can they be so different that you can't take them in among you?"

"Their beginnings and ours differ," Nenisi said. "Around the onset of the Wasting that ruined the world of the Ancients, there was made a place called the lab, where the government men tried to find new weapons for their wars. We don't know just what they were looking for, but we think it was mind powers, the kind that later got called 'witchery.' The lab men—and lab women, who had learned to think like men—used females in their work, maybe because more of them had traces of the powers, maybe because it was easier to get them with so many men tied up in war."

Alldera tore at the grass with her hands. "Nenisi, is

this going to be another tale of slavery?'' What she
wanted to say, and could not bring herself to say, was
Why did you hide my cub, and why did they say you
mate with horses—Barvaran had said that too, once.

"It's all right, this story has a happy ending," Nenisi
said softly. "The lab men didn't want to have to work
with all the traits of both a male and a female parent, so
they fixed the women to make seed with a double set of
traits. That way their offspring were daughters just like
their mothers, and fertile—if they didn't die right away
of bad traits in double doses.''

"I don't understand," Alldera said. "How could
they do that?''

"Who knows?" Nenisi sounded a little impatient.
"No one denies that the men of those times were clever.
It was the combination of their cleverness and their
stupidity that caused the Wasting in the first place.

"Now, in the lab, the change of trait-doubling was
bred into the daughters, to be passed on ever since.''

"To you.''

"Yes. The daughters got together and figured out
how to use the men's information machines. They
found out all about the Wasting, the wars and famines
and plagues going on outside, and how the lab could be
made self-sustaining if things outside collapsed completely. They laid plans of their own.

"They got the information machines to give a false
alarm warning of an attack in the offing and ordering
the lab men to rush off to the Refuges and save themselves. The lab men believed the orders; they knew the
leaders were already hidden in Refuges made for themselves and their helpers, and the lab men had high ideas
of their own importance. So off they went with great
speed and excitment.''

She paused. Alldera thought, giving me time to take it
in, treating me like some stupid hulk of a free fem.
"Tell me the rest, please," she said, to show that she understood.

Nenisi cleared her throat. "I'm used to talking about
this with young girls just out of the pack. I hope it

doesn't sound childish to you.

"Anyway, the first daughters sealed themselves up safely in the lab and using the information machines began to plan for after the Wasting. They took the lab animals and tried to breed them to be ready to live outside when the world was clean again. A lot of animals were let out too soon and died. The sharu were bred up from some tiny animals the men had been using to find out about ferocity, and once let out they flourished—an unhappy surprise, but not bad in the long run. Sharu have their place too."

Alldera had seen sharu tracks, the splintered bones of sharu kills, the torn-up areas which they had stripped even of grass roots in their voracity. They horrified her, and she could not imagine what sort of "place" they could have.

"There were horses at the lab for making medicines with their blood. Some of the lab men had also kept good horses of their own in the lab stables. But the horses' chances were poor. They bred slowly, and they were delicate from living so many generations with humans to take care of them. The daughters made them tougher and faster-breeding without worrying about their looks, and the horses came out and flourished too—a happy surprise."

"And what did they do for themselves, these great witches," Alldera said, "so that they could breed without men?"

"Not witches, but dedicated and intelligent women," Nenisi continued carefully, almost formally. "They perfected the changes the labs had bred into them so that no men were needed. Our seed, when ripe, will start growing without merging with male seed because it already has its full load of traits from the mother. The lab men used a certain fluid to start this growth. So do we."

Simple and clean, compared to rape in the Holdfast. No wonder jealousy drove the free fems to slander. "Nenisi, why do you keep me with you? I'm no more like you than those other fems are."

"You brought us a live child. Only one other fem did that, and that child we couldn't save. Your child is alive; that makes you kin to us."

Her slim fingers brushed Alldera's very lightly. "We change little, do you understand? Some, of course: the Wasting left slow, strong poisons in the earth and water of the world. They sometimes alter a child from its mother's traits. We don't try to judge whether a change is good or not. The child survives the childpack or not, that's all. Sometimes a cousinline, even a whole Motherline, is lost. No new ones are gained, only variations of the old."

"Then my cub—"

"New seed, new traits, the beginning of the first new Motherline since our ancestors came out of the lab. That's how important your child is to us. My ancestor, a woman almost exactly like me, stepped out of the lab and lived, and now though she's generations dead there are many of us Conors. So it will be for your child's blood descendants."

She sounded moved by what she said, and still she was blind to how every word she spoke folded in Alldera's child but shut out Alldera herself. Alldera turned on her in the darkness: "But it's a Holdfastish cub, with dam and father! How can it be like you? You're raising a free fem among you, that's all."

"No, we don't think so. When you came to us, that child was still forming inside you. We made you sleep to rest and strengthen you both. We fed you the milk of our breasts and the food chewed in our mouths, the food of Motherlines that we feed our babies. We fed your child, through your blood while she was still in your womb. We think she's become like our own children. We still feed her—that's why we do all her nursing. You see how healthily she grows, how fast, just like other babies here. We don't have our forebears' wisdom or the wonders of the lab to change her to be like us, but we've tried to do it with what we have."

"So you hid her from the free fems." Why did that make Alldera uncomfortable. The women had saved the cub's life, they had fed it their food, they had made it theirs.

Nenisi said, "What sort of life would she have among a dying race?"

"Well, what life will she have with you if she turns out to be barren without men, like the free fems?"

Nenisi answered quickly, "It would still be better. There are those among us who have no children, out of necessity or by choice. They still have relatives, sharedaughters, kindred. Do you see? Does that satisfy you?"

Alldera could not explain without sounding selfish and ungrateful; if she had known about the free fems sooner, she would have had a chance to consider the cub's future as if there were choices to be made about it. The women had not kept the free fems' existence secret from her, exactly; their plans as Nenisi outlined them were clearly good ones, probably the best choice that could have been made anyway. Alldera saw no way to voice her unease, nor even exactly what there was to object to.

Nenisi got up. "Come to the tent soon, there are sharu wandering tonight." She left.

The stars threw a dim light by which Alldera could dimly see the wide tents. The fems' wagon was invisible. Their fire had gone out. It was true, she thought, their road came from destruction and led to destruction, and if she found herself fortunate enough to be on another path, why turn back? She reminded herself of the prime lesson of a slave's life: protect yourself, be selfish.

Next morning she put on her belt with the knife sheathed in back and she said, "Nenisi, will you teach me to ride?"

Nenisi grinned. "I was afraid you'd never ask."

Alldera, responsible today for raking out horse dung to dry into usable fuel, was late to the chief tent and had to sit outside with the overflow. They were debating not the usual personal complaints beyond the abilities of the families and Motherlines to settle, but a diplomatic matter: whether or not to accept the offer of some grazing rights from neighboring Red Sand Camp. Women feared that Red Sand would come around later—as they had done to another camp in the past—and say the grass had been a loan, and demand repayment. In such a discussion Nenisi Conor would surely speak.

The tea bowl was handed round; Alldera sipped and passed it on. Listening was thirsty work. Sometimes she thought the Shawdens were chiefs because they could afford to serve endless rounds of tea to half the camp day after day. It was certainly not because they took the lead in anything.

The slow, oblique movement of debate was mesmerizing. She remembered the way the men—and fems, imitating men—had decided things, quickly, by command. Here, anyone with something to say could speak, which made for long hours of exhaustion or entertainment, depending on the interest of a given case. Their ease at speaking their minds still awed her. She sometimes spoke herself now, of grass and horses, over the evening tea fire; she sought to share their free flow of conversation.

She nibbled at a callus that had formed on her hand from the pressure of the rein. Many months' work had made her a decent rider, but she was not yet familiar enough with horses to make one lie down and doze, like that Faller woman over there, so that she could curl up against its flank and stay warm. Never mind, by midday the sun would strengthen and they would all be shedding headcloths, shirts, breast wraps.

At last Nenisi arose. No one interrupted as her calm, reasonable voice recounted the history of feeling between both camps. She said, "Sharu have ravaged our northern pasture. What will you do when you hear your horses wandering and calling in hunger at night in the Dusty Season? Our friends and sisters and cousins, our daughters and mothers in Red Sand Camp say, take this gift of grass.

"Now, is Red Sand Camp the same this season as the

Red Sand that broke down the walls of new wells sunk by Steep Cloud Camp because those wells were too close to Red Sand grass? Or is it the same as the Red Sand that gave forty horses to Salt Wind Camp the year that poison grass wiped out half of Salt Wind's herds?

"There are new families in Red Sand since both those times. How many here have sisters and other close kin now in Red Sand Camp that did not have them there five years ago; two years ago; last year? A woman is constant in her actions through her life according to her traits until at last she dies. But a camp changes all the time as its women come and go, and it lives forever."

When she drew her headcloth about her and sat down again, no one applauded. But speaker after speaker got up and gave another version of what she had said, until those opposed to accepting the gift gave in and made the same sort of speech themselves. One woman next to Alldera shook her head and murmured, "Those Conors are always right."

Alldera sat straight and smiling, warm with admiration, rejoicing in her own unbelievable good luck in having Nenisi for her friend.

Walking with the black woman later—Nenisi was cutting reeds for arrows—Alldera said, "I'm proud to hear you speak at the chief tent. I wish you did it more often."

"Oh, women are perfectly able to do without the Conors' nagging most of the time, and we don't believe in wasting our influence or growing self-indulgent by too much talking. We take care to be selective. I could have mentioned today a time when Stone Dancing Camp women themselves behaved very badly toward a neighbor camp. Of course there was the excuse that we hadn't yet recovered from one of the earth tremors that give this camp its name, but it was long before my time and no one really knows for certain what was in women's minds. . . . Anyway, bringing that up just would have caught everyone up in an old argument, and nothing would have been decided about Red Sand for days yet.

"I see you sitting at the chief tent often these days, as I pass by on other business."

"I like to hear women talk about family situations," Alldera admitted. "In case. Well, in case Sheel's nastiness gets unbearable. I want to be able to go and speak there for myself."

Nenisi straightened from examining a strand of reeds. "Tch," she said, "you've been managing her meanness very well lately, it'll never come to that."

As she cut the reeds she began singing her self-song, addressing the reeds as if identifying herself with them.

> You know me.
> In the Gather of the blind foal year I put eight arrows into the air, one behind the other, before the first fell to the ground.
> You know me.
> My mother Tesh Periken taught me to bite out a colt's balls with my good front teeth. The horse scarcely swells, the wound never festers, but I'm one of those whose teeth hurt her a lot. Is it the geldings' revenge? I say, do your own gelding, but use your knife.
> You know me.
> If you offer me sausage of fine fat and berries, I'll eat it all up and leave you nothing but my belches.
> You know me.
> I helped Tomassin Hont to cure the finest sharu hide she ever took, I put my scraper right through it, I was so much help.

There was a lot more; Alldera found herself laughing. "How can you say such things about yourself?"

"The Conors may be always right, but I don't mind reminding everybody that Nenisi Conor can be as wrong as anybody else." Nenisi handed her more reeds. "Every woman needs her own personal history."

Alldera looked over to where the grazing horses were visible, drifting against the skyline that ran forever, flat and broad.

"In all this space," she said, "I suppose everything that helps tell one person from another or one place from another is very important."

The black woman straightened again and smiled. "It's good, the way you see in fresh ways the things that are old to me. But things which unite us in all this space are also very important." She wiped her knife and sheathed it. Then she took off her belt and dropped it to the ground. "Come sit here." She pulled Alldera down on the sand beside her, pushed away the bundle of reeds, and, laughing, slipped her arm around Alldera's neck.

Alldera yielded uncertainly, was pressed to Nenisi's sharp-boned side.

"Don't be nervous," Nenisi murmured. "We're together, that's all; friends. No one is master of the other. We do what we like, and we stop when we like. No need to be shy about your scars—give me your hand. A sharu sliced my ribs once when I was being foolish, and feel this great ridge I'm left with! We Conors can't hide our mistakes, we scar badly; no wonder we try not to make any." Now when she laughed the sound was richer, roughened with excitement. "You and I will learn to cherish each other's faults."

They made love together. Alldera asked no questions. She had felt shut out from the women's constant patting and clasping and stroking of one another; at the same time their closeness had offended her.

Now she wanted nothing to intrude on the joy of touching and being touched, freely and sensually. It was a triumph to feel Nenisi's cabled body loosen and flow as she held it. Her own limbs slackened and trembled when Nenisi stroked her, seeking out the sensitive places that turned the light tickle of fingers into a deep, sinking sweetness almost too intense to be borne.

That night she lay awake in Nenisi's bedding, warm and drowsing, for a long time. As she snugged herself close against the smooth curve of Nenisi's back, she thought of the Holdfast fems. There had been some moments of passionate contact, usually in a corner of the crowded room that served as night quarters for the members of her master's femhold. She remembered tension, haste, the need for silence. The others would thump you in the head to keep you quiet so that they could get the sleep they needed for the next day's work . . . bad dreams out of a hideous life, but rich with excitement and danger.

She remembered a pretty fem, only recently demoted from pet status for some trifling error or other, the only really pretty partner Alldera had ever had. In the dark tangle of their embrace, this one had thrust an object into Alldera's hand, begging her in a smothered voice to use it, to root in her body with it like a man. Alldera had tried to break the wooden phallus against the bars of the window. Others had pulled her down; don't let the little pervert upset you, they'd said.

That memory had no power to hurt her. She was a woman now. She pressed her cheek to the back of Nenisi's neck, breathing in the faintly musky scent and feeling the giddy joy of her own liberty.

In the Holdfast Alldera had been a messenger trained to run. She had not run in some three years now. That Cool Season she took it up again. It was hard. Months of riding had firmed up new muscles and slackened others.

She ran with the horizon flowing past on one side and the tents of camp wheeling by on the other, and she thought of other runners she had known in the Holdfast; like great Kanda of the long, thin legs who ran with a tireless, bounding stride, her hands flapping loosely at waist height as if she exerted herself no more than the wind does when it blows. Not thought of in all this time; dead now, probably.

Women came to look as Alldera ran, clearly not comprehending her devotion to this outlandish way of making herself sweaty and exhausted on her own two feet. Sometimes she pushed herself, happily showing off for them.

6

In time her gladness dimmed.

"There has been strain between us these past months," Nenisi said one morning.

Alldera said nothing. She had felt the safety and happiness of their closeness wearing away for some time, and had not known what to do.

"The Rainy Season is nearly over," the black woman continued. "The seed grasses are tall in the gullies. Leave your running for a while, and come grain gathering with me. We need some time alone."

That would be good, Alldera thought gratefully. She would be happier not having to share Nenisi with others. Nenisi's apparent unfaithfulness with women of the camp had been weighing on her mind.

Trailing their spare mounts and pack ponies they rode together into the vast quiet of the plain.

On the first morning, Alldera brought herself at last to speak. She wished that her cheeks would not grow so hot with embarrassment. Taking the tea bowl that Nenisi offered, keeping her eyes on it, she said as quickly as she could that she appreciated so much having Nenisi to herself finally, knowing there was no other bed waiting to be warmed by Nenisi's body.

Very quietly Nenisi said, "Alldera, I want you to understand something about us here. It's a sickness to fix on only one person and keep everyone else out. It's as if to say, only I and my lover are true women, the rest of you are false and worthless.''

"You think it's sick, but—"

"Listen. You should find some other women to love, too. Do you want me to wear myself to nothing, trying to be all the women in the camp to you?''

"I don't want all the women in the camp."

The black woman sighed and drank from her bowl. "You will have to learn, but not from me. For us two to talk about this will only lead to quarreling. But I will show you how we think of love so you can see it, all right?'' She made a scooping motion over the surface of the ground by her knee and thrust out her hand, showing a little clutch of pebbles in her dark-lined palm.

"Look, here is womanness. Why should we separate from each other two by two? What makes it right for two to be alone, when it's not right for one to be?''

There was some sort of sense in it; if one bit of smooth gray gravel stood for Barvaran, say, then another just like it would be Barvaran's mother, and another her daughter. The rest would be cousins in her Motherline, all alike. If someone—if Nenisi—loved Barvaran, how avoid loving all the others?

"It's different where I come from," Alldera muttered, and was relieved that Nenisi did not press her.

The women liked to make noise out in the open, Alldera had noticed, asserting themselves against the emptiness. Nenisi sang and talked incessantly as they rode. Eventually Alldera plucked up the courage to try on her the self-song that she had composed:

I don't look like anyone here.
    Where I come from there were many like me, sweating fear.
    That's left behind, but I lived it.
    Our heads were bent because we couldn't look our masters in the eyes. We just sidled by, nursing our lives along.
    That's left behind—

*   *   *

Nenisi said suddenly, "No, that's not the idea at all. That song is all about fems, not about yourself."

"I was trying to please you," Alldera said. She wished she knew why things kept going wrong between them.

Day after day they rode the muddy watercourses, shaking the heavy seed heads from the grass on the banks into baskets fastened over their horses' shoulders. One afternoon Alldera spoke of the fems of the Holdfast, harvesting hemp plants under the whips of their overseers.

Again Nenisi interrupted her: "Why think about that? It's over."

"Nenisi, no one ever asks me about the Holdfast—very considerate of them all; or is it that nobody is interested? It is part of my past, part of my life."

"No. This is all of your life." Grass stems bent, heads of grain rattled into the baskets. The black woman said, "I hate to see you unhappy. I think that maybe I treat you a little like a child sometimes, and you don't like it. That's good, that you don't like it. Only to me you are still something of a child. While you drifted in healing sleep, you sucked milk from me like a baby. And you are not done learning to be a woman. Look how well you ride, better all the time; and Barvaran is making a stronger bow for you when we get back, instead of that child's bow you've been using."

"I wasn't wakened from a nightmare, you know," Alldera said. "The first life was real too. It's as you say—like being born twice."

Nenisi looked at Alldera sideways from her eyes with the warm-stained whites, the centers like wet dark stones. "I'll try to remember that you're growing out of your childhood."

When the deep arroyos were swept clean Nenisi refused to work the shallow ones on foot. "Leave something for the sharu," she said.

The trip to the granaries, low buildings by the Dusty Season wells, took days of driving the laden pack horses before them. Then they had to fill the granary bins and baskets with the gathered seed heads.

"Won't the sharu dig their way in here?" Alldera said, kicking at the thick mud wall.

"Sometimes they do."

"You could have someone stay here to keep them off. And then you'd have seeds enough to plant—there's plenty of water on the ground in the Rainy Season—and grow more grain."

Nenisi threw out her hands in a gesture of incomprehension. "More for what? We gather enough seed heads for the horses and for our flour. If we had more—well, there'd soon be too many horses to feed and care for and milk. Women aren't slaves to tend the earth. We just live here as best we can."

"It's stupid to do things this way when there's a better way."

"Make your suggestion at the chief tent," Nenisi said, thrusting out her dark lips in irritation. "As a woman does."

No woman would let Alldera give to her. Angrily Alldera slammed her shoulder against the wooden door, wedging it tightly into its frame to keep out the animals that would only burrow in under the walls instead.

Close to Nenisi that night and fearful of sharu—for they had found recent sharu sign at the granaries—Alldera shivered.

"Cold?" Nenisi said, turning toward her.

"This isn't cold," Alldera said. "I'm scared of Sharu. Let me tell you a story now about real cold, Holdfast cold. One winter evening I went to a certain company in Lammintown on my master's business. Out in the icy pen by the men's hall the company fems piled together to sleep under the stars, and I was put in with them. It was near the shore, and all night a raw wind blew. In the morning two fems were found frozen, hugged in each other's arms, by the gate. They must have hoped to get at the soup pot first in the morning. Mother Moon, how my master lit into the young men in charge of the fems for putting his trained runner in danger of freezing to death!"

Nenisi said, "Why didn't all you fems break into the hall and throw the men out to freeze?"

There just wasn't any point in trying to explain. Alldera turned over and tried to sleep.

When they got back to Stone Dancing she found that something important had happened in their absence. Every year the women held a Gather of all the camps. When pressed, Barvaran said it was a sort of social meeting, with games and political arrangements about horses, grass and water, and so on. Alldera had gone through her first Gather all unknowing in healing sleep, and last year only a few families from Stone Dancing had attended, for some reason too complicated and obscure for Alldera to unravel.

"Not everyone in a camp can go every year," Barvaran said. "There are always other things that need doing around the same time."

And that was all that she, or anyone, would say about it.

She came fighting out of sleep to find the tent shaking with the aftermath of swift action. The poles were quivering, but no one was left inside in the dim predawn light but herself and old Jesselee. The others were nothing but faint cries and a dwindling drumbeat of hooves.

"What is it?" Alldera stood in her bedding, her knife in her hand, her pulse ringing in her head, thinking of Holdfast men swooping down on the camp to take slaves—

"Raiders," said Jesselee. "It's got to be a party from White Wind Camp. I heard that Poleen Sanforath of Steep Cloud Camp is visiting family up there—did I ever tell you how she hid a prize mare in her tent one night, when she and what's her name, from down at Towering, were raiding rivals? She's been after that red stud of Sheel's for years. I wonder what else they got?

"Well, there are chores to be done. Leave the child with me, you go on ahead and pull the bedding outside to air."

Alldera guessed the old woman had noticed how little

interest she showed in the child. Well, it was their child; Nenisi had made that very clear.

Returning from work at midday Alldera found meat, milk and flour noodles stewing in a pot over the fire. She filled her bowl half full. It was early in the Dusty Season, and already women were eating small while waiting for the first rains and their supply of fresh milk. Alldera no longer accepted oversized guest portions.

"You eat like a Riding Woman," Jesselee said approvingly. "Now you won't weigh down your horse."

"What difference does it make?" Alldera said moodily. "When it's something important like a Gather or a raid, I get left behind."

Jesselee shifted the child in her arms. It was long-limbed now, a heavy burden. It belched and muttered sleepily to itself. Jesselee said, "I wish I could have gone too, but it isn't fair to load down a pursuit party with a rider who might die on them."

And what about me, stuck here with all the work and an old woman's ramblings to listen to?

"I'm getting weak. Your baby has more teeth than I do and better ones too. It's a sad thing to have to ask other women to chew your meat for you because you can't manage for yourself any more."

Alldera swished water in her bowl and drank. "Then you must be farther gone than I thought," she said brutally, hoping the old woman would retreat into silence.

"I make my way along, not too fast or too slow." The creaking voice took up the theme, sounding calm and even contented. "After I live my life and die, I'm still part of my Motherline, with women of my flesh before me and behind me. Death is nothing to get excited about.

"I remember, I can still hear the Hanashoshes who fought against their own deaths, every one of them screaming and yelling like gutshot sharu. Strange women. They said they had the right to act how they liked about their own deaths."

Alldera warmed to these women who had insisted on meeting death their own way, no matter what other women did. "Are they those yellow-skinned women, there's one now in Calpaper Tent?"

"No, no, that's a Tayang. The Hanashoshes died out." Jesselee snickered, as if the hard diers' dying out amused her.

The stillness of the camp played on Alldera's nerves. She looked outside angrily. "Almost everyone's gone. The raiders could double back and attack the camp; there'd be hardly anyone to defend it."

Jesselee grunted, chewing slowly and loudly. "Don't be foolish, who'd attack a camp? Where's the honor in stealing other women's cooking pots?"

"Well, they still didn't all have to run off and leave us everything to do here today."

"What do you expect? Women get itchy after several Dusty Seasons without a single raid. Did you think we lived such a quiet life all the time?"

Women get itchy, and I get to do the tent work, Alldera thought. Well, I won't. She said, "I heard that the raiders came and went before moonrise last night. How can our riders catch them?"

"Things are dry enough so the raiders will have to stop to water the horses. Our women will try to get to the wells first, on the raiders' way home, and hold them up—our horses back in exchange for water."

Jesselee put the child in the cradle and with a little urging was soon absorbed in working out for Alldera the likeliest route to White Wind Camp. Alldera got it all, maps in the dirt and even a history lesson: "Right here it was, I got caught sneaking up on Red Sand Camp all by myself, trying to grab Meryan Golashamet's prize dun mare, and oh, she gave me such a licking—! I was an arrogant child, I wouldn't promise to give up on that horse."

When she knew all she needed to know, Alldera grabbed up food and water, weapons and tack, and ran outside to saddle the one horse left with them, Dark Tea. Jesselee shouted after her, but she rode away.

From a long way off she saw them, two rough lines of women brandishing their broad-bladed knives at each other over about thirty meters of bare ground. Behind one of the groups the stolen horses were being held by two riders.

Someone dashed out into the open space between the two lines of women. Alldera, galloping down a long roll of grassy ground, heard the voices shrilling high and the whickering of horses.

The lone rider curvetted her mount there in the open, standing in her stirrups to yell at the smaller group, the raiders. She rode up and down between the two ranks, she flung down her knife and threw out her arms, shaking her fists. Shouts, whistles, some movement among the White Wind women. The rider leaned down and scooped up her weapon and rode back to her own line.

Alldera thought of her bow, but the range was too great for her from a horse's back.

Someone had seen her, rode hard to meet her—Nenisi, her dark skin smeared with dirt and sweat. Pulling up beside Alldera in a flurry of dust she cried, "What are you doing here? You shouldn't have left all the tent work on Jesselee's back!"

"Why do I have to be the one to stay behind?"

"You're not fit yet to fight women!"

Swallowing anger and disappointment, Alldera shot back. "You aren't fighting either, and we outnumber them."

"Of course we're fighting! Sheel has already taken Noralen Clarish captive—see her, she's that one that's almost as dark as I am. They had a fine fight, you'll hear all about it tonight in the chief tent." Nenisi looked wild with excitement, her eyes flashed wide.

Below, two riders now circled each other between the opposing ranks, guiding their horses with their legs, buffeting and cutting at each other. One had a small hide shield; the other had whipped off her headcloth and wound it around her arm, and she deflected blows with that.

"You stay here," Nenisi commanded. "I'm going back—the raiders are tired and thirsty, they'll break and run any minute."

Down below, one of the fighters' horses stumbled to its knees but she pulled it up again and rode back into her own group.

Eager now herself to join in, Alldera said, "I'll string my bow and pick them off from here as they run."

Nenisi drew rein so suddenly that her horse reared, and a gout of foam from its mouth landed wetly on Alldera's knee. "Never!" said Nenisi in a furious voice that struck Alldera silent. "Do you see a bow in my hand, in any hand down there? What kind of coward are you, to suggest cutting down women from a safe distance?"

"But they're enemies," Alldera cried, shrinking back.

"What enemies? Those are women. What could you do with a bow except kill dishonorably and bring a feud on your line? That's what a bow is for—a feud; or for the borderlands."

Then Alldera remembered Barvaran in the desert that time years ago, raising a bow toward her before realizing that she was not a man but a fem. She wanted to speak, but she was flooded with confusion.

In a roar the women of Stone Dancing charged. Nenisi whirled her mount and raced away, angling to cut off a fleeing White Wind rider.

Alldera sat where she was while Dark Tea blew and sighed beneath her. She watched the sprawling indiscipline of the battle with slow-dawning bitterness. These were not warriors destroying enemies who had treated them unjustly, but wild women brawling over prizes.

The struggling mass broke into small skirmishes and pursuits. The stolen horses, unheeded, streamed down into a gully and away. Within moments of the charge only one pair of riders was visible, locked together and heaving at each other while their mounts plunged under them and carried them out of sight behind a fold of land.

In time women came drifting back toward the well, several of them riding double on droop-headed horses —captives, Alldera assumed, or tent mates picked up after being unhorsed. Some riders drove horses before them. One woman rode in holding her bloody arm and reeling in the saddle. Her friends closed in quickly to support her.

Alldera turned Dark Tea back toward camp, hard-handed with anger so that the horse fought the bit. How could they shut her out of this game, she who had fought real war all her life?

Riding alone, she made speeches in her head till her throat was raw with the parching from her breath, and her eyes pricked with tears: who has more courage, who has endured more? While you rode and hunted and hugged each other here, men beat me and starved me, a man threw me down on my back in the mud and fucked me and made me eat dirt to remind me how much power he had over me. I fought back when I could, I escaped. How many of you would have killed yourselves or gone crazy with despair?

But there was no one to make speeches to, not unless she wished to go address them that night when they reveled in the chief tent. The drumming and shouting rang right through the walls of Holdfaster Tent, where she stayed, thinking, arguing with herself.

After a while she went to join them, whether to speak out or not she did not know.

Just outside the chief tent someone touched her arm and said, "Wait, we want to talk to you."

Four women surrounded her. By the dim glow coming through the chief tent wall she recognized a young woman of Barvaran's bloodline. Another was a blotch-skinned Monotay, and she did not know the other two.

One took her arm. "You showed a keen edge, Alldera Holdfaster, riding to our battle. You're not the dry old stick we took you for."

The Monotay whispered, "Come into the long grass with us tonight." There were sounds of approval from the others.

Someone slid an arm around Alldera's waist; she stiffened.

"You're shy," the Monotay said admiringly.

The young one who looked like Barvaran said in a coaxing voice, heavy and slow, "Come on, Alldera. Nenisi has told us what a fine, sweet lover you are."

Alldera pulled free and fled. She ran to Holdfaster Tent, rolled herself into Barvaran's empty bedding and held very still. Someone entered, went over to where Alldera normally slept, and left again. Alldera heard the sound of a muffled conference outside, and that was all.

Come to me, Nenisi—the threads holding me here to you are breaking, she wept.

The winds of the Dusty Season blew hot and hard; there was not going to be enough grass for all the horses. The women could not wait and let some horses starve. They had to butcher some while they were still fat, to save more grass for the survivors and to get the most meat from the slaughter for themselves. It was like this most years.

"I want you to come help me with this," Nenisi said to Alldera. "I think we've been leaving you out of too much of our lives."

Sadly and tortuously the women of Holdfaster Tent debated which horses to slaughter. They chose males and weak or barren females, animals that could not help increase the herd again when times were better. They chose many, and Alldera saw how it hurt them. She asked at one point why the women did not get their meat by killing sharu instead.

There was an appalled silence. Alldera did not wait for Nenisi to step in on her behalf, but said as calmly as she could, "I think I've said something wrong. I apologize for my ignorance."

She had the satisfaction of hearing old Jesselee mutter, "Well said," but Sheel snarled, "No one eats sharu but the filthy free fems. They eat the flesh of scavengers because they're scavengers themselves. Go to them for a taste."

"Heartchild," Jesselee chided mildly, "you speak like a lesser woman than Alldera." To Alldera she added, "The only meat we eat is horses' meat. We eat no sharu because the sharu eat our dead.''

Alldera could not hold back an exclamation of revulsion, and was instantly ashamed. Jesselee expounded thoughtfully on the ability of sharu to find and dig up anything edible that had been buried, and the foolishness of wasting scarce fuel to burn corpses; and Jesselee was nearer than any of them to having her body left for the sharu to devour, thought Alldera, shuddering.

With the other sharemothers Alldera helped to make killing hammers, choosing carefully the stone heads, the wooden hafts, and the sinews to fasten both together. On culling day she went with Nenisi from the place where the herds were being held. Nenisi rode bareback on a colt to be killed. Alldera, on a stolid gray, carried the hammer and a leather bowl. She was apprehensive but reassured herself that a fem from the Holdfast could take any harshness that this plains life had to offer. They went to a sandy dip below a ridge spined with brush. Alldera was instructed to tie her horse securely behind the brush, upwind. Then she walked back down to Nenisi with the tools.

"The hammer," Nenisi said from the colt's back. She took the hammer in both hands and set the colt trotting in a tight curve past Alldera. She was speaking as she rode, addressing the colt in a low, grave tone. Alldera could not hear the words.

Suddenly, all the cords in her arms standing with effort, Nenisi whipped the hammer down on the horse's head.

Even before he stumbled, muzzle to the ground, she was off him and drawing her knife. She threw her weight against his shoulder and he fell heavily onto his side, his breath rushing out in a thick sound, his tongue dragging on the sand. Swiftly she cut into the base of his throat, threw down the knife and reached for the leather bowl, which she held to catch his blood as it streamed from the wound.

Crouching there inside the curve of his neck, still murmuring to him while she bled away his life, she seemed to Alldera to enact an obscene parody of a woman resting curled against her prone and trusting mount. The colt made no further sound at all, but subsided into a graceless, ugly heap.

On shaking legs Alldera walked back to her own horse, to try to soothe its nervousness while she waited for Nenisi. She felt sick and miserable and could scarcely meet Nenisi's eyes when the black woman came up and told her they would leave the dead horse for the team that would come and drag it off to the butchering site. They rode out double on the gray horse to catch a lame mare next. The hands clasped around Alldera's waist were the hands she had just seen wiped clean of blood.

It was as if Alldera was suddenly touched by some raw, cruel current hidden till now under the sunlit surface of the women's lives.

At another dip in the land Nenisi killed the lame mare the same way. She looked up from scrubbing her knife clean with sand and said sharply, "What's the matter? It was a good kill. The next one will be harder—that starfaced gelding." She shook her head. "I helped to get him born, turned him in the womb where he was lying crooked. I nearly got my arm squeezed off doing it."

"Then how can you kill him?" Alldera protested. "Bleeding them to death—"

Nenisi did not look up from the knife again, she did not help. She gave no sign that she hated this horrible work.

As they walked to where Alldera had tied up the gray, Nenisi said at last, "We need the blood, and we use it; it is dried and kept for making broth later in the year. You've drunk it, remember? The death itself is pretty painless, and never carelessly inflicted. Bones, hide, hoofs and hair, nothing goes to waste, and we're grateful for it all."

There was one more horse to kill. Each woman of the tent had one or more assigned to her to slaughter, and Nenisi was doing Alldera's killing as well as her own. Holding the nervous gray, Alldera kept thinking, that

woman loves the horses but she doesn't hesitate to kill
them. I don't love them, and I can't bear to watch.

After the last kill they rode back toward camp to
prepare for a turn at butchering the carcasses. Nenisi
said without emotion, "Do you want Sheel to see you
looking so stunned? Get hold of yourself. You'll kill a
horse yourself, in time."

As Alldera stripped down in the tent, she became
aware of a rider galloping through the camp shouting.
She rushed out and saw the sky above the butchering
ground black with smoke. Grass had ignited from one
of the fires there, the women were yelling. If the wind
shifted, the camp itself would be in danger. Even if not,
vital ranges of grass would be burned.

She helped Nenisi to drag out all the tent's bedding,
ride to the rock pool the camp was using for water, and
throw everything in. Other women were doing the same,
jumping from their horses' backs to trample the
blankets and leathers into the water and get them
saturated. Then with sodden bundles heaped before
them they galloped for the butchering ground and into a
pall of smoke and flying ash.

The soaked blankets were snatched by others who
used them to beat on foot at the margins of the fire.
Everywhere among cooking pots and bones and heaps
of meat and offal, women raced.

"Like this!" Nenisi shouted. She clamped a shank of
rope between her thigh and the saddle, and Alldera did
the same with the rope she was handed. "Ride with me,
keep up, a woman's length apart!"

Leaning against the weight they were hauling, the two
of them fought their horses into a gallop along the edge
of the fire where the beaters had fallen back. The flames
were not very high but they threw off such intense heat
that Alldera felt her lashes and brows curling. Looking
back, she saw what it was they were dragging: the carcass of a horse, split open down the belly and spread
wide to suffocate the fire with its moisture and its
weight. Along the path the carcass made, women on
foot rushed in again with blankets.

The smoke gradually thinned, the fire's roar diminished to a spiteful crackling. Confined within charred boundaries, beaten back from all sides, the flames shrank and spat.

Alldera's horse staggered. She turned over her drag rope to another rider and went off slowly with a load of scorched bedding that needed soaking again.

On her way back with the heavy blankets she saw Nenisi trying to mount a fresh horse, a sidling, rearing mare bridled only with a rope. Alldera hesitated: it was, she knew, something of an insult to help a woman with her horse. But the black woman seemed to be having trouble. Something was wrong with the saddle, and she wound the bridle rope around her wrist to secure it so that she could use both hands on the girth.

The horse shied and leaped, pulling the woman off her feet, and it tore away over the blackened ground dragging her under its battering hooves.

Alldera's howl of anguish was lost in the cries that went up. The fire beaters hurled themselves at the horse, grabbed at the taut rope and were knocked away. Alldera flung down the blankets and galloped after, sobbing, lashing her mount. Her vision was filled by that dark figure jouncing and twisting at full stretch of the one entangled arm.

She heard a whining sound and saw an arrow strike the runaway on the neck, slowing its wild career. Someone raced in ahead of her from the side and with the flash of a knife parted the horse from its dragging burden.

Alldera looked down past the heads of the women standing gathered there. The blackened shape left lying wound in rope was not Nenisi. This was a Calpaper woman, long-limbed like the Conors, dark-skinned and frizzy-haired, made black by soot and now blacker still with char from the burnt stubble over which she had been dragged. The ropes trailing around the sprawled legs were not ropes. They were guts, torn out by the pony's hooves.

The raw, ugly underside of things again. It could have

been Nenisi; she had imagined this corpse was Nenisi, she had nearly burst with terror for Nenisi. Now she burned with resentment, as if her love had been offered all along to a false image—to matchless Nenisi, revealed today as a hard and bloody-handed slaughterer.

Alldera brooded on this often in the weeks that followed, tormented by her sense of having been betrayed. Brutality she had known in the Holdfast; in that life she had been cruel herself by necessity. Here she had thought herself free of that necessity, because she had not seen cruelty among the women.

Now to find brutality in the person she respected most horrified her and made her feel cheated—cheated of the free, clean life she thought she had found.

She had wanted the women to be perfect, and they were not.

She watched Nenisi take chewed food from her own mouth and poke it between the child's lips. Almost too large to carry now for any length of time, the child still nursed but had begun to accept solids. It had been Alldera's own head against that dark, smooth breast once—in her healing sleep when the women had fed her and through her fed her unborn baby. The thought gave her feelings too complicated to unravel, sweet and sour at the same time like everything here.

She studied Nenisi's face, freshly scarred pink over the brow. One of the new ransom horses had snapped at her and broken the skin of her forehead as she jerked back out of the way. Alldera's resentment had faded. Looking at Nenisi, hearing her speak, was what Alldera stayed for these days.

Barvaran was saying something about the next Gather, and spoke Alldera's name.

"Not her," said Sheel firmly and loudly. "That fem is going to the wells."

"To the wells?" Alldera said. "What for?"

"Our ropes drag loose the stones along the tops of the walls. They need mending."

Alldera protested, "Last year I went grain gathering. It's someone else's turn to miss the Gather."

Sheel said, "This year you're one of the well menders. It's not a big job." She did not bother to look up. She was painting in the bodies of running horses that she had first outlined on a pegged-out skin with a burnt twig.

Heatedly Alldera said, "How long are you going to go on maneuvering to keep me from your precious Gather, Sheel?"

"As long as I can."

No one else spoke. Alldera looked at Nenisi, who silently rocked the sprawling child. Sheel's brush dragged on the leather.

They all went out to a shooting contest next day except for Nenisi, who stayed behind with aching teeth. Alldera gave up the place in the contest that she had been practicing hard for and stayed with Nenisi. They talked about the argument of the day before.

"I told you I wouldn't treat you like a child any more," Nenisi said. "You can't fight this out with Sheel, she's in your family. Have you thought some more about bringing her persecution of you up in the chief tent?"

"Not unless I know what a Gather is all about. What happens at the Gathers that Sheel thinks I shouldn't see?"

Nenisi took another mouthful of pain-killing brew and spat it out again. The medicine steamed in a pot between them under the tent fly, souring the air. Finally she said, "You must have guessed. Matings happen."

Alldera frowned. It was a hot day; she wiped at her neck with her headcloth. "What do you mean, 'matings'? You told me that you used some fluid to start your seed."

"The fluid comes from a stallion. We mate with stallions."

Alldera was stunned. She could not think. From where they sat they could see the women out beyond the edge of the camp, shooting at leather targets pegged tightly to the ground. A flight of arrows winked in the air. A moment later came the sounds of impact, like drops of hard rain on a leather wall. Nenisi could not be talking about the archers.

Shakily Alldera began, ''Come on, Nenisi. That's just a thing women tell the fems to shock them, Barvaran even said it to me once—''

''Yes, she told me; she'd forgotten how it seems to strike fems, and she was afraid she'd embarrassed or upset you, so she let it drop. But what she said was true.''

''It doesn't make sense,'' Alldera objected desperately. ''Nenisi, I know that a stallion's cock is as long as your arm. You'd have your guts shoved right out through your mouth if you let one—do that to you.''

Nenisi rubbed at her jaw and said reasonably, ''That would be true, for fems. This is our way; it was worked out for us by the first daughters. They saw that after the Wasting there wouldn't be any places like the lab, and we would need some way to breed simpler than the lab way. So these lab-changed women designed their daughters' reproduction to be set off by the seed of a stallion. Take Shayeen; she has a bloodchild over in Floating Moon Camp. The horse she mated with is not that child's sire; his seed only started Shayeen's seed growing, and Shayeen's seed was complete with Shayeen's traits, no room for any others. We are not half horse, as ignorant free fems tell each other.''

Alldera sat silent, her hands on her knees, looking out at the shooting. She tried, but she could not make sense of what Nenisi said. This horse mating was like a river that Nenisi and the others had just crossed on an inexorable journey that they were making away from her into a mysterious and incomprehensible distance. And not the first river; there had been others, now she recognized them: the childpack, the Motherlines, love without bonds, the brutal killing of horses, warfare as a game, the leaving of the dead for the horrible sharu whom women hunted but also fed. . . . She began to be afraid that all the time she had thought she was catching up with the women, they had been leaving her farther and farther behind, that she would never be able to reach them.

She knew the relaxed pitch of Nenisi's voice was intended to calm her: "Why don't we drop this for now. You could go and watch the shooting."

"I need to understand this," Alldera insisted.

Nenisi cleared her throat. "Let me try to explain. We make the mating as safe as we can. There's a lot of size difference in any generation of colts. We choose them small and arrange things so that full penetration is impossible. Thickness is more the danger than length. As young women we train and exercise beforehand to stretch ourselves. The horses hardly ever tear us."

Alldera felt stifled by this dreamlike amiability of Nenisi. She shut her eyes and saw her beautiful lover coupling with a horse. She saw it as she knew a Holdfast man would see it: as something titillating, Nenisi's dark legs parted by the long pink shaft of a stud reared up and shaking the brambles of his mane above her. It was unbearable to think of Nenisi as gross and comical, she whose body Alldera had stroked and kissed.

"But sure," she stammered, "surely you could—you could get the stallion's seed without—without—and put it in—"

"We don't have such fine lab ways; and if we could do it another way, then it wouldn't mean the same thing. Sheel doesn't want to keep you away to spare your feelings, though we all know how upset fems get about this—you're different anyway, you've lived with us a long time, you'll understand eventually."

She spoke as though in the chief tent, winding up a long debate. "What Sheel says is that you have no place around a mating because you have no bond with the horses. We do have a bond, of our bodies and theirs. The balance of all things includes us and acts on us, and animals—even the sharu in their way—are our links with that balance. We celebrate it every year at the Gather of all the camps, where young women mate.

"The Gather is part of our bond with each other too, you see. Every woman has trusted herself to a horse this way, or is blood kin to another woman who has. Sheel says you can't go raiding either because you might kill someone, and no woman knows what would happen to the spirit of one of us killed by a stranger." She laid her slender hand on Alldera's knee. "You see what I mean by 'stranger.' It would be like—like being killed by some man from the Holdfast. Maybe you shouldn't do your own horse killing either. It's going to take us time to decide."

The more she explained, the more she seemed to recede from Alldera. Gravely, imperturbably, she went on. "You're not bound to us to begin with by being part of an old Motherline, and you won't be truly bound until your bloodchild mates. Shayeen says that meanwhile you should open to a horse yourself even with no chance of issue, but that's absurd, you're not young and flexible enough any more to safely—"

"No, I can't," Alldera gasped. "Why are you talking like this to me? Don't you see I can't follow?"

"Are you worried about your child's mating?" Nenisi said with concern. "Don't be. The stud doesn't attack anyone, he means no harm, no abuse or degradation. He's innocent. He has to be led and coaxed and trained to do his part, with our help. It's nothing at all like a man overpowering a fem just to show her who's master. You've heard me mention my sharemother Sayelen Garriday, who was jumped by her gray stud once, but it turned out—"

Alldera felt as if she were wandering in the Wild again, mystified by a monster's footprint. In a small, exhausted voice she said, "Nenisi, please stop, it's no good. I think it would be better if you would just tell me how to find the free fems."

III
Free Fems

7

Daya loved the sweeping yellow plain. Yet she always enjoyed returning to the tea camp in the foothills. The space and silence of the open country was pleasing only up to a point, for she had lived her whole life among other fems, first in the kit pits and later in her master's populous femhold. Conversation, lively companions and the pleasing tension of intrigue made up her natural surroundings. Her periodic excursions with the trade wagons were passages in a special dream life of loneliness and survival amid elemental forces.

Today the tang of wet weather was in the air, and clouds stood on one another's shoulders obscuring the mountains. She looked forward to the comforts of the tea camp and to seeing Elnoa again. She would be warm with Elnoa, and generous. She could always extend herself to her conquests.

The wagon she walked beside was a sturdy openwork structure of wicker and light wood pulled by a crew of twelve fems. They did not sing as they leaned into the ropes and straps of the harness. They had sung at work as slaves in the Holdfast, and they were free people now. Daya missed the old music.

In the quiet of her own mind she sang a load-carrying song as she walked looking for seasoning plants for the stew pot.

*   *   *

> See how the muscles run in our arms,
> See how the strength swings in our stride.
> What is the weight that we could not carry?
> Where is the riverboat we could not haul?
> Mother Moon, send us a task fit for our power.

Not that Daya herself had ever been a labor fem. She was too small and slight. But she remembered the labor gangs' voices.

Again her thoughts turned eagerly toward camp. Perhaps she would find a tense scene in Elnoa's wagon: she pictured fems' faces lighting with relief to see her, for there lay Elnoa prostrate on the edge of death —losing weight—insisting that to none but Daya would she reveal the hiding place where she hoarded her treasure of precious objects, to none but Daya would she relinquish her great leather account books. . . .

The first free fems to settle here had grouped their wagons under the trees by the spring that flowed down the heart of the narrow valley. The abandoned hulk of an old wagon still marked the spot, a trysting place Daya had often used. By Elnoa's time the camp had been moved to an elevation backed by the southern hills, overlooking the spring and much of the valley. Signs of an effort to build walls of fired mud brick on the hill remained. Daya had heard a tale that the move and the attempt at fortification had been a response to a period of especially tense relations with the Mares.

Elnoa had entrenched the free fems in their higher location. Under her direction they had begun to park their wagons to form a hollow square and to mount a patrol of sentries on the perimeter. Broken-down and tenantless wagons, now used for storage, were interspersed with occupied ones. The spaces between them and the gaps left by wagons gone out trading were filled with temporary walls of rock and brush. This patch-work parapet enclosed a wide, bare yard in which the free fems lived and worked, either in the open or under awnings stretched from the wagon roofs to poles planted in the dirt. There were no trees. Elnoa's own huge vehicle, holding the center of the yard, dominated everything.

On a wet day like this the place looked dead, and Daya quailed a little at the sight of it. What have I come back to? she wondered. Awnings of oiled leather were stretched over racks of smoking tea, some stacked tea bricks, and a pile of raw leaf. The heavy weaving looms were similarly sheltered, looking like big-boned creatures standing gloomily together out of the wet.

While the crew pulled aside a mound of brush to let their wagon through, Kobba, the crew boss, entered the muddy, deserted yard. She paced about heedless of the rain. Daya had noticed that no sentries were walking the perimeter or the skyline above and behind the camp. She knew Kobba would have grim interviews with those she had left on guard. Some would soon sport black eyes and swollen lips. There were always fems foolish enough to ask Kobba what there was to watch for. The Mares patrolled the borderlands to the east, so the men of the Holdfast could never spring a surprise attack. Kobba always said she was not interested in what the Mares did, she was interested in what the fems did, particularly about their own security.

Swiftly the crew parked the trade wagon, checked the lashings of its cover, and climbed into their friends' wagons for shelter, hot beer, and a night of talk.

Elnoa's own wagon was walled with solid wood, elaborately carved and stained. Its immense weight did not matter, since it was never moved. Under the shelter of its eaves Daya wiped the mud from her legs, wondering who would be the present members of the favored circle that Elnoa admitted to her wagon. There were sure to be changes since Daya had left with the trade wagon, two seasons ago. There were always new members Elnoa had introduced, others she had unpredictably discarded.

Beside Daya, Kobba tugged vainly at the knotted thongs of one of her sandals. Rain had swelled the leather. Daya knelt to help. She liked touching Kobba.

Kobba was tall, lanky in the limbs, and blessed with well-formed hands and feet. The skirts of her smock clung wetly to her long, powerful legs. Her belt—a wide strap of leather with an unpolished metal disc for a buckle—fitted slant-wise from one shoulder down between her breasts to her hip, where her hatchet hung on a leather loop. The brim of her broad hat cut on an angle across her face half hiding the ruin of one cheekbone, smashed long ago in a fight. Like most free fems she wore her hair long, flaunting the freedom to grow it for her own pleasure rather than for the profit of a master who sold it to the fur weavers of the Holdfast. Daya kept her own hair shorter, more in Marish style, because it was flattering; but she found a heavy mane like Kobba's attractive.

What a pity Kobba was so uncompromisingly faithful to Elnoa the Green-Eyed. Elnoa and Kobba were long-term lovers despite their separations in the cause of trade. Elnoa indulged herself with others; everyone knew this. No one, not even Kobba, held it against her. They accepted as her natural prerogative the sexual appetite, nourished on power, which they derided in others—Daya, for instance.

Daya went up the slippery steps first and parted the bead curtain in the doorway. Voices from within greeted her as she tried to adjust her vision.

As always, coals glowed in ceramic bowls around the inside of the wagon; Elnoa was easily chilled. The air was thick with aromas of tea and perfume. Elnoa insisted that her people wear strong scents in her presence. She held that freedom meant, among other things, the privilege of breathing air that did not stink of sweat.

Windows of scraped thin leather let in little light and less sound. Daya had helped Elnoa design her quarters to mute the noise of the tea camp. Layers of blankets hung on the walls, masking the sleeping platforms that were raised against the paneling during the day. More blankets carpeted the floor deeply enough for the foot to sink in them. Any wood that showed was so intricately carved that it could scarcely be recognized as a hard surface. The chests and wicker baskets set around the long central space were heaped with pillows of the deep gold and orange tones Elnoa loved. Seven or eight fems, Elnoa's current circle, reclined among them and waved greetings to the newcomers.

Daya took a pillow from a pile by the doorway on her way in. The heat, the syrupy air, the rich colors welcomed and delighted her. She almost forgot, as one was meant to, the outer casing of wood and moved into a warm, cushioned world of hushed voices and languorous privilege. Even the chiefs among the Mares did not live like this. In the Holdfast itself only rich old men could afford to surround themselves with comparable luxury.

Elnoa had been lying on her stomach for a massage. Moving slowly and with great sureness, she sat up and tucked the hem of her embroidered smock down around her legs. Her shape was not flabby but thick and cylindrical, and she leaned on her couch of pillows like a monumental tower against a bank of cloud. Even in the soft, flattering light her skin showed creases at the corners of her mouth and eyes, and gray streaked her hair. In her broad, handsome face her eyes were perfect, brilliant and enormous. Daya envied her those eyes. She did not envy Elnoa's eminence; influence, she knew, was subtler and more versatile than authority.

Elnoa's greeting was in handspeech. Decades ago when she had first bossed her master's femhold, one of the fems under her command had argued and denied a charge of theft instead of taking her punishment with her mouth shut. Following tradition, the master had ordered Elnoa's tongue removed to impress upon her that she was responsible for the silent submissiveness of those she bossed.

"This is a special day, my friends," said Kobba, translating Elnoa's hand signals in a mellifluous, formal tone that she reserved for Elnoa's words. She was Elnoa's voice, a conspicuous luxury since every fem

knew handspeech. "I'm happy to see my friends Daya
and Kobba again. Let them come sit beside me and tell
us the news of the plains."

They talked plains gossip, camp gossip. A fine set of
glazed spitting cups, everyone's favorites, was brought
out. Emla, the masseur, took a bar of fresh, pungent tea
from a storage chest and sliced it. The slivers were
strong-flavored when chewed. Because of the scars on
her cheeks Daya could scarcely chew solid food, let
alone chew tea, without lacerating her own flesh with
her teeth. She tucked her portion into her belt pouch.
Elnoa's tea was good currency.

It pleased her to note that Emla was looking sulky.
She thought, in Elnoa's wagon Emla and I are like two
pans of a scale, one swinging high and the other low,
and then the reverse. Emla, high now, sees me here and
feels the balance shifting.

Mean-mouthed Froya was here, she noted resignedly.
Old Ossa of the milky eyes was still here, homecoming
after homecoming. But not the cheerful, eager fem who
had sung so sweetly and whom Daya had made love to
the night before leaving camp with this trade wagon.
Fems died off year by year, and no new runaways had
come over the borderlands recently to fill the gaps.
Elnoa chose her intimates from among ever smaller
numbers.

Like addicts turning to their drug, the free fems fell to
discussing the plan. The great plan. It was Elnoa's idea.
According to her, the free fems would one day slip past
the Mares' patrols and return to the Holdfast, where
they would infiltrate the population and take over, capturing the men and freeing the fems enslaved there.
Kobba's scouting parties, under the pretense of searching out the best growth of wild tea plants, had
penetrated the borderlands as far as the desert, which
they were secretly mapping. Elnoa's stores of food,
clothing and weapons were essential. When the time to
go drew near, the scouts would distribute Elnoa's stores
in various caches intended to provision and sustain the
whole band of free fems on their route homeward. Just

how this was to be done without drawing the attention of the Marish patrols was not, it seemed to Daya, very clear. The free fems did not have a high opinion of Marish intelligence.

Daya suspected that she was not the only one who thought the plan absurd. The Mares had patrolled the borderlands for generations, preventing the men from learning of their existence and coming over the mountains in force. Marish patrols had never once let a man come as far as the Grasslands; surely they were capable of preventing fifty fems from returning to the Holdfast.

Moreover, those fems who had come out of the Holdfast most recently—years ago now—had brought news of dreadful carnage there as men struggled with each other over ruinously small food supplies. In the years since, no more fems had escaped.

Yet Elnoa's followers chewed tea and discussed their return as if they would find life there much as they had left it.

To Daya it was all a game, but she did not disdain the plan. On the contrary, she admired Elnoa for knowing a useful illusion when she saw one. Elnoa was far too ungainly and soft to make that crossing ever again. She never talked about her own part in the later stages of the plan, and no one ever asked. Daya did not believe for a moment that Elnoa would give them her substance and wave them goodbye, remaining tamely behind to explain their disappearance to the Mares.

But what a fine player the great fem was! She read in signs now from one of her leather books of records, leading off the reports of progress on the plan. She listed how many baskets of dried milk and meat she had added to the permanent stocks from trade with the Mares since her last accounting; how many metal knives and spear points, how many light cotton smocks and leather tunics, how many pairs of thick-soled sandals.

Everyone had a place in the plan. Froya, long-faced and supercilious-looking with her drooping, bruise-colored eyelids, recounted the exploits of her troop of scouts. "We walked farther into the southern section of the desert than ever before,'' she boasted.

There was a report on a new design of water bottles for the homeward journey. Old Ossa spoke quaveringly of her efforts, aided by others whose eyes were better, to make colored maps of the Holdfast so that each returning free fem would have a good idea of the territory in which she was to rouse the slaves.

''What about fighting practice?'' said Kobba.

She got an account of their sessions practicing with spears and hatchets. Daya hid a yawn.

''And running?''

We have a new teacher of running, Elnoa signed. One who came to us just after your wagon left, having at last escaped the Mares who were keeping her among them. Where is Alldera the runner?

''Alldera the crazy,'' muttered old Ossa, and she spat tea juice into her cup which she held up close to her seamed face. ''She's out running in the rain again.''

''Or doing witchery,'' someone else said. ''Who knows what secret magic she learned while she was with the Mares?''

Another: ''She still won't wear sandals as we do. We keep telling her only slaves go barefoot.''

Elnoa signed firmly, Alldera has a skill—her running. That makes her more useful to the plan barefoot than some others who go shod.

So the ''prisoner fem'' had gotten free at last. Daya wondered how she had managed to make enemies here so swiftly.

''If Alldera wanted to be useful,'' Ossa growled, ''she could have brought her cub here to us.''

''A fem cub,'' someone else sneered. ''What use would that be?''

''As much as a male,'' retorted another. ''By the time a boy cub got old enough to fuck, how many here would still be young enough to bear? We're none of us kits, you know.''

A free fem with a cub! Daya, astonished, leaned to hear more, but Elnoa moved her hands and Kobba translated, "The cub is not in the plan; the runner is."

The matter was closed. They began to talk about "the clowns," fems who were to concoct a diversionary ruse to draw off Marish patrols at the outset of the expedition. Kobba pulled back the blankets from a section of the floor so that, using soot from a fire bowl, she could sketch maps of the foothill trails.

Daya did not pay attention. She was intrigued by the bizarre complications that had come with the runner Alldera, and a little put out by the feeling of having missed the camp's newest sensation.

Meanwhile, here was Elnoa—bored to death with the others' plan talk—making furtive signs to her, commenting sarcastically on each speaker, berating Daya for having abandoned her to go tramping the plains. She forgot very easily that this had been at her own order. Finally, during a pause while Kobba rubbed out some error in her map, Elnoa signed broadly to Daya, You have not satisfied our curiosity about life cooking for Kobba's wagon crew. Surely you had time at least to make up some new stories.

Well, it was about time. Daya said modestly, "I speak only what I know of what I hear. I did hear some strange tales out there. There was one in particular—no, you'll call me a liar."

They flattered her and cajoled her. She loved the coaxing, which was, after all, her due.

To warm them up she told a quick story of Little Fist, a free fem whom she had invented years ago, now the subject of a hundred anecdotes. Shrunken to tiny size by a bolt of plains lightning, Little Fist had wild adventures wandering the Grasslands in her tiny cloak, sneaking into the Mares' camps, encountering ghosts and demons from the past in the Ancients' ruins.

Today Daya told how Little Fist was hunted remorselessly by a vicious sharu fifty times her size, and how she had pinned its tail to its nose with a cactus spine so that it ran in circles till it died. Then Little Fist did a victory dance on her tiny cloak—

"Enough tiny-headed nonsense. Tell a tale about the Holdfast," Emla drawled. "Something we haven't all already heard, if possible."

Her bitchiness did not matter. A story lay ready for them in Daya's mind, clearly and wholly visible now like a white stone at the bottom of a bowl of water. With a nod at Emla she began.

"The free fems return across the mountains, and they stop on the edge of the Holdfast and see that something strange has happened there: earth and sky are bound in a great stillness. The clouds hang in the sky without changing shape, and far away they can see that the sea itself lies still, neither advancing nor retreating along the shore.

"Elnoa signs for a brave volunteer to go down into the lower hills and find out what has happened. One fem goes, spear on her shoulder, hatchet in her hand.

"For a long time she meets no one. Her legs seem to carry her no further toward the sea. The river beside the road she follows does not move between its banks.

"Suddenly she sees a figure ahead of her on the road. Drawing near with great effort, she comes upon an old fem in a ragged smock trying to lift a huge wheel of white stone that has fallen on its side, blocking the way. The old fem straightens, wipes her wrinkled face with the hem of her smock, and says to the free fem, 'Come help me raise this stone, for I must roll it down to the sea.'

"The free fem looks at the old fem, all scarred and dirty with the sweat and dust of labor, and she says, 'Tell me what has happened here, why the Holdfast is so empty and still.'

" 'Help me,' the old fem says.

"The free fem gets angry, she thumps the butt of her spear on the ground and cries, 'I have come home to conquer, not to work!'

"At this, the old fem shrinks away to nothing and vanishes, and the free fem thinks, very well, I have vanquished some evil phantom that would have bewitched me.

"But she finds that the white wheel has grown so huge that she cannot climb up over it or even walk around it, and she is forced to return to where the others wait. So Elnoa signs for another volunteer, and another free fem goes, spear balanced on her shoulder, hatchet in her hand.

"She walks beside the still river and under the still sky, and she seems to make little headway. Then she sees the old fem before her, bent and straining to lift the wheel of white stone. The old fem calls to her, 'Come and help me raise this stone on its edge so that I can roll it down to the sea.'

"The second free fem says, 'First you tell me what's happened here, why the Holdfast lies so still and empty.'

" 'Help me!' the old fem commands her.

" 'I won't!' the second free fem cries, raising her hatchet to the old fem. 'I haven't come home to follow anyone's orders, I've come to give orders—so get out of my way!'

"At this the old fem shrinks away to nothing and disappears, but the second free fem finds that the white wheel has swollen so big that she can't climb over it or walk around it to continue on her way; so she has to come back too.

"The third volunteer is a fem named Semda, who walks and walks till she comes upon the old fem and her stone wheel, and the old fem looks up at her and calls, 'Come and help me raise this stone on its edge so I can roll it down to the sea.'

"Semda looks at her and thinks, if I had not had the luck and the strength to run away from the Holdfast, I would have withered early like this old fem. And she says, 'I'll do what I can.' To her amazement, she no sooner sets her hand to the stone than up it springs to stand on its edge in the middle of the road.

" 'Now, help me roll it down to the sea,' says the old fem.

"That's a long way, Semda thinks. But she looks at the old fem and she thinks also, I was not here to be beaten, but how many blows has she taken? So she says, 'I'll try.'

"She finds that the wheel rolls true with the two of them pushing it, and as they walk the old fem says, 'Waiting is more tiring than working,' and Semda says to the old fem, 'Why are you doing this job alone, an old weak fem like yourself?'

" 'Because it is my job and always has been my job and always will be my job,' answers the old fem.

" 'Under the orders of what master?' says Semda.

" 'Under no orders, I mark out the time,' says the old fem, and Semda realizes that this is Moonwoman herself. In fear and shock she jumps back from the white stone wheel, which immediately tumbles into the river. The old fem falls in with it. But when Semda runs to look she sees the stone wheel floating on top of the water; and the old fem, standing on the floating stone, shouts to her, 'Jump on!'

"The water is flowing very fast, and Semda is frightened, but she jumps and the old fem catches her. They go whirling down the river so fast Semda can hardly breathe, but the old fem is laughing and shouts to her, 'I thought the right one would never come. When we reach the coast, jump off again. You will find a ferry boat beached there. Go strike its side with your hatchet, and you'll have your reward.'

"Semda soon smells the sea, and she leaps onto the shore at the river's mouth. There is nothing to be seen on the coast but saltgrass and sand and, canted on its side, the great bleached hulk of one of the coastal ferry boats.

"The old fem is still riding the stone wheel, which is shooting out to sea. 'Use your hatchet!' she calls.

"Semda walks up to the silent wreck and taps on the wooden wall. Nothing happens. She takes a strong swing and chops right through. A whole section of the hull breaks away, and out of the opening fems come walking, rubbing their eyes, yawning and looking around in astonishment. Moonwoman had hidden them there while she killed the masters.

"Among these fems Semda sees a lover whom she thought dead and others whom she knows were once lovers of her free fem companions—lovers long ago given up for dead. She embraces her own lover, and their hands are very soft on one another, and the ocean begins to roar to the beach and the bright moon rises, round and white as a polished stone, to float in the sky."

They gave Daya a tribute of spellbound silence, and then Elnoa leaned forward and threw sweet-smelling powder on the fire. They all drew together into a tighter group, leaning toward the smoke. The hemp plant, called "manna" on the other side of the mountains, grew here too, though in less abundance. Daya did not care for manna, which produced in her a languorous slowing of the senses. When she took manna she could not concentrate to tell stories.

A new person entered the wagon. She sprinkled people with water as she tossed back her rain-wet hair from her face. She was a stranger to Daya and not pretty. Her eyes were small and the bridge of her nose was flattened so that the nostrils seemed by contrast to flare like the nostrils of a horse. She looked to Daya like the kind of fem who liked to fight. Such spirit could be attractive to Daya.

The newcomer glanced at Daya and did not bother to hide her contempt. Daya faced that contempt all the time, a prejudice against those who had been the favorites of their masters, coddled for their manners and their looks.

The newcomer sniffed the air of the wagon and withdrew into the rain without a word.

Daya guessed, "Was that her? Alldera the runner?"

Kobba was already leaning over the fire, breathing in the drug fumes, and did not reply. But old Ossa, who clearly disliked the runner, circled Daya's arm with her bony hand and hissed, "That's her. She's just as standoffish as when she came, would you believe it? That was at the beginning of last Cool Season, a little after the wagons had left. Roona's wagon had no sooner gone

than it was back again. This fem had come to them
while they were trading at Red Sand Camp, and Roona
thought they better bring her back fast so she could tell
us things about the Mares she'd lived with.''

Ossa hooted. ''A lot of good that was! Alldera hardly
talks about the Mares. She's scared we'll see how sorry
she is that she left them. The only thing she told us was
that she'd borne a cub and left it with the Mares—can
you imagine? There was a to-do over that, I can tell you.

''She never even brought her horses to the wagon with
her, the ones she'd ridden from Stone Dancing to Red
Sand. Said they weren't hers, left them in Red Sand. She
never stopped to think Roona's crew might like a feast
of fresh horsemeat for a change instead of dried sharu.''

''She won't get herself liked that way,'' Daya said
guardedly.

''She doesn't like any of us. She's young all over,
never a thought for anybody but herself. Staying so long
with the Mares made her too good for us. We don't
measure up.''

''Who says so?'' Kobba snarled. She took a breath of
smoke. ''Not me!''

A few of the fems cheered her sleepily. Most were
dozing among the deep colored cushions, their faces
gilded by the light from the fire bowls. Daya had to
shake her head to dislodge the shimmering waves of
color and distortion that the manna poured into her.
Kobba's words seemed to be rocking the wagon.

''The Mares are strong, but we're stronger. They live
on their horses; they travel only where this barren country gives them food for their beasts. We live on foot, go
where we like, make the Grasslands support us. We each
came over the borderlands. You have to be tough to do
that, and they know it. They're scared of us. They know
if we ever gave them a fight for their water and grass
and herds, they'd lose it all. But we don't want what
they have.''

Then Kobba rocked to her knees and pushed among
the pillows so that she could stretch out behind Elnoa
and enclose her bulk in her arms. Elnoa shifted to lie

against Kobba. Her face half hidden in the fall of her heavy hair, she gargled in tongueless sounds.

Kobba mumbled above her drooping head, "She wants Daya too."

"I'm here," Daya murmured. She moved Emla's slack body aside so that she could curl up and pillow her own head on one of Elnoa's enormous thighs.

When the rains stopped and the Cool Season began, the trade wagons were ready to resume their journeys out onto the plains. This time it was Emla's turn to travel, and Daya saw to it that everyone knew Emla was leaving with one of the crews by order of Elnoa.

Daya hung about all day when the last wagon was being packed for its journey. The crew stacked it full of chests of wooden tools, ornaments, and great odorous piles of tea brick. There were boxes of small goods, too, utilitarian items like buckles and fine glazed beads. Holdfastish products, Daya thought approvingly, for the wild, ignorant Mares.

It was the wagoneers' custom to travel all the way west to the Great Salty River during the cool weather while there was water to drink in the slowly drying rain pools along the way. Then they would trade tea for salt from the Mares of Salt Wind Camp. Turning, they would work slowly back eastward trading tea, salt and other goods in the camps on the way back for meat, milk, leather and metal. As the Dusty Season advanced the camps of the Mares homed to their wells and so were easily found.

"Daya, you can still come with us if you want to." Kobba looked up from her tally during a pause while the crew was busy picking up and recoiling some rope that had dropped out of a wicker chest. "Your cooking kept my crew happy on our last trip."

"Come along, Daya!" shouted Kenoma. "I'll keep you warm. It'll be like old times."

Times, a year or so back, best forgotten, Daya thought. Yet she would go if she could. With longing she pictured the huge, high-clouded sky of the Cool

Season, the broad golden land patched with shade and bright sunlight. Kobba was a good boss, scrupulous about rations and work loads. She did not permit much fighting. There were others along besides Kenoma to choose for protector and bedmate. Tempting—only Daya was not really in a position to go. She was not about to give up this time in camp with Elnoa that she had intrigued all Rainy Season to obtain.

Watching Emla helping to buckle the hauling harness to the wagon, she began to feel quite cheerful. The masseur's fortunes at Elnoa's side had sunk while Daya's, carefully tended, had risen. Emla's turn would come again if Daya meddled too much in camp affairs. and Elnoa sent her traveling again. Daya intended to hold her place this time.

While the crew drew the oiled cover over the wagon frame, Kobba had her final consultation with Elnoa. Daya made herself busy on the porch of Elnoa's wagon to watch and listen. Kobba wanted Alldera to be added to her crew. She said it would do the runner good to take orders with others instead of leading them out running as she had been doing. "She must sweat with the rest of us."

She is out running now, Elnoa signed. Your crew will do better without her discontent. I will keep her busy here.

Daya had heard Alldera say that the tea camp sometimes seemed just like a big femhold with Elnoa as master. Did Elnoa know that? If not, there might be a profit, sometime, to be made out of the runner's imprudent statement.

For the present, there was something else to pursue. One of the crew fems had left a request that Daya speak for her with Elnoa while the crew was gone. The present of a bag of first-quality tea shavings assured that Daya would make a strong case for her.

Later, inside the big wagon when the traders had gone, Daya murmured to Elnoa, "Poor Suda is having a terrible time with a debt she can't pay. No doubt you know all about it already, but maybe you hadn't heard that she was drunk at the time they were gambling or she wouldn't have risked so much. Now if she doesn't pay up out of her share of this trip's profits—''

Elnoa signed, Not yet, tell me about that later. Tell me now why you like it out on the plains.

Daya began to speak softly about what it was like out there. Elnoa sat looking through her current volume of accounts, occasionally smiling and looking up when something Daya said particularly pleased her. At such times Daya thought of herself as the tender guardian of some wealthy invalid.

Mornings in the Cool Season, old Ossa hung around the cooking pots to keep warm. Daya was cooking up the rare treat of a fresh meat stew—someone had speared a sharu at the spring the day before—and she found Ossa flicking out chunks of meat with a sharp stick and popping them into her mouth. Furious, Daya slapped her away. Ossa made a great show of falling down, and shrieked at her in a voice that could be heard all over camp:

"Be careful, you stupid, clumsy bitch! Do you want to kill the first child conceived by a free fem in the Grasslands, the daughter of Moonwoman herself?''

By noon the old creature was the talk of the camp. She claimed she had spent the night of the previous full moon outside and Moonwoman had magically impregnated her. Her cub was to grow up to reproduce merely by willing it. That was Moonwoman's promise, and everyone had to acknowledge, however snidely, that Ossa's wrinkled belly had begun to swell.

Daya smiled with the rest. This was not the first false pregnancy to be known in the tea camp, only the most grotesque and unlikely. It soon came to an end. Ossa drank another fem's ration of beer, "because it was good for the baby's hair." She got kicked in the belly for it, and the swelling vanished.

Then, around the cooking kettles behind Elnoa's

wagon, Daya heard Alldera being blamed for Ossa's misadventure: "Ossa says Alldera killed the child by witchery."

"What's the witchery in a good, hard kick?"

"Who knows what the runner learned, living so long with the Mares."

"What would you say if Ossa accused Froya, there?" Laughter.

"But it's Alldera, not Froya."

"The runner should have brought us her cub. What right did she have to decide to leave it?"

"Ossa's right about that. Alldera never talks of the cub. We're only fems, you know, not good enough to hear about the cub she left with the high and mighty Mares."

Daya noticed that the runner's name came up in conversation often, and usually with disapproval. There was a mad tale of her trip out, before Daya's return to camp, with a mapping party headed by Froya. The group had dragged home days overdue, still streaked with desert dust, and complaining bitterly that Alldera had gone off alone into the desert so that they'd all had to troop after her to bring her back.

Taxed with endangering the entire expedition and reminded that the free fems could ill afford to risk losing anyone, Alldera had defended herself by saying she had thought they were to go into the desert, not just along its edge making drawings of what they could see from there.

All very true, Daya reflected, if one insisted on taking symbolic action for the real thing. This was a distinction the runner seemed incapable of learning. No wonder she had enemies.

Not long after Ossa's "pregnancy," Daya heard that Alldera was asking Elnoa to discipline fems who did not turn out for running practice. Daya had to put up with Elnoa's subsequent ill humor, which included thrown objects, bursts of incoherent and ugly noise when mere gestures would not carry the weight of her anger, and sometimes—praise Moonwoman's mercy—merely the sulks. She had her work cut out, restoring Elnoa to a decent frame of mind. She wondered how people here could think a pet's life was all sweet drippings from a master's plate.

Couldn't Alldera see that the tea camp went slack when Kobba was gone with a trading crew? Elnoa worked everyone very hard at weaving and dyeing but did not interfere at all with what else they did. Her business was the accumulation of goods. Kobba's job, when she returned, was to slam on the discipline again and push ahead with the plan.

If Alldera had not worked that out for herself, she was heading for disaster. Daya saw no reason to enlighten her. She knew the type: proud, demanding, impatient, withdrawn into herself out of disappointment with others, but lacking inner resources, particularly imagination.

Only action would suit her, and she was not going to get the kind of heroic nonsense that she wanted. Not here. Daya could have told her.

Someone came pounding across the yard shouting, "It's a Mare! A Mare's come to the valley!"

Roused from a slumbrous afternoon in the big wagon, Daya went with Elnoa to the perimeter of the camp. A Mare as dark-skinned as the horse she rode was down by the spring, in plain sight of the sentries, if there had been any sentries. There was no telling how long she had been waiting there till someone noticed her.

Elnoa had Alldera sent for.

Daya's head was full of wild suppositions. She stared down at the rider, fascinated. She had never been this close to one of them for this long with nothing to do but look. She thought the Mare's appearance rather grand.

Under the back-thrown headcloth the Mare's face was an unreadable darkness lit by the glint of her eyes. She led two spare horses by ropes on their necks. How obedient her horses seemed, how patient. Her mount leaned down in a leisurely fashion to rub its head on its foreleg. All of them lacked the scruffy flash of wild horses. Daya wondered what the Mare had done to tame them so completely. They did not look scarred or starved.

Alldera appeared below, padding swiftly down the trail to the spring.

The yellow tones of the plain, visible beyond the mouth of the valley, had faded as the days lengthened and heated toward the early Dusty Season. Daya imagined the bold Mare riding alone through that landscape, as it was gradually leached of color by the increasing power of the sun. . . .

The Mare leaned down and as she spoke touched Alldera, a swift flicker of the hand. While trading in Marish camps Daya had often seen them do that among themselves, casually, as if they owned each other. One of the led horses stepped forward and put its nose against Alldera's shoulder. Alldera laid her hand on its flat forehead. The watching fems stirred.

For a moment Daya wished strongly that she were down there too, and she was almost jealous of Alldera. What did it feel like to be touched by a woman as black as char and to stroke a creature that was not even human at all?

Alldera and the black Mare talked in distant voices. The runner's voice seemed choppy and hard, the Mare's richly liquid. An experienced storyteller's voice, Daya thought, and what an attentive audience she had in the fems strung out along the wall of wood and brush and stone on the hillside above. She was so black, a dramatic shadow-person; she gave Daya the shivers.

Alldera nodded curtly to the Mare and turned back up toward the tea camp. All the fems began to talk excitedly at once. The Mare gathered her headcloth about her shoulders and rode away down the valley with her horses.

When Alldera came to Elnoa she said, "That was someone who looks after my cub for me. She says that the cub has gone into the childpack of Stone Dancing Camp. They always tell the bloodmother. It's a custom."

What are you supposed to do? Elnoa signed.

Alldera shrugged. "Nothing. I'm just supposed to know."

Froya said in a skeptical tone, "You told us the cub was nothing to you."

"It's important to Stone Dancing Camp that I know," Alldera said, speaking directly to Elnoa. "The rider comes of a bloodline that cares a lot about doing what's right."

"If the Mares did what was right," Froya sneered, "they would have brought your cub to us. If they did what was right, they wouldn't let their horses screw them." That raised a snicker among the others. Froya never knew when to quit. "Do you think she's fucked with that brown one she was riding?"

"Idiot," Alldera said with contempt, "she was riding a mare. Can't you tell a male horse from a female?"

Froya's cheeks patched red over the high, narrow bones. "From this distance only an expert could," she retorted. "Someone who knows them as well as the Mares do."

Alldera dropped into a fighting stance, and Froya jumped back with a shout, "Oh no, I know your fancy kicks; you could put my eye out while I was watching your hands."

The runner straightened and said angrily, "It's not my fault that you don't know how to block a kick or throw one. I offered to teach kick fighting, remember? Only some people decided it was too dangerous."

Daya let out her breath, watching Alldera stalk away. What a foolish thing to say, since word was that Elnoa herself had forbidden those lessons, probably rightly. The free fems quarreled frequently among themselves and were too few to add new risks of serious injury.

This Alldera was no realist. She was nervy, though. You had to grant that—always remembering the foolhardy ones were just the sort that got themselves killed by irate masters in the end.

Kobba's wagon came home late in the Rainy Season,

battered by a flash flood that had caught it in the foothills. Emla had almost been swept away in the flood. A white swatch in her hair, just noticeable at her departure and now wider, was suddenly being attributed to the accident. She took her time recovering from the shock, Daya noted, indulging freely in fits of nervous tremors and weeping, keeping weakly to Elnoa's wagon. She was, unfortunately, far too distraught to help Daya with the cooking and cleaning.

Elnoa played along with the act. Probably she was angry because Kobba's poor judgment had cost most of the cargo. Solicitude for Emla, poor victim, seemed to Daya a neatly calculated way for Elnoa to continually remind Kobba of her mistake. Of course, this was only Daya's suspicion. There was really no telling with Elnoa.

Daya was bored. The months since the Mare's visit had rolled uneventfully by. Getting Emla displaced from her new closeness to Elnoa seemed a diverting and useful project.

She decided that Emla's weakness was her greed. The masseur liked to wait till she thought no one saw and then grab an extra pot of beer or a bar of Elnoa's own best tea. She tried to be the last one to leave a wagon, and might slip into one while all its inmates were away. Caught, she would say, "Sorry, I thought I heard voices inside."

It was all small-scale pilfering. Elnoa surely knew, but chose not to punish.

All that would be necessary would be to raise the suspicion that Emla had found the hiding place of Elnoa's private treasure trove. Each of the free fems had a secret cache hidden in the hills. The whole area was planted with belongings of the living and the dead; sometimes fems died without revealing their hiding places. More than one member of the tea camp had been hurt or even killed because of the suspicion that she had found—by accident or by craft—another's hiding place.

Elnoa surely had the greatest fortune hidden and the most to fear from a thief. It was Daya's business to know secrets, and she had known for years the location of Elnoa's treasure cave, though she had never entered it herself.

Pity she could not come up with some really original plan; but old tricks work best.

Elnoa had recently given Emla a bracelet of blue gems set in fine braided leather. It was perfect for Daya's purpose. It had no catch and tied on. Emla had complained that the knot worked loose so that the bracelet kept dropping off and getting lost. No free fem who found that bracelet would dare to keep it for herself; she would recognize it and remember its august source.

It took three days of careful observation to discover where Emla kept her bracelet. She had wound it around the catch of one of the unused sleeping platforms. Daya pulled out the spare bedding from all the platforms to be aired, and in the process she slipped the bracelet down into an opening in the hem seam of her smock.

Then she left camp early with her herb basket for the part of the hills where she knew the tea cutters would be working that day.

There was no way of knowing just what Elnoa would do if Daya were caught at this. The risk made her heart speed with excitement. The voices of the tea cutters rang in the sparkling morning air. They were catching up with her. She could see their heads bobbing above the tea bushes and hear the blows of their hatchets. A long arm flashed as someone reached for a promising-looking branch.

Daya set the bracelet in a tea bush right over the concealed entrance to Elnoa's treasure cave, positioned as if it had caught on a branch there. Then she slipped back to camp and waited. Oh, there would be a furor, everyone asking angrily what the owner of the bracelet had been doing out among the treasure-laden hills when she was supposed to be in Elnoa's wagon, laid up sick with nerves.

The scene later in the wagon began the way Daya had imagined it, right down to the outrage in Emla's scratchy voice. Emla said exactly the right things, at

first—about thieves, a cherished possession never
carelessly worn, and how she was too feeble these past
weeks to move far from her bed—She hunched up in her
blankets trembling, making the most of her weakness.

Elnoa sat amid her cushions with the bracelet on her
massive knee, chin sunk on palm. Daya knew Elnoa
could not show her full anger and alarm, for then other
fems might guess that the bracelet had been found near
her own secret location.

No more, Elnoa sighed, the bracelet's blue stones glittering now in her moving hand. You have not always
been in my wagon. You have been out.

Naturally Emla had been out; Daya had guessed that
too. Emla had certainly pilfered from the cargo of the
unlucky wagon. She must have made at least one
stealthy trip to her own treasure with her takings. To
pretend otherwise was a mistake.

"I did go out," Emla admitted, "to see to my own
property. But why accuse me? We all look after what
belongs to us. I know one person who wanders the hills
constantly by herself, no matter how many times people
have warned her. She hasn't lived with us long enough
to have amassed any wealth of her own. She's smart and
secret and neither labor fem nor house pet. Alldera the
runner has stolen my bracelet and lost it in the hills."

The unpopular newcomer! Daya had forgotten her
completely.

"I saw her trotting off alone only two days ago,"
someone volunteered anxiously, and suddenly everyone
was talking. At Elnoa's command two of the tea cutters
hurried out and brought the runner back with them.

It seemed to Daya that she had a reckless look these
days, which did not help. Surrounded by the silent,
resentful group, Alldera listened to what Emla had to
say. She laughed at the charge. In an angry tone she
said, "You can't mean you believe I did this."

Someone shouted, "Why not? You haven't had time
to build up a treasure of your own, except from our
belongings. Why do you keep wearing that Marish shirt
of skins instead of a good smock from our looms?

Maybe you like those pockets they wear in front, maybe they're handy for putting stolen things into?''

Alldera said furiously, "I don't like to wear a slave smock as if I were still somebody's property back in the Holdfast, that's why!" She stared desperately from face to face. "I can't believe this. It's as if I'd never left the Holdfast at all—fems spending their lives laboring for someone else's profit, squabbling among themselves over trifles—"

They murmured; some faces showed uncertainty. Then Emla yelled, "Thief! Where did you get that hair binder you're wearing?''

"I traded Lora a bag of pine nuts for it." Alldera was looking over their heads now as though disdaining their questions, but Daya saw the sweat gleaming on her face. "Go ask Lora."

Seeing her fully on the defensive now, the fems pressed in, demanding, accusing. Elnoa was obviously just letting the tide of anger roll; Daya, appalled, could think of nothing to do. Now everyone was hostile to Alldera, and the runner seemed unwilling or unable to placate them. When faces grew red and fists were clenched, Elnoa sent for Lora. But by the time word was brought that Lora was out on sentry duty, it was all over. Only the question of punishment remained.

Elnoa signed her judgment: Alldera is confined to camp. No more running at all.

"Who are you to give me orders?" Alldera blazed. "You're not my master! I've stolen nothing. Prove that I've taken anything from anyone!''

Elnoa stared at her. The bracelet of blue stones was wrapped around her thick fingers like a weapon. Go away, she signed. You are lucky not to be treated more harshly. Perhaps you have done this, perhaps not. You are an arrogant young know-it-all. I think you would like to take our goods and run off to be rich among your Marish friends.

Alldera rejoined fiercely, "At least my Marish friends had some notion of right and wrong—"

Edging closer to her, Daya whispered in anguished

agitation, "Go, you're in danger here! You've really made her angry!"

Spinning on her heel, Alldera pushed her way out through the crowd. The others shuffled after her, taunting her for a thief.

Now Elnoa's eyes were fixed on Daya's face. Clumsy with nerves, Daya began to straighten the floor blankets rucked up by trampling feet. Don't panic, Elnoa knows nothing, she only suspects, she told herself. The wagon smelled of sweat now, and cushions lay tumbled everywhere.

Emla leaned at ease among her pillows. When she met Daya's furtive glance she smiled.

Elnoa isn't through with me, Daya thought wretchedly. She had an instinct about these things.

The next morning she woke early and could not get back to sleep. She crept outside and stood on the back porch, trying to rub the tension out of her neck and shoulders. The wide yard lay empty all around her under a drift of mist, and she could see no one stirring at the wagons in the perimeter. She wondered what she could do so early for distraction from her worries, thought about going back in for a blanket—it was chilly out—but shrank from the possibility of waking Elnoa, seeing that massive, brilliant-eyed face turned coldly toward her in the gloom. . . .

A sound made her look up. A knot of sentries was coming down from the hills behind camp where they kept watch, now that Kobba was home. Two leaned on the shoulders of their companions as if they had been hurt. In the center of the cluster was Alldera, head lolling and feet trailing, being dragged into camp like a trophy.

They brought their prize and their injured to the steps of the back porch. Lexa, head of the watch, rapped on the rail with the shaft of her spear.

Elnoa and Kobba came out. Kobba had a blanket in her hands. She stood behind Elnoa and folded it around the big, soft shoulders. Shrunk into the corner of the porch, Daya noted this indication of renewed warmth between the two. In the quiet she could hear clearly the painful breathing and low groans from the injured.

What do I see here this morning? signed Elnoa.

"A rebel and a thief," Lexa said, shaking Alldera's slack head by a twist of her long hair.

Free fems had begun to drift over from the other wagons. One asked, "What did she steal?"

Listen or disperse, Elnoa signed; and at her shoulder Kobba said forcefully, "Listen or disperse."

Lexa said, "She said she was just going running as usual, but when we said no she tried to get by us. There was still mist on the ground. If she'd slipped past us, she'd have been hard to find. She could have looted every cache in the hills and been on her way—"

"How did the sentries get hurt?" Kobba demanded. "Were the Mares waiting out there to help her?"

"She was just going right by us as if we weren't there," Lexa said resentfully. "She said we'd had time to dig new holes like the sharu do—that's what she said, ask the others—so our treasures were safe and she wasn't going to sit around and get fat because we were afraid.

"Anyway, poor Soa shoved her back a little, you know, not hard, just a warning. She gave Soa a terrific kick. I think Soa's knee is knocked right out, she can't put any weight on it at all.

"Well, we went at her. Nobody used a weapon, you can see that, but I think she's got some cracked ribs. She hurt us, and we hurt her back."

Elnoa signed, Go and take care of your injuries and Alldera's injuries too. You sentries were right to stop her, but rougher than you should have been. We do not use the masters' ways here.

The sentries turned Alldera over and carried her away by shoulders and ankles. Daya saw the dirt and blood streaked over her face and chest. Her head hung back, eyes closed, in that horrible, loose way Daya remembered from the days when the men of the Holdfast used to bring in captured runaway fems and give them over to be hunted through the holiday streets to their deaths.

*   *   *

The need to make presents to Elnoa was mortifying, but
Daya had to do something to melt the frost between herself and her patron. It was weeks now since the bracelet
incident.

It did not help her feelings to be stopped on the back
porch by Emla, who insisted on sorting through the box
Daya was carrying and opening the bottles it contained.
These were perfumes that Daya had selected over the
years from the best stocks of Fedeka the dyer.

The tea cutters were all out, the camp lay quiet. A few
fems tended fresh-cut tea that was laid out on long racks
over fires to be dried. A solitary figure sat nearby with a
blanket draped over her like a Marish headcloth.

Emla glanced that way too and said slyly, "Too bad
the runner no longer runs—except to fat."

What Alldera the runner did these days was drink.
The battering she had suffered at the sentries' hands
seemed to have broken her. She moved slowly about the
camp, bent as if in pain. Daya heard people say Alldera
had brought it on herself, but their hostility was
blunted; there were rumors that certain unnamed free
fems privately agreed with some of her assertions. A few
openly pitied her and blamed Daya, who knew that her
part in the affair was common supposition. The whole
situation was unjust. It was not Daya's fault.

"She certainly is the poorest drunk I ever saw," Emla
said, turning a small stone bottle in her supple hands.
"More than a single bowl of beer makes her sick. She is
stubborn, you have to grant her that. Did you see
her—or rather, hear her the other night? Throwing up
and cursing all evening, trying to keep enough beer
down to knock herself out! Hasn't she come begging for
beer? No? She stays away from you, I notice.

"Ugh, this smells awful, what was Fedeka thinking
of?"

"Why, of you, sweet friend," Daya said instantly.
"She told me especially to give that one to you from
her." The lie pleased her. She smiled her rare smile,
feeling the scars in her cheeks ruck up the skin into

hideous lumps, making of her smiling face a fright mask.

Emla recoiled and said venomously, "Don't show that nightmare face to me, Daya. I've put worse scars than that on the faces of fems who crossed me."

Daya deftly snatched the box of scents and stood up. "I'll take these in now that you've inspected them."

The masseur would hardly wrestle with her for the gifts here in front of everyone. She gave Daya a freezing glare and went rapidly in ahead of her, no doubt intent on dropping a nasty word or two in Elnoa's ear.

Glancing back over her shoulder, Daya saw that the lumpish figure of Alldera had not stirred. The sight of the runner's pain-cramped body brought back the pain of her own maiming, the desolation of her beauty destroyed.

Even the best wagons leaked in a night of hard rain. Spreading damp blankets to dry on the porch rails was not suited to a pet, but it was work Elnoa appreciated having done. The sun was out this morning. Elnoa sat in her wide chair, one of her ledgers spread open on her lap. Emla stood behind, pinning her hair up, preparing her for a massage.

A fem came to the porch steps: Alldera, wrapped in her grimy blanket, steaming odorously in the sunshine. Her hair hung lank. Dirt outlined the nails of the hand that clutched the blanket. Her light-colored eyes seemed to have retreated into darkened sockets, and there was a half-healed scab on her broad lower lip. She looked old.

Why does this coarse creature keep intruding on my life? Daya asked in silent irritation. She moved away a little down the porch.

Alldera said in a flat tone, "I want to go out with one of the wagon crews."

Lips pursing like a tea bud, Elnoa shut the leather book, opened it again to shake straight the limp pages, and put it aside. She beckoned Alldera to join her on the porch.

Drink and inactivity have ruined you, she signed. Hauling is hard work.

Daya heard Alldera respond, "I know the Mares. I could help the wagon crew bargain with them."

The inner bark of certain foothill pines, baked underground for a day, became a sweet and crackly candy. Daya brought some of these crisp, sticky sheets out on a tray. Elnoa took some. Alldera shook her head.

Elnoa signed, Some people would object that you might run away from the crew to live with the Mares again. She slipped her smock from her shoulders, and Emla began the massage with her oil-shiny hands.

With a jerk of her head Alldera indicated the fems at work at the tea-drying fires. "I don't think they'd miss me."

Patiently Elnoa signed, We are both free and few. Everyone is worth something here. Take some sweet.

Daya extended the tray again but Alldera ignored it. She moved her body uncomfortably, as if her injuries still pained her. Suddenly she burst out in a low but intense tone, "I'm rotting here. I need something to do, work to keep my head thinking."

Elnoa tilted her chin, stretching the line of her neck under Emla's hand. She signed, You have sometimes expressed a strong dislike of the way we do things.

Alldera did not speak. At least she was learning when to keep still, Daya noted. She hoped Elnoa would grant the runner's request to go out with a crew. She did not want Alldera around forever, a living reminder of her own disastrous miscalculation.

Elnoa signed, Maybe you can still learn to fit in here despite your strange background. I will see what my crew captains say. Come back and we will talk about this. Daya heard her suck on the sweet fragments stuck to her teeth—a revolting habit.

Alldera returned to her place across the yard and sat down again slowly.

Exasperated, Daya slapped another blanket over the railing. She knew the signs. Elnoa was in a playful mood; she would keep Alldera begging, never refusing

outright, never agreeing. Perhaps she was taking
vengeance for the runner's criticisms of her. Daya could
see the complacent smile on Elnoa's face as the big fem
leader leaned back and let the weight of her shoulders
rest against Emla's oiled palms.

Later, when both had gone in, Daya crossed the yard.
She knelt near Alldera and began pulling twigs and
branches out from under the wagon, selecting fuel for
cooking the day's meals.

Softly she said, "Elnoa isn't going to let you go with a
wagon. Hard work like that isn't what you need
anyway. Go to Fedeka the dye-maker, she's healed
people hurt worst than you are. You've heard of her?
She travels across the plains gathering plants, getting
her supplies from wagons that she meets with out there.
You've crossed that country with the Mares, you can
find your way. After the rains Fedeka moves south to
avoid the colder weather. She should be down near the
wells of Royo Camp soon."

"You think I should run away?" Alldera's tone was
neutral, unreadable, and she did not look up.

"Lots of fems have gone to Fedeka for help. That's
not running away; and you can slip off easily. No one
watches you any more."

Alldera did not answer.

Daya left her in a damp cloud of tea pungence and
smoke. It was the runner's mistake if she chose to ignore
such a good suggestion. She and Alldera were quits
now.

At the old tea-camp site, screened by trees near the
spring, Daya took leaf fragments from the pouch at her
belt and chewed them. She undressed and anointed herself with the leaf saliva. Shivering slightly in the evening
chill, she smeared her nipples, the insides of her thighs,
and her vulva, making them fragrant.

She did not do this for Elnoa. For some time Elnoa
had not sent for her. She slept these nights with Tua, but
she did not sweeten herself for Tua either. They bedded
together only because each of them was partnerless. She

prepared so elaborately to make love because she knew she excelled in this preparation, and she was proud of her skill at it.

Then she lay down in her blankets under the shelter of the abandoned wagon. She had not trysted here since going trading—two years or more? Too long. She looked out at the clouds piled deep into the darkening sky, preparing new assaults on the mountains. Good. When making love she liked the drumming of distant rain and the drama of far thunder. She enjoyed seeing her companion's eyes glinting greedily in the flash of the lightning. Let the rest of them keep to the stuffy wagons, descending to the floor to make love while others peered down at them from the sleeping platforms above. Though that was exciting in its own way, to know people were heating themselves on your own heat. . . .

Tua stood above her in the twilight, and Daya raised up on one elbow to greet her and draw her down.

"Listen," Tua said eagerly, "what do you think I just heard—Alldera's left camp!"

Daya caught at her hand. "Come here, I'm ready for you."

"Imagine!" Tua breathed, holding back still. "Bet she's gone back to the Mares. What's Elnoa going to say? What will Kobba do when she finds out?"

"She'll have a cub." Daya was vexed. "Lie down with me."

"But this is important! Aren't you excited?"

"Yes I am; and this is what's important." She drew Tua's mouth to her breast, and the two of them sank down. With the ease of long practice, Daya slid her knee between Tua's legs, and she lay back with a sigh of anticipation as Tua rolled on her with her good, warm weight.

Daya had never known the rains to last so late into the start of the Cool Season. A Generation Feast was always held shortly before the first wagon was scheduled to leave on its trade journey. This year the feast began in a rainstorm. Daya and those assigned to help her prepare food worked all day sheltered by awnings, cursing the leaks and the muddy footing.

Daya chose and combined the ingredients of the stew kettles, then left the tending of the cooking to her subordinates. She reserved for herself the oversight of the little covered pots that steamed all day over small fires. Each pot was filled with a fertility douche concocted to a formula of Fedeka the dyer's.

By evening the rain had stopped. Satiated with food and hot beer, the fems assembled quietly in the yard. Kobba stood on the porch at Elnoa's right hand. Tonight she spoke to them not in Elnoa's voice but in her own, that clanged like iron bars over the crackling from the fires and the desultory dripping of rainwater.

"We gather tonight, fems," she said, "to try once more to find a starter that will make new life in us. The Mares conceive without men, and so will we—but we won't turn to beasts to do it.

"Now, you may say—some say it every year—why do we want cubs at all? Once we made them for our masters, just like we made cloth or food or furnishings—for their use. And if the cubs weren't perfect, the men killed us for it. Even at best, with so much breeding it was awful for us. All of you remember old fems so torn from cubbings that they went raw-legged and stinking because they couldn't hold their piss. I myself have wondered, if cubs don't come to us in the course of things, why run after all that pain again?

"I'll tell you a story, friends.

"Back in the Holdfast I worked in the mines. The ore was crushed machines that the Ancients had stored away in stacks underground. The pieces were big, they could tear loose under a miner's foot and smash the people lower down. We had to be strong and light-footed. You see my hands, my feet? No calluses, no scars. We miners were given shoes and gloves so we wouldn't slice ourselves on wire and jagged edges or get acid burns. That's how valuable we were. I went through a dozen pair of palm pads a month.

"It was always damp down there. We worked by lamplight. The rust cough ate out everyone's voice in the end. But I didn't stay till the end.

"Everytime I came up from the mines I smelled that good clean smell coming east on the wind. I knew our side of the borderlands because I'd been marched up and down in the scrubby trees there with a search gang, looking for new mining sites. When the time came, I ran west laughing.

"A man came after me, one of those drug-mad Rovers that used to guard the old men's lives and their goods and chase down runaway fems for them. I hid. I jumped out when he passed me and I broke his neck. I rammed his chin up so hard I almost tore the head off his body. I'd never thought to do anything with my strength before but beat on the metal heaps and on any fems who bothered me. I never saw how easy it would have been to smash the life out of those men that stood around telling me what to do all my life.

"I see now. But it may be a long time before I get home, and by then my best strength will be gone. By then there may be only twenty of us going back, not fifty. We'd be weak.

"Unless we have some cubs. We can't let our numbers drop or age cut us down. We should go home a conquering army, or why go home at all? If we find the men all dead, that's all right too—we should have young fems there with us to help us break the men's bones and their buildings and trample everything of theirs and bury them in a foot of sea salt, so our cubs will know what their freedom is. If Moon-woman wills it, nothing will be left to show that men ever lived in the world, but our cubs will be there to show that we did."

The response was a collective sigh from the assembled fems and the sounds of a few sobs and snuffles. Kobba's voice, hoarse with emotion at the end, moved them this way every time.

Then the fems came in pairs—except Kobba, who came alone, for herself and Elnoa—and to each pair Daya gave two pots of douche and a syringe to take into one of the wagons. The syringe was to draw the douche and use it in the partner's body. The fems' faces were bright with hope that this time one of the douches would work.

Daya did not believe this would ever happen, but she was pleased to be the dispenser of Fedeka's mixtures on these welcome days of feasting, love, and hope. At least Fedeka knew the plants of the plains so well that the douches were sure to be safe. Free fems no longer poisoned themselves in their efforts to conceive, as in the past.

Personally, Daya had no particular wish to become bloated with pregnancy ever again, whether from a man or one of Fedeka's brews. She did like the warm flooding of her body. It was a feeling that no man with his imperceptible squirtings of lukewarm stuff had ever induced. She even enjoyed the feel of the syringe itself. Early on in the Holdfast she had seen that a pet's life included a lot more fucking than the life of an ordinary labor fem; she had made herself enjoy, and had later come to crave, the sensations of penetration.

There were those, she knew, who found her desire to be entered perverse. She could only be sorry for them, wretches whose experience had been limited to monthly battering by men pressed to do their copulatory duty in the Holdfast breeding rooms. Men who liked the bodies of fems were rare in the Holdfast.

In Tua she had found a friend who knew how to serve her tastes without open disgust. When the others were all gone, Daya and Tua found a corner for themselves in one of the wagons. Daya lay with her upper body hugged between Tua's legs while Tua worked the syringe pipe slower or faster, at a deeper or shallower angle, whatever pleased Daya, until Daya lifter her hips from the rumpled bedding and rode the flooding instrument to her climax.

The syringe, filled from Tua's bowl, was pressed into Daya's hand. She turned, gathering the body's heavy center in her arms and gliding her cheek up Tua's soft inner thigh.

Before dawn she was wakened by obscure discomfort. It was not, as she had thought at first, something bad in her gut. The sensation was of a burning in her lower belly and vagina.

The wagon was full of the sounds of sleepers. On the floor a fem gasped her way laboriously toward orgasm—probably old Ossa, who always went back for a second round of douche. If no one could be induced to lie with her, she would manage by herself, fingering her own body to its climax.

The burning feeling flickered out. Daya settled herself in her bedding, which was still damp from the douche.

By morning she was feverish. She curled, moaning, around her pain. She felt people handling her, trying to straighten her limbs, washing out her vagina and lifting her onto a pile of soft blankets at the back of Elnoa's wagon.

She tried not to cry out. There was Tua standing over her, weepily repeating that it could not be her fault. Then Tua was gone, sent away. Elnoa could not bear whiners.

They did not abandon Daya in her trouble. Someone was with her all the time, burning sweet-scented herbs in the fire bowls, gently restraining her when she sought to dig the pain out of her own body with her nails. It was she who, because of the wandering of her mind, felt herself leaving them.

As she lay burning it seemed to her that her head was swollen vast enough to contain whole populations; she could not understand how the wagon held her. She kept hearing the cracking of the short, split-ended switches that young male overseers used to drive labor fems. She smelled the scents that had mingled in Master Kazzaro's private chamber. She tasted the flavor of someone's body—her old lover the pet Merika, coming to her to receive solace. Or maybe it was the limping fem, name forgotten now, who had taken Daya under her protection down in the kitchens; she had applied salves made of cooking oils and spices to Daya's cheeks, vainly trying to repair the jagged holes torn by the broiling spit.

The pain in her body was surely the pain of cubbing, but this place was not the Holdfast hospital. There was no screaming here.

She was fed broth. She thought hazily, How sorry they are for me, how angry with the unknown fem who's killed me.

Someone was bending over her, mumbling, breathing on her, tugging at her legs—

Ossa. Old Ossa was dragging at her. At first it seemed like another vision. Daya pushed at Ossa, but the old creature slapped her hands away and continued dragging her toward the far end of the wagon.

Looking up suddenly, Ossa smiled at someone behind Daya and panted, "Oh, good, she's too heavy for me. Help me drag her over to the door."

The other person leaned down to take hold of Daya's shoulders. It was Kobba. She said, "Why are you pulling at Daya like that? What are you trying to do?"

"Tip her out, get rid of her," the old fem whispered, tugging alternately at Daya and at Kobba.

"I'm sick," Daya moaned, shrinking against Kobba.

Kobba hissed, "She's sick, you old fool!"

Daya was terrified that between them Kobba and Ossa would pull her into pieces. Her inflamed flesh would part with a sickly tearing sound and a release of stinking gas—

"Yes, yes, she's very sick," Ossa replied. "She's breathing sickness on us all. Help me toss her outside. Can't you smell it? Her decay makes the whole wagon stink."

"That's the smell of all the medicines we've been trying on her. Let her go!" Kobba commanded.

Ossa backed off, panting distressedly between her crooked teeth. As Kobba lifted Daya in her arms, the old fem whined, "I have to guard my health. Nobody looks out for me. They pinch me and abuse me, they say

I don't work to earn my food. It's not my fault my sight is going. Spoiled little pet. It's all very well for you, Kobba, you're still young and strong." She rubbed her hands on her wrinkled flanks as if to get rid of the touch of Daya. "Man slime." She wept a little, sniffed, and shuffled off.

It was good to have strong friends who could drive away one's enemies with a frown and a sharp word. Daya watched Kobba's squinting face floating above her and prayed to Moonwoman for an end to her pain.

Kobba's voice said harshly, "Fems are saying you'd rather see your pet dead than send her to the Mares."

Daya turned as much as the pain would allow. Kobba was standing near her, rolling up a leather window to let in daylight. Elnoa reclined on her couch of cushions. No one else was there.

Elnoa signed, She may after all recover.

"She'll die. You must send her to the Mares now. Maybe they can cure her, maybe not, but if she dies here people will say that's what you wanted because she was annoying you. If she dies with the Mares, the blame falls on them."

Elnoa signed something Daya could not see; her vision kept washing in and out of focus. Her throat was burning. She could not understand why they went on talking, ignoring her, when she needed something to drink so badly.

Kobba said, "Is this how you would act if she were the property of your master in the old days?"

Passionately Daya explained to them that she was too valuable to be let die. It came into her head that she had offended them with her scarred smile, that they did not want to look at her. She promised not to smile again, ever.

No one seemed to hear her. Kobba went on talking, louder and louder, until darkness enfolded and protected Daya from the sound.

Why were they moving her, didn't they know how she

hurt? She wept and flinched from their hands.

"Hush," Tua whispered in her ear, "we're trying to help you."

Deftly she wrapped Daya's hands in a strip of cloth, binding them together forearm to forearm beneath her breasts. Someone else was there, putting things into a wicker box. Was that Emla, sneaky fingers pawing through Daya's clothing?

"Don't let Emla," Daya moaned.

Tua patted her, smiled at her, and lifted her up. She was carried to a trade wagon and nestled into a hammock, separated only by a curtain from stacked bricks of tea.

Elnoa came in and lowered herself onto a bench beside the hammock. She had brought a cushion with her, which she tucked behind Daya's head.

Elnoa's lips trembled slightly as though she were trying to whisper. She leaned forward, doubling the rolling flesh of her body over her thighs. Her eyes were wide with emotion, green like sea waves standing toward the beach. The eyes seemed to speak almost as much as the hands, as if hands and eyes were the living spirits of that huge bulk.

I have been consulting my ledgers, she signed. Someday civilized people will find and read them, and they will learn from them what our lives were like and how we ended, cubless and dwindling away one by one to nothing. Did you think I wrote only figures, totaling up my wealth for my own amusement? I write everything there, all that I know—what I remember of life in the Holdfast, what I know of life here. Your stories are fancies, Daya, that will vanish when you do. Nothing will be left of you, for all your fine imagination. In my ledgers the facts are written.

All our works will disappear—the wagons will rot, and the tea will grow wild over us. Only what I have done and thought, sitting quietly and using my mind while others used their muscles, will last. It is in my ledgers, and my ledgers go year by year, volume by volume, to safety in a dry place in the hills where they wait for discovery in the future. My voice that has not spoken for decades is in them and will outlast all your loud talk, your whispers, your singing of songs.

The words made no sense to Daya. She knew they should. She wanted to smile at Elnoa, but remembered she had promised not to.

Meanwhile, Elnoa continued, the past recorded in my books is useful to me. The past tells me that nothing pleasing should be wasted, not even when it is also a troublesome nuisance—which is what you are, Daya, with your intrigues. It is something, too, that though the masters took your looks from you, here in the Grasslands you have more lovers than ever you had at home. You and I are alike in that; we two have subdued adversity.

The actual signs she used, Daya saw, meant simply, "we both have beaten bad luck." But with Elnoa's handspeech, grander and subtler interpretations invariably suggested themselves, overwhelming utterly the blunt common equivalents of her gestures. Daya thought, what a good friend, to come and soothe my feverish vision with the cool, deft dancing of her hands.

So let no one say, she was signing, that I am like a bad master, that I neglect those who belong to me. I am sending you to the Mares to see if they can cure you. You are no burden to the wagon crew, though they complain—you have grown lighter than dry grass. They will do as I have told them, and take you to the Mares and pay the Mares to do their best for you.

I will write down what I have done for you, and perhaps a few of your stories, if I can remember them.

Touching her fingers first to her own mouth, then to Daya's, she patted her smile onto Daya's burning lips in place of a kiss.

IV
Fedeka's Camp

8

I could kill her, Alldera thought grimly, looking at the pet fem's scarred, sleeping face: choke her, slice her throat. Her little game with Emla's bracelet wrecked me. Without even meaning to she did it. She sent me here to Fedeka (out of guilt; it cancels things out). And she came here nearly dead herself (that cancels things too).

Alldera sat sewing strips of colored cloth together. The outside walls of Fedeka's small tent were covered with similar strips that had been dyed in Fedeka's battered dye pots and fastened on with a stitch or two to weather and fade. They fluttered outside in the breeze like faint voices.

Alldera worked close to the fire. The Cool Season was well advanced and the morning sun brought bright light but little warmth. She wore a cloth tunic under her leather shirt and kept her feet curled near the flames. There was no room to stretch her legs. With two guests and Fedeka's bundles and pouches and baskets cramped inside, the leather walls bulged. Sometimes Alldera took her blankets and slept outside in spite of the cold, just for the freedom to straighten her limbs.

Her ribs still ached in the mornings when she got up: Daya's fault. Even Fedeka could not promise complete recovery, for Alldera was no youngster any more—a disquieting surprise, to realize that—who would heal easily and completely.

If this pet bitch says the wrong thing when she wakes up I'll wring her neck.

The needle jabbed and Alldera yelped. Then she saw Daya's eyes open just a line and Daya's leg strain furtively to loosen the blankets in case she should have to run. Let her try. It felt good to see the pet fem afraid.

Alldera said briskly, "Fedeka's out. She says your danger's past, so she's left you with me for a while."

Daya's eyes, enormous in her wasted face, opened wide. "What will you do?"

Plain scared of me and straightforward about it, Alldera thought. "I'm going to stay with you. I'm a grateful patient and a guest in Fedeka's tent. For her sake, I won't do you any harm. She seems to consider you valuable. I saw how she fought to get you from the wagon crew. She just wanted some supplies from them, but there you were in the wagon, and she wouldn't hear of letting them take you on to the women.

"She says, by the way, that there was nothing wrong with any douche made from her ingredients. Somebody must have doctored yours. I suppose you have a lot of enemies."

Daya licked her lips nervously. "Maybe Emla had it done. Clever bitch. Maybe because she was annoyed with me over the bracelet."

"I'm surprised you didn't foresee that."

"There are always risks," the pet fem murmured dreamily. "No one can foresee everything."

Well, you certainly could not fault the bitch for nursing a grudge.

Daya said drowsily, "You're sewing those strips to your pants. . . ."

Carrying cactus pads in her hat, which she held upside down by the cord, Alldera trudged home to Fedeka's tent. She could see the two of them together outside, Daya's slight form reclined next to the leather groundsheet that Fedeka had spread out to work on. Fedeka sat sorting through piles of dried plants, crumbling them thoughtfully in her fingers, smelling them. She had only one arm, having lost the other to Holdfast machinery.

As Alldera drew nearer they looked up at her and let their conversation trail off. Talking about me, she thought. She was surprised by Daya's easy intimacy with Fedeka, whom Alldera had come to regard as a person of energy and determination. What could such an individual find in Daya the pet?

Alldera put the hat down and squatted to build a fire with twigs from the fuel pile.

"How does your side feel?" Fedeka asked.

"Doesn't hurt."

"Did you run at all?"

"You said I shouldn't rush things." Alldera was afraid of how badly she would run, like a cripple. With flint and metal she struck a spark into the little tower of dry sticks and grass she had made. She took a green stick and held it out toward Daya. "Run some of those pads onto this so we can roast them and get the spines burnt off."

Daya obeyed silently.

Fedeka took her portion of the evening tea and tucked it into her cheek. Alldera had not been able to wean her from the revolting femmish habit of chewing the stuff instead of drinking its juice. Fedeka shook her head over Alldera's careful brewing procedure.

"The things people will swallow to relieve thirst! Somebody once told me that Ossa actually guzzled down one of my douche mixtures one time because it had been in the shade and was cooler than the water in the water bottle."

"Let me tell you about a master I knew," Daya said, settling herself more comfortably by the fire. "He used to put earth into his beer before he drank it. Well, you can imagine what kinds of dirt his fems found for him to use. . . ."

She was full of stories. Alldera had to admit that she told them cleverly; but how repellent they were. Alldera could never enjoy them as the tea camp fems had. She thought about it, sitting back from the fire and deliberately not listening to Daya's words. Maybe, she thought, it was because she had tasted real freedom among the Riding Women, while the others had simply run from Holdfast slavery to a more comfortable bondage in the Grasslands. The same stories were told here as had been told in the Holdfast. Yet Fedeka listened and laughed.

Alldera had not presumed to approach Fedeka's bed, but Fedeka slept with Daya as if it were a matter of course.

"What are you doing out here?" Alldera snapped. Daya was sneaking around after her.

"Looking at the country," Daya said. "It's beautiful."

Relenting a little, Alldera said, "I never saw a dry riverbed before. How does Fedeka know that a river really ran here on the plain in Ancient times?"

"She hears all sorts of things from the Mares."

"Everything dried out, and the rivers vanished," Alldera said. "It's hard to imagine." She turned her head, alert to a sound out on the plain east of them. Darkness was drawing on.

"It's Fedeka," Daya said quickly. "She's gone off to pray."

Restless, Alldera got up from the smooth-sided boulder she had been sitting on. "I thought nobody paid attention to Moonwoman here."

"You'd have seen a different side of things if Fedeka had shown up in camp." Daya's voice softened and took on warmth. "When she arrives, suddenly everyone starts saying prayers at meals and making water offerings and everything."

"Because she's different from them, she's free, and they respect her."

"Oh, yes. Fedeka is the freest of the free fems. She keeps her own ways, gathering her dyes and potions. There's not a growing thing in all the Grasslands from green threads finer than your hair to spiked bushes thick as your wrist that she hasn't gathered, dried, and boiled up."

Alldera said abruptly, "You've traveled with her before, she says."

"Yes. But she's most comfortable alone, so I never stay long. Even her interest in a skillful pet fem dies down pretty quickly. She has another lover. She gives her body to Moonwoman out there in the dark."

Was that the only way to find your strength if you couldn't find it among your own kind—to give yourself up to something greater? The sound of Fedeka's prayer came distinctly through the evening air. Her voice was strong and unselfconscious:

Pour into us through the thickest walls of our prisons;
Grains of silver, to bend to any pressure;
Strength of grizzled iron, to bear any blow;
Fastness of rock, to outlast them all.

Alldera groaned under her breath. Daya asked her what was the matter.

"Where was this great Moonwoman when we were living our wretched lives back there and dying our terrible deaths?"

"Fedeka says she was in our minds, giving us strength to exist."

"Strength to work and strength to die, you mean," Alldera said bitterly. "An ally of masters, not of fems."

Alldera ran, feeling full of power. Sometimes she crossed the blurred tracks of laden horses, and the sight of them gave her the most peculiar, wrenching feeling. She remembered the days with the Riding Women when it had been the impressions of femmish wagon wheels that had caught her eye.

She was surprised when Daya asked to go running with her. The pet fem soon gave it up. She was not able to mask her disgust at filthying herself with sweat and dust.

Alldera still went with Daya in search of plants for

their meals, or to scrape up the white salt crusts the dyer used to fix her colors in cloth.

Skimming this white mineral off the sand one morning, they found tracks and droppings of sharu. Daya jumped like a startled foal and looked anxiously around. This wandering life had thinned her down and browned her until she seemed to suit the land. It was hard now to picture her in Elnoa's rich nest.

"Don't worry," Alldera said. "The sharu have come and gone."

"I'm wearing my bleeding cloth. Couldn't they smell me and come after us?"

"They won't." She pointed to the tracks. "There's only this one around here, left behind because she's old or sick, maybe. Don't you know why the sharu never bother Fedeka? The plants she looks for are weeds that take root where the earth has been disturbed and the grass roots broken up. That's the way the sharu leave land after they've foraged over it. So Fedeka ends up trailing behind the sharu around their feeding range, following them by a growing season or two."

"Mother Moon, the things you know!" Daya exclaimed.

Alldera almost laughed, the pet looked so astonished; half an act of course, but that made it funnier. "I'm tempted to show off when you don't know."

Daya did not defend herself. She looked pensive. She said, "Don't tell Fedeka; what you just said, about the sharu."

"As long as she doesn't tell me that Moonwoman keeps her safe."

Alldera said nothing to Fedeka. How could she? She admired the dyer too much for her ability to live alone, her harmony with her life.

Gathering brush for fuel along a dry watercourse, they startled wild horses that fled in a flurry of dust. Alldera recognized a brown stud that had driven off two of the Calpapers' mares one year when she had been in the women's camp. Transported for a moment back into

that existence, she felt her loss of it. All that seemed
long gone now, another life outgrown.

She told of the brown stud.

"Imagine a wild horse stealing from the Mares,"
Daya said in obvious delight. "It must be pretty clever
to set the Mares' horses free."

"They're not free. A bunch of wild horses is mostly
mares, all of them the property of the stallion, their
master. He sires all the foals, he bullies and bosses his
mares and fights off other studs. Just like in the Riding
Women's herds."

Daya looked up from tugging at a stubborn dead root
that projected from the earth bank. "Doesn't that
bother the Mares—to see female creatures harried and
owned by males?"

"Women say that animals live as they must. They say
women live as they must too, but also as they think
right, which is what makes them more than just
animals." She could not keep from adding bitterly,
"What the free fems seem to think is right is to make
one of themselves master and serve her. How could the
Riding Women think well of them?"

"That's what you really care about, isn't it," Daya
said. "What the Riding Women think. Well, maybe
we're not good enough for them, but you aren't either,
or you'd still be living with them."

"They didn't send me away. I left. To be with my
own kind—who make themselves slaves when they
could be free—to be part of their stupid plan, that
miserable lie—"

"You don't know that the plan won't happen."

"I know," Alldera said with disgust. She snapped off
branches of the brush that straggled like dry, tangled
hair down the side of the gully and she threw the pieces
into the rope net on the ground. "I know. I'm a fem
myself."

Ah, this quarreling is bad for me, she groaned inwardly.

Daya said, "Who are you, to demand that we all act
as you'd choose for us to act?"

Alldera stood over the hoofprints of the wild horses. Trying to sound reasonable she answered, "I just want to see the free fems break out of the old order, not make it all over again here. Some of them know it, but they haven't the courage to act. They should live, grow, become something besides playthings or drudges for Elnoa. Anything would be better than the way you plod along letting that gross creature dominate your lives." It sickened her to recall how she had begged Elnoa to send her out trading.

"If you had your way," Daya replied, "we'd become your slaves and drudges, doing what you want instead."

"Maybe that's the only way to get you all moving, to make you all alive." Alldera felt angry and out of control.

"I see," taunted Daya in an oily voice. "You'd like to astonish us all, both Mares and fems, by seizing the initiative and driving us all before you to go save our people, like the hero of a Holdfast story. I recognize the pattern. It's a compelling story; I've told it often; but it isn't life. You have to wait till you're dead and gone before your doings can take on the shape of such lying legends."

"You're like the rest of them," Alldera burst out. "The free fems will never follow me or anyone home, they'll just sit around making excuses for their cowardice until they die!"

Tears appeared in Daya's eyes. "We did more for ourselves even in the Holdfast than you think; the masters could never completely crush us."

At this Alldera closed in on her: "Oh, yes, you and your stories of clever fems outwitting their masters! Your romances of the past are as false as your romances of the future. We were slaves. A few of us, fems like Elnoa, were smarter, better placed to protect themselves, or luckier. Even when those tales are true they don't mean anything. We were slaves. That's our real history. Better to fight and die." She snapped a bundle of sticks over her knee with a downward plunge of both fists. "You are everything slavish about us, everything I hate."

Daya stood sideways to her, twisting a piece of wood in her hands, crying. "Most of us burned out our courage crossing the borderlands. What great task must I now perform to satisfy your standards?"

She threw the wood at Alldera's feet and said, "Of us two, I'm not the one who's ashamed of who she is."

The hot weather came full strength. "Now I'll take you to a place north of here," Fedeka said. She led them to a small, grassy valley among the foothills. She had dug a well there and transplanted trees to shade it. They put up the tent under the trees and drew out Fedeka's great simmering-pots from the brush shelter she had made for them.

Alldera woke the next dawn, while the others still slept. She walked the cool slopes alone and looked down on their little encampment, feeling rested but not calm. Her spirits rode high on a tingling wave of anticipation: then the meaning of this place grew clear.

Fedeka had made this, a retreat such as no slave had ever had. But she did not hide here, growing fat and easy. She always returned to the plain with its dangers and its beauties. Because—it must be—out there, alone, was where she had found the strength to make this.

As quietly as she could Alldera got out water bottle, hip pack stuffed with dried food, rope; but Daya heard, raised her head, and said in a voice husky with sleep, "Where are you going?"

"I'll be back before the dust storms start."

Running toward the plain Alldera felt light and swift and tireless, at her best.

9

Daya steadied the great pot as Fedeka levered sodden cloth out of it with a pole. Her muscles taut, the dyer transferred the dripping weight to another vessel full of the steaming, smelly solution that fixed the color in the fibers.

The trees had fruited with fantastic colors and shapes: Fedeka's bright pennants hanging up to dry. Daya resented Alldera's escape from all the work there was to do: drawing water from the well with the creaking windlass, tending the fires under the dye pots or scouring out the pots to clean them for new colors, setting out cloth to dry or taking it in.

Was Alldera dead or alive out there, near or far off on the long, flat, empty horizon of the plain? It was months now. The figure of the runner stayed in her mind's eye.

While they worked Fedeka listened with bursts of appreciative laughter to Daya's anecdotes of tea camp life.

Daya sighed. "You're my best audience, as always. I think I miss you a lot when I'm back in the tea camp."

"Me too," Fedeka said. "Pity we're not better suited. But my nature doesn't much suit anybody in the long run, so it's a good thing I suit myself." Fedeka sat with the pottery mortar locked between her legs, grinding dried plants to powder with a strong, patient motion of her single arm.

"What kind of company was Alldera before I
came?"Daya asked idly.

"Quiet company." Fedeka dipped a finger into the
mortar, withdrew it, and spat on the film of dark
material on the tip. She peered at it, and at that moment
Daya knew herself to be forgotten.

To get the dyer's attention she said, "I'm completely
healed now, thanks to you; but am I sterile, do you
think?"

"Not if you've attended to your prayers." Daya knew
that Fedeka really believed that someday, if it were
Moonwoman's will, a free fem would conceive without
a man. Her fertility solutions were, to her, merely in-
struments of the deity.

"Do you think Alldera is alive out there?"

"If she's attended to her prayers, yes," Fedeka said.
Sometimes her piety could be irritating. Now she
frowned, grinding the pestle round and round. "I can
see why she had trouble in the tea camp. Nothing suits
her, she has no place else to go, but she can't seem to accept herself and the life around her. It's a sickness I
have no medicine for."

Daya said, "She takes everything too seriously,
starting with herself. That's her trouble."

Fedeka gave a decisive shake of her head. "She
doesn't see. Moonwoman could help her see. When I
first saw one of those Marish drum heads of leather all
covered in designs rubbed in with red willow juice, I
started to see color everywhere; that was a gift from
Moonwoman, a great gift. Eyes that always look inward
miss everything."

Eyes that always look upward at the moon or down at
color plants don't see everything either, Daya thought;
knowing and liking Fedeka well, she did not speak her
thought out loud. She found with surprise that she was
missing Alldera a little. Arguing with the runner could
be painful, but it was not as monotonous as discussion
with Fedeka could get once the name of Moonwoman
was invoked.

*   *   *

Among the rocks topping a knob at the mouth of
Fedeka's valley Daya searched for a yellow herb. She
paused a while to watch the dust storms drift above the
plain like dirty finger smudges on the sky. It was a hot,
bright morning.

She saw someone approaching over the plains on
horseback. Thinking it was a Mare come looking for
Alldera, she ran down the hillside shouting to alert
Fedeka. She saw the visitor gallop into their hollow,
fling herself from her mount and stride forward to meet
the dyer.

It was Alldera, her leather shirt scraped and rent, her
hair matted and her lips blackened and split, her teeth
white as salt in her brown, grinning face. Her stench was
so strong close up that Daya could hardly breathe. She
had ridden in on the bare back of a gaunt, shaggy brown
horse, trailing two others that followed her like the
docile herd beasts of the Mares.

"You've been to the Mares," Fedeka accused. "And
what have you brought back? Horses! Mares' mates!"

One of the horses lifted its head, made a low, breathy
sound, and took a step forward. Fedeka bent to snatch
up a stone.

"She's not after you," Alldera said. "They smell the
water in your well. Let me see to them, and then we can
sit in the shade and talk, if I can keep awake. I rode all
night to avoid the heat."

She twitched on the rope that she had tied around the
head and jaw of her mount, and the horse followed her.
The other two fell in after it.

Daya could not stop staring at her. How strong and
brown she looked, how effortlessly she commanded the
horses. Her eyes were bright with excitement, and she
grinned and grinned like some exuberant spirit. Daya
had never seen Alldera like that.

Alldera drew water for the horses and tied their front
feet loosely together with leather to keep them from
straying out of the hollow. She pulled off her tattered
clothes and sluiced herself down in cold water. Then she
settled under the trees draped in a blanket. Brewing up

tea, she told them what she had done. She kept laughing in the middle of what she said and reaching to clasp their hands as she spoke.

"I never went to the Mares, that wasn't the point at all. These are my horses. They were wild. I caught them, I tamed them."

Daya marveled. She basked in the vitality of Alldera's muscular body. She had an urge to touch Alldera, to hug her around the waist.

Alldera had gone from watering hole to seeping spring, all the places where water somehow persisted through the Dusty Season weather in amounts too small for the herds of the Riding Women but enough for a wild band. Where she found recent horse tracks, she waited.

The wild horses, a roaming troop of fifteen, returned to drink. Scenting her presence, they ran away. Alldera followed. She did not need to keep them in sight. She had only to jog along on their tracks until she came upon them where they had stopped to graze. At the sight of her they bolted again. Again she followed, and so it went for a number of days.

"But a horse can run faster than a person," Fedeka objected. "Why didn't they just run right away from you?"

Alldera shook her head. "No horse without a rider covers great stretches at speed. It's only an animal, it runs until the danger is out of sight and then forgets and gets back to its business of eating. Besides, these horses were in poor condition. Even the women have to harden their horses for long trips in the Dusty Season.

"But I was in good shape, and I could eat enough on the run to keep me going and drink water that I carried with me.

"The horses got sore-footed and sore-muscled, and they couldn't get enough to eat because I was always showing up and scaring them off. I know where the water holes are, so I could figure out which water the stud was headed for, cut across to get there first, and scare them off before they drank.

"Mind you, I guessed wrong twice, and had to go track them down again to different watering places. Otherwise, I would have been back long ago!

"I never changed my clothes or washed myself. They could recognize me from a good distance if the wind was right, and they began to get used to my smell. They learned that though they let me get closer and closer, nothing bad ever came of it. A day came when even the old stud could hardly drive them to run from me, they were so tired and gaunt and bored with running away from something just as familiar and harmless as a clump of grass or a rock. It was the morning after that that they came down to drink, even the old stallion, though I was right there at the spring.

"When they left, I left with them; just walking, wandering along on the outskirts of the band at first, but later right among them. There was a roan mare that acted as if she'd been gentled before; stolen from some women's herd by the stud, probably. I cut her some grass and she let me handle her a bit. By the time the horses were rested enough to make it hard for me to keep up with them, she let me ride her. I just lay back on her rump at first, until she and the others accepted what I was doing. Then I sat up and rode properly. What luxury, to be carried after all that walking! But I only did enough riding to keep up. I didn't want to wear her out.

"Meanwhile I began working on some of the others, the way the women gentle their horses: riding alongside and rubbing their backs, leaning my weight on them, getting them used to being handled and laden. Most of the band were scrubs, not worth taking. The old stud, while I was working on them, got into the habit of snoozing all day and leaving the job of lookout to me.

"Signs of sharu or fems or women were all signals for me to give the alarm, just as if I were really a wild horse myself. It didn't happen often. Traveling like that out there, you'd be surprised how few traces of human life you come upon. I talked to the horses sometimes, though I knew words meant nothing to them.

"I brought these away with me. They don't look like much, but they'll fill out, and there's plenty of grass here for just three."

Fedeka eyed her curiously. "You never thought of staying out there, living on your own with the horses?"

Alldera sipped tea from her bowl. She said, "Let me put it this way. One morning the old stud wanted to head the bunch in one direction, and I wanted to go in another. I was riding that dun mare at the time. I had my knife. I could have given the stud a fight and whipped him, too. He stood there snorting, pawing the ground, throwing his head and swelling his neck to threaten me, and I thought it would give me pleasure to beat him, considering how he bullied his mares.

"Then I thought, suppose I drive him off or kill him, what do I win? The leadership of a bunch of horses. So I grabbed up a handful of stones to sling at him if he chased me, cut out my three head, and left.

"And that's all there is," she finished on a note of happy satisfaction. She yawned.

"But what did you do it for?" Fedeka looked around at the horses in dismay. "What's to be done now?"

"I wanted to see if I could do it. I'll take care of them, don't worry."

"One thing I want to know now," Fedeka said, lowering her voice. "This old stallion, the leader of the herd—did he ever think you were another of his herd? The Mares get male horses to mate with them; weren't you afraid what the stallion might do to you?"

Alldera blinked at her. "I didn't say I got to smell like a horse, only like myself," she protested. "I never gave off the right odors to rouse the stallion. I don't think a horse has any choice about mating, when the time comes. If I had smelled right, he couldn't have helped it, he'd have had to try to mount me. Since I smelled wrong, I never feared to turn my back on him. The women are right—horses may do things that look like what humans do, but the meaning is all changed." She stretched. "I'll go sleep now. I can hardly sit up."

Daya could not bear to lose contact with her. "I'd

like to come with you," she said shyly.

After a moment's hesitation, Alldera laughed and pulled her to her feet. Into the tent they went together, getting in each other's way as they laid out Alldera's long unused bedding.

Their lovemaking was not a great success for Daya. She needed to feel overwhelmed by a force of-nature, swept to a place of infinite security and delight where she could safely let herself melt. She found Alldera a conscious sort of lover, possibly self-conscious to an added degree with a partner whom she knew to be unusually experienced. Daya could feel her thinking all the time.

It did not seem to matter much. They fell asleep hugged tight together and breathing each other's warm breath.

10

"I hear Alldera doesn't fit in with her own people any better than she did with us." Sheel and Nenisi sat together in a sunny patch outside the tent of Nenisi's cousins, where Nenisi was staying during the Gather. Nenisi looked just as she always had. The dark-skinned lines hardly aged at all, Sheel thought. She added, "They say you go and visit Alldera among the free fems."

Nenisi groaned. "You and I have been out of touch, Sheel. Don't provoke me here at the Gather. My teeth are already sore enough. I went only once, after the last Gather, to tell her that our child had joined the child-pack. She said when we send for her to attend the child's coming out, she'll come."

"So," Sheel said. "What of it?"

"Someday at a Gather like this it will be our daughter, and hers, mating with a stud horse. I know it's hard to think about any daughter that way when she's still only a wild creature running with the pack. But look forward a little, Sheel: when this child comes out, we won't be much help to her as mothers if our feelings about her—and about her bloodmother—aren't warm and loving."

"Loving!" Sheel snorted. "I hardly think about the man-used bitch now that our tent family has separated, and it's never with love."

The women of Holdfaster Family had gone traveling

after the years of staying at Stone Dancing Camp to tend their baby. They would reassemble to welcome the child when she was ripe to emerge from the childpack. Meanwhile Shayeen kept Holdfaster Tent running as a shelter for visitors unable, for one reason or another, to stay with their own relatives in Stone Dancing.

Nenisi said, "What will you do, Sheel, when the family comes back together for this child's coming-out ceremonies?"

"I'll help," Sheel said promptly, "but nothing we do will place that child properly and securely among us."

Nenisi slapped the hard ground between them. "Why not? Why do you say that?"

Sheel frowned, considering. She disliked talking about ceremonial matters, but it was a long time since she had seen Nenisi and she wanted to be understood. She explained slowly, picking her way. "We are in touch with strong currents that hold all the things and beings and forces of the plains in balance. Any woman here can be helped to find that balance, or to regain that balance if it's been lost. We help. The horses help. But you can't put in balance something that never belonged at all."

"We'll make it work, if we try hard enough," Nenisi insisted. "We will make that child into one of us, complete with relatives, duties and honor."

Sheel studied her and saw in the dark, smooth-planed Conor face that tightness of anxiety she had noticed so often in Nenisi since the fem had come among them. Easy enough for me, she thought now; I just hate the fems, no complications. Nenisi's feelings are all gummed up with rights and wrongs. Does she know how she really feels?

She saw Nenisi's pride, the Conor pride in being right. It was a Conor trait and part of Nenisi's beauty. Once Sheel had been comfortable with Nenisi, before Holdfaster Family.

"The horses won't dance with her, Nenisi. Her mothers won't be able to bring her out properly. It can't work."

*   *   *

Next day the huge camp of the Gather, a camp composed of all the women's camps, was quiet. The games and the races and the settling of quarrels were all over; the time for the mating drew near.

Women filed in and out of the sweat tents all day long. Sheel sat quietly cleaning and repairing the belongings of her tent with other women. They all went inside during a brief, hard shower of rain at midday.

In the afternoon Sheel, among the last women to use a sweat tent, walked out toward the great dancing ground outside camp. She shook out her clean wet hair and swirled her long leather cloak in elaborate passes. The sound of the capes whishing through the air drew the women from their tents. Talking and laughing, they joined the growing procession flowing out of the camp.

Looking back, her arms already aching from wielding the weight of the cape, Sheel saw the sailing cloaks like a camp of tents taking flight over grass still bright with beads of rain.

The childpacks of the camps swarmed among the women, circling, piping and screaming, ducking under the billowing leather, diving into gaps between the walkers. Around and around the dancing ground the procession flowed until it formed a noisy wall of women ringing the flat space. Overhead great ragged cloaks of cloud streamed slowly across the clean blue sky. The moon, a mere edge away from full, was a fragile white disc against the blue.

In a little while the first childpack went racing away from the dance ground, scattering out on the plain. Others followed. Several packs sorted themselves out of a whirling free-for-all and ran in another direction. Too excited by the procession to stay afterward for a dull dance, the children preferred to ambush each other over the thick southern turf or harry the horses left unattended. If they returned too soon, there were women stationed outside the dancing ground to turn them away, with whips if necessary.

As the early risen moon grew more substantial, a

channel opened through the women's ranks. Horses poured into the circle, all stallions, nervous at having been separated from the mares. Those women who had walked the horses to the dancing ground closed the gap, penning them in. The horses milled inside the human enclosure, calling, darting one way and then another.

Her arms linked in those of the women on either side of her, Sheel whooped and stamped with them when the horses ran near her sector of the crowd, and the beasts whirled back the way they had come. Her voice skirled joyfully in her throat, she threw her fresh-washed hair from side to side as if it were her mane. Let the land stretch dry and dusty over the rocky bones of the world; the horses were a tumultuous river flowing past her, rough, swift, life-sharing.

Now the young women who had been working with the horses for months had their moment. Dropping their cloaks, they stepped from the crowd and ran naked among the horses. Amid the plunging shadows they swung up onto the studs' backs, where they balanced or leaped. A young woman sprang over a dark colt's back, just touching him in passing, and landed on her feet. Another, a bright-haired Salmowon, stepped from the dipping back of one horse to the back of another as lightly and surely as if crossing a stream on stones.

Sheel remembered, her whole body moved with remembering. Every childpack danced the horses. You skipped over their backs, leaping, vaulting to touch the ground an instant before bounding back up onto another horse's back. Around you and beneath you ran the horses in a chaos of dust and din. You played them until they moved as a group, until they learned the game, you danced them to a lathered standstill. Then next day you laughed at the adults' dismay at finding their horses worn out.

When you were grown you danced the stallions under the round moon before all the women. You felt your strength flow to the horses, and then back again to you, made stronger. All beings found their rightful places in these exchanges, and the balance of all things was re-affirmed.

A young Hont woman came whirling out of the mob, a bay horse with her. It curvetted past her, rearing and shaking its head, and then turned back to come to her shoulder and rub its knobby face against her. The Hont's mothers came out to lead her and the lathered horse quietly away, both to be prepared for mating tomorrow.

By dawn the last stallion and the last dancer had been escorted away, the dust had settled, and the bedding chute was built. The Hilliars had put it together this year, in the neat, casual-looking way that they did everything. Some called it "the saddle" because this was the horse's turn to ride.

It was a rectangular box with three closed sides, an open top, and a high floor. The insides of the floor and walls were padded with leather cushions. Arched across the open top and joining the two long walls was a carefully padded superstructure to take the weight of the stallion and the grip of his forelegs. It would suspend his body over the young woman lying inside the box. There were ropes to release an escape trap for a woman whose mating went wrong and endangered her.

The women assembled as they had for the dancing, forming an oval of spectators surrounding the bedding chute. Here a voice rose in song, there another. The members of each Motherline sang all the self-songs of the past generations of their line. The singing of each Motherline unfurled like a banner against the paling sky.

"I crossed the Sunset River to raid my enemy's herds," sang a yellow woman next to Sheel. That was an old song from the days before the camps had discarded streambeds as boundaries because they were places of confrontation and fighting.

Sheel sang the song of her own bloodmother. It was composed largely of affectionate descriptions of the horses the woman had taken during her lifetime of

raiding, and the names of women she had faced in feuds
and duels. Sheel sang it with passionate pride.

The moist wind stirred the hair of the young Hont
candidate who stepped first into the open. She was
thickset like all her line, but the simple leather cloak she
wore disguised her body's lack of grace. With her clean
golden hair falling down her back, she looked her best.
You forgot the big-featured Hontish face.

Sheel approved, and found the Hont's showing off
appealing. The youngster strolled the circumference of
the dance ground, smiling, waving to women who called
her name in the midst of their singing.

Someone slipped an arm through Sheel's: Barvaran,
her red face shining with happiness. She herself had
been to the stud horses three times, and she had three
living bloodchildren as robust and good-natured as herself.

Sheel thought of her own two blooddaughters, one
lost in the pack and the other to an epidemic of fever.
She no longer grieved for them or for her own failure to
bring adult daughters to her Motherline. It was true, as
women said; no one rides only one horse on a long journey. There were all the daughters of her sisters and her
cousinlines, young women as like to her own dead
bloodchildren as they were to Sheel and to each other.
She sang a brief self-song for the child which had lived
long enough to come out of the pack, and then her own
self-song of hunts, raids, and the deaths of men.

The Hont climbed into the chute and lay down on her
back. One of her sharemothers got in with her to en-
courage and caress her so she would be moist and open
to her stud. Sheel remembered well feeling the smooth
wooden rests against which she had braced her bare feet
and watching the support frame dark against the sky.
Poli Rois, her friend, had lain down with her, kissing
her neck.

Poli was gone now many years, struck dead in her
saddle by lightning while still a youth.

Into the circle of onlookers came two of the Hont's
family. The bay stallion stepped along neatly between

them. They walked with their hands on his withers and
his neck. They talked into his flicking ears. Small,
sedate, groomed so the sunlight shimmered on his hide,
he was scarcely recognizable as one of the wild-eyed
studs of last night's dance. His feet were filed and oiled,
and ribbons of dyed leather were braided into his mane
and tail. He was called Tiptoe, and was bred from the
home herd of Salmowon Tent in Melting Earth Camp.

Sheel's first stud had been a nameless chestnut with a
lop ear. She had looked up and seen his familiar
crooked silhouette and the little beard of whiskers on his
jaw, so well known to her and so ridiculous that all her
fear had dissolved. Awe and joy had filled her, that the
instrument of her own joining with the great patterns of
the world should be so ordinary a creature. Well, so was
she, yet both she and the stud embodied the dependence
of all beings on each other and the kinship of creatures.
That was the mystery of the mating, its beauty and
necessity.

She had spoken softly to him above the singing voices
of the gathered women, and he had entered her as
smoothly as the staff of oiled leather with which she had
stretched herself in practice for him. After the culling
that year his flesh had gone to help nourish the child he
had started in her belly.

Her second stud, a barrel-bodied gray, had sired a
number of fine foals after mating with her. She had ridden him for years until an infected sharu slash had made
it impossible for him to keep up with the herd any more.
It had taken two hammer blows to drop him for
butchering. Poor Cloud.

The singing had sunk to a soft murmur. The faces of
other women showed Sheel that they too were thinking
of the dead; dead horses, dead children, dead women
who had bled to death after bad matings.

The handlers rubbed the neck and chest of the little
stallion. They stroked his face and nostrils with pads
that had been run under the tails of mares in season. He
began to throw his head and snort, and within a few
moments they had him erect. Under the touch of hands

well known to him he reared high and clamped his
forelegs on the padded support frame. He gripped the
leather roll at the chute's head and rattled it with his
teeth. Standing outside the chute, the handlers stroked
his sweating neck and shoulders and bent to guide him.

Suddenly he thrust forward against the wooden
braces which prevented him from entering fully. He
oscillated his rump, snorting loudly, and his tail jerked,
marking the rhythm of his ejaculation. Within seconds,
it seemed, he pulled back and stood dark with sweat,
droop-headed, quiet.

The handlers praised and patted him as they led him
away to rejoin the herd. He left between them as
modestly as he had arrived.

Others of her family reached to help the young Hont
up, but she was already on her feet in the chute. She
swung her robe about herself with a grand gesture that
showed as well as anything could her triumphant success. They closed around her, checking her for injury,
mopping the milky overflow from her thighs. With her
arms on the shoulders of two of them, she walked
briskly from the dance ground.

A new candidate had already stepped out from the
crowd. A sorrel horse, thick-maned and heavy-headed,
came into the circle. Snorting at the crowd, he bounced
along half sideways. Sheel knew that horse. She had
taken him from the herds of Chowmer Tent in Windgrass Camp last year. She hoped he was smoother as a
rider than he was as a mount.

She thought angrily of Nenisi. The black woman was
mad to insist that the child of a fem could lie down for a
stud like a woman. Holdfaster Tent was just a dream
anyway, Nenisi's fantasy of righteousness.

There was a story about a free fem, long ago—she
had been taken up briefly by the Golashamets because
she had looked so much like them. She had attended a
mating, just once. Women said that after the first stud,
the fem had turned and vomited on the woman next to
her.

11

When the cool months started the three fems returned to
the plain. They brought the horses that Alldera had
caught. Fedeka's open dislike of the animals abated
when she saw that not only could they help carry
baggage from campsite to campsite, but they could bear
many more than the number of plant samples that she
normally packed on her own back.

For Daya, their presence was magical; she rode
whenever she could. She had begun, timidly, to learn
how under Alldera's tutelage and had discovered a
horse's power to transform its rider.

Alldera had made Daya a saddle of padded leather
sewn wet onto a wooden frame so as to shrink as it dried
to make a strong seat. The saddle was trimmed with
straps and strings to lash on bottles, blankets, and other
equipment. The leather required frequent applications
of soap and oils to keep it supple and uncracked. Daya
used the heavy saddle gladly on long rides, but she loved
better riding bareback, seat and legs fitted to the horse's
body, wearing pants cut off at the knee so that she could
feel the living flank of the horse along her calves.

The dun mare had a big, ugly head and at rest its
lower lip drooped and exposed its yellow teeth in a
comical, foolish-looking manner. But it was responsive,
almost tireless, Daya's favorite mount. Alldera said
with a trace of jealousy that Daya was a natural rider.
She admitted to Daya that she herself did not love the

horses; what she loved was having the mastery of them. Daya loved their rich appeal to her senses and the joining of her own meager strength to their power. Crouched on the shoulders of her galloping mount, she reveled in the ecstasy of speed. Alldera often had to remind her that the Mares did not gallop everywhere and that Daya too should practice the slower, less wearing gaits.

Riding under drifts of illuminated cloud, Daya dreamed of tearing down the far side of the mountains scattering terrified men, battering them down with the shoulders of her mount and pounding them under its hooves. Her horse was invincible. She heard in her mind the thudding of heavy, blunt blows on flesh and the crack of bone. Or she dreamed of nothing at all, but lived totally and raptly in the warm, driving reach of her horse under her.

On foot little changed for her. She still spoke softly, moved automatically out of another's way and shed tears instead of shouting when she was angry. She knew these ways were forever part of herself, not to be changed by her joy in the horses and the new strength that they had lent her.

As she rode with Alldera, Daya began to talk about their former lives and even to ask questions about Alldera's adventures with her two outlaw masters in the last days of the Holdfast.* Alldera seldom raged against Elnoa's free fems any more. Now when she spoke of them it was painfully, questioning earnestly why they were as they were. Sometimes she would ask Daya for an opinion and then ride silently a while before replying, if she replied at all.

They slept together only occasionally, yet Daya felt them growing closer, knit together by quiet conversations and companionship. The gradual weaving of this connection delighted Daya and frightened her; it

*The story of Alldera's escape is told in *Walk to the End of the World* by Suzy McKee Charnas (Ballantine, 1974); Berkley, 1979).

was new, an unreadable part of the mystery of the horses.

Sometimes they talked about Alldera's years with the Mares.

"They'll send for me when my blooddaughter, my cub, is ready to come out of the childpack," Alldera said once. "The sharemothers come together to receive her, and stay together for however long it takes—a few months, even several years, depending on her maturity—to prepare her for her mating and the forming of her own family."

"Will you go when they send for you?"

"Yes. Now I have some horses to give for the tent herd. I'll leave the dun mare with you." After a glance at Daya's face she added hesitantly, "Unless you'd consider coming with me?"

They were watering the horses. Sitting on the dun mare's back, Daya looked down at the sunlight breaking on the water and spreading in circles from the mare's hot muzzle. Her hands moved over the sleek shoulders, feeling the glide and pull of muscle under the skin as the animal stepped forward, lifting its dripping mouth. A tightening of the rein, a tap of the heels, and it would move on obedient to the will of the small, weak creature on its back.

A person with this power would not be just a runaway fem among the Mares. If riding were all there was to it. . . .

"There's what you call a family waiting for you to join it, Alldera. What would I be, among the Mares?"

"I've thought about that. You'd be my cousin Daya. As my relation, you'd be their relation."

Daya thought of the tea camp; her place by Elnoa was occupied, but surely not if she chose to return and claim it. It would be dreadful to be abandoned among strangers once Alldera had settled with the Mares again and wearied of the novelty of showing off her pretty pet friend.

She said, "But what sort of position would I have, myself, with the Mares?"

Alldera looked impatient. "They have no positions, only relations. You don't need a position when you have kindred."

Yes, now Daya remembered: waking among the Mares years ago after her own rescue by a patrol and her own healing sleep, and being unable to work out who was important among those who tended her.

"I won't know anyone there, Alldera. You wouldn't—drop me, and leave me on my own?"

"No," Alldera said. "I promise."

"I never thought you'd want me," Daya murmured.

By the time the Dusty Season came, Fedeka was talking with undisguised anticipation of the rendezvous with one of the trade wagons toward which they slowly made their way. She had been acting more and more distant, and Daya knew that with Fedeka it could not be jealousy. Probably the dyer was just tired of company and hoped that her two guests would join the wagon and leave her to wander on. It seemed to Daya that Alldera was not likely to find a welcome with the tea fems, but there was no point in talking to Fedeka about that.

The trade wagon was not at the wells of Steep Cloud Camp where they had expected to meet it. Fedeka glared with frustration at the stubbled flats.

"They must be still back at Royo Camp," she said. "I need tea. I need cloth. They have to pass this way. We'll wait."

The hot, dry days dragged past. No one talked about what was to happen when the wagon finally did arrive, and this increased the tension of waiting.

Alldera and Daya endured it, riding out daily in search of grass for the horses. They were returning one evening, discussing the possibility of trading for grain from the Mares to sustain their animals, when a sudden rush of hoofbeats engulfed them. The dark heads and shoulders of running horses dodged around them.

The dun mare bolted, throwing her head forward so suddenly that she jerked the rein from Daya's hand. For thirty long strides, gasping in fear and exultation, Daya clung with her fingers twined in the dun's mane. Then something slammed at her body. Off-balanced, she jumped for her life, rolling like an acrobat when she hit the ground so that she ended up standing on wavering legs.

The dun ran on in the dust of the other horses, holding her head high and to one side so as not to tread on the reins hanging from her mouth.

A rider came toward Daya—Alldera, surely.

Two riders, three, half a dozen; all in a rush they flowed around her, a wall of horses, faces peering down at her past the horses' necks and heads.

"Who's this on foot?" rang a voice she did not know, a Marish voice, rich and imperious. "Who unhorsed you, woman?"

A new rider galloped up, leading the dun mare. She stood in her stirrups. "Where is she? Stand back, I knocked her down and I claim the capture!" She pressed past the others and with a swift gesture threw the slack of her bridle rein around Daya's neck. "I claim ransom! How many horses have you at your tent to give to Patarish Rois of Windgrass Camp?"

Daya was paralyzed by fear of them and dizzy with their stench of sweaty leather.

Someone said in a puzzled tone, "Looks like one of the Carrals to me, but she hasn't got a big enough behind."

Then a rider raced up behind the others, leaped from her horse, and rushed into the center on foot. It was Alldera. She snatched the rein from around Daya's neck so fast that it burned Daya's skin.

The first speaker, bending deeply out of her saddle for a closer look, whooped, "It's that fem Alldera Holdfaster that used to live in Stone Dancing Camp! This must be another one. You've caught two fems, Patarish!"

One woman laughed. Another cried, "Sorry, fems!" Wheeling their horses they rode away, calling to Patarish Rois to follow them.

She did not. She hung darkly above the two fems,

smouldering with outraged pride. Daya moved silently behind Alldera, sheltering from the Mare's rage.

"What are fems doing on horseback?" cried the rider. "No fems own any horses that I've ever heard of, and any Riding Woman who lets fems ride her mares deserves to lose them. You know who I am. Let the woman who lent you horses come to me to claim her property if she dares!" Her mount danced and snorted. The dun mare tried to break away from its captor, lifting its head and tugging at the reins in alarm.

"No," Daya whispered, clutching Alldera's arm. The tears of anger welled in her eyes.

Alldera grasped the woman's rein just under the jaw of her mount. "That dun horse belongs to us."

"Nothing on the plains belongs to a fem! Stand aside, I'm taking the brown horse too."

Like a whip lashing, Alldera struck. She spun in the air so that one foot shot high above her own head, and she landed crouched to kick again. There was no need. The Mare's horse had bounced sideways with a terrified snort, and the woman fell like a sack out of the saddle. Alldera caught the woman's horse and stood clutching the stirrup, as if holding herself up.

"See if she's all right, will you?" she said in a strained voice. "I haven't done anything like that in years. I think I've ruptured myself."

The high hoops of the long expected trade wagon loomed beside Fedeka's fire. As they rode in, Roona's crew sprang up. Daya saw faces well known to her from Elnoa's camp. It occurred to her that the crew fems may have expected fems on horseback, but never a Mare riding with them. These closed, defensive masks that greeted her must be what fems often presented to the eyes of the Mares. Now she sat a saddle herself and looked uncomfortably down at her own people.

The captive woman ignored them all. She dismounted stiffly after Roona invited her to. She politely tasted everything they offered her to eat. No one spoke to her. When she went to lie down a little distance off, curled in her blanket beside her hobbled horse, the fems all crowded into the wagon.

Roona turned at once to Daya and said, "What is this, Daya, what's happened?"

Daya told them. The fems grew furious at Alldera: what would the Mares do in return? they cried; what would happen to the trade, the fems' welcome here? Roona kept pulling off her leather cap, polishing her bald head with her palm, then jamming the cap on again as if she had come to a decision. But all she said was, "No one has ever done such a thing before!"

Alldera sat on a bale of hides massaging the long tendons of her groin and thighs and the base of her belly. At length she said, "Listen to me, everyone. It's no use for you to try to figure out what to do. No one is going to be put at risk with the women on my account. I'll see to this myself.

"In the morning I'll start for Stone Dancing Camp with my guest—which is how this young woman is to be treated by all of you. At the first camp I'll stop and have her relatives send word of what's happened to her home tent. It will be up to her own Motherline members and her family at Windgrass Camp to gather horses from their herds and deliver them to me as ransom. They'll object, but in the end they'll pay, and I'll leave the prize horses in the herd of Holdfaster Tent. That way the free fems won't be involved, since no horses will come into your hands."

Fedeka asked urgently, "But why go? Turn the woman loose, forget it ever happened, and hope they'll be willing to forget too."

"I can't. If I just let her go it would mean I thought she was without value, not worthy of a ransom, and I'd be giving her and all her relations a deadly insult. The other way is much better. It's getting near the time my cub should be coming out of the childpack anyway. I'd already decided to go back for that. I'll just start for Stone Dancing Camp earlier."

There were protests: the Mares would be enraged to see fems on horseback, let alone with a woman prisoner.

They would take it out on all the fems. A few said darkly that the whole thing was a trick of Alldera's, too complicated for them to understand. Others, their first panic eased, spoke in tones of shy admiration.

Fedeka gripped Alldera's hand and pumped it to punctuate the single point she made over and over. "I don't like to see you return to those wild people. They don't believe in Moonwoman."

She gave up and retreated into silence when Daya admitted that she was going to Stone Dancing Camp too. The atmosphere in the wagon became quiet, but distinctly strained.

Daya went outside to see that the horses were securely hobbled for the night. Clouds masked the moon's bright face, and all the sky seemed crowded with heavy shapes edged in brilliant light. There was so much life in the sky here, she thought, even at night. She went to the horses and stood among them, rubbing their soft noses and lips and the muscles behind their ears, grateful for their undemanding warmth.

The hostility she had felt in the wagon worried her. Maybe she had made a wrong decision. But she did not want to go back with Roona's crew to the tea camp. She did not want to have to figure out—for her own safety—who had tried to poison her in that whirl of passion and intrigue around Elnoa. The suspicion and self-absorption of the wagon crew tonight had struck her as strange and unpleasant.

Now that she rode a horse herself the idea of staying a while among the Mares seemed less alien. She would have to be careful not to use the insulting term "Mares" in their hearing, though.

In the morning Fedeka was gone. She had left the gear and belongings of Alldera and Daya in a neat heap on the ground. The horses grazed nearby.

Alldera packed up. Daya did the same. The dark young Mare, Patarish Rois, sat watching in the shadow of her horse while working at her kinky black ringlets with a wooden comb. The fems watched from the wagon.

Daya said, "Alldera, a couple of the crew fems came to me early this morning and said they would like to go with us."

"What for?"

"To see what it's like with the Mares. To learn riding."

"No!" Alldera busied herself knotting the saddlestrings around one end of her roll of bedding. "We have no horses for them. Besides, it would make more bad feeling than ever between us and the tea camp if we ride off with part of Roona's crew." The horse swung its head and nipped at her shoulder. She slapped it over the nose, and it jumped. She said, "What did they pay you to get me to agree?"

"Some good tea," Daya said, gauging the distance between them in case she should have to duck a blow.

"You'd better give it back to them, then."

"They paid me for my effort."

"I thought we knew each other pretty well by now," Alldera said, mounting and looking down at her. "I hope I wasn't too far off the mark about you."

"There's always more to know," Daya said. You had to keep a little distance from strong people if you were not to be mastered by them.

Two fems from the wagon crew trotted after them for some little distance, shouting abuse. Before turning back one of them threw a rock.

Patarish Rois rode with her eyes fixed politely straight ahead. She did not, during the days and nights that followed, try to take the horses and run away or cut the fems' throats while they slept. Alldera's confident courtesy toward her was at first hesitantly and then routinely returned. The Rois was soon talking animatedly with her, waving her dark hands in this direction and that as they discussed how to thread their course among the women's migratory routes.

They expected Alldera's camp to be on the move in the early rains by the time they reached its range. Their first stop on the way for food, water and grain was to be Singing Metal Camp.

On a hot morning they topped a rise overlooking the
Singing Metal herds. They paused, wiping the sweat
from their faces, adjusting their gear, clearing their
throats of dust. Their own horses, footsore and thirsty,
pricked up their ears and neighed to the horses of the
grazing herds. The hot wind blew in their faces, tearing
away the sound.

The women of Singing Metal Camp, according to
Alldera, had a special hostility toward fems. They resented the femmish contention that the women's skills
at working Ancient scrap had been learned from fems
rather than from the ancestors of Singing Metal women.

Daya was not reassured by the way Patarish Rois sat
tugging nervously at the fringes of her sleeve, or by
Alldera's silence. They had no choice, however. They
needed the use of Singing Metal's wells.

Patarish Rois led them down. They did not make
directly for the tents but circled to approach from the
side opposite to the grazing herds. Alldera explained.
"We don't want to seem to be sizing up their stock for a
raid later on. This young Rois has a lot to lose if we're
treated badly or laughed at, so she'll help us. Don't
worry; this is going to go well."

Daya was not convinced. She felt very vulnerable,
riding among the Mares' tents. Women peered out at
them as they moved toward the largest tent. Tethered
horses lifted their heads and whinnied. Someone was
working at a forge, throwing out an irregular, clinking
rhythm.

Two people stepped out of the big tent as they drew
near, handsome look-alikes with coppery skin and black
hair.

"Bawns," Alldera breathed. "We're all right.
Shayeen, one of my own sharemothers in Holdfaster
Tent, is a Bawn."

There was nothing about the two, no insignia or
finery or attendants, to show that they were chiefs. They
were smiling, but did not speak. They were so clearly at
a loss that Daya was embarrassed for them.

Alldera dismounted, took a breath and announced

herself. "Alldera Holdfaster, of Stone Dancing Camp. This is one of my femmish kin, Daya. And this is my guest, Patarish Rois of Windgrass Camp. We're going home to Stone Dancing to see to the horses that Patarish's kindred will be sending to us there, as soon as they hear that she and I are related by the rein." Meaning, Daya remembered, by Alldera's having captured her.

The younger Bawn looked as if she had been struck.

"Welcome," the older one said at last. "Come out of the sun and take tea with us."

The younger one added nervously, "Come tell us your news." As if the greatest of their news was not already told.

The older one embraced Alldera, and Patarish Rois jumped down from her horse and hugged the other. Alldera drew back, signed to Daya to dismount, and said firmly, "Will you greet my cousin Daya?"

The Bawns hung back, almost visibly trying to work out in their heads the consequences of any action they might take. Alldera they plainly knew by name if not by appearance; she was a relation, though a fem. Daya, in a femmish smock and Marish pants like Alldera but without headcloth or boots, was so obviously a wagon fem that the Bawns did not seem to know what to make of her as a relative.

Finally, with a gusty sigh the elder Bawn hugged Daya too. Enveloped in a muscular grip and a smell of horse sweat, smoke and the lingering pungency of tea, Daya said through dry lips, "Cousin," as Alldera had instructed her to do. She averted her face, hating the scars on her own cheeks.

The younger Bawn took charge of their horses. Daya watched jealously, noting how the woman eyed the dun as she handled it.

In the coolness of the Bawns' wide-winged tent some twenty women of Singing Metal Camp were gathered, and the guests were invited to sit with them. More women arrived, murmuring greetings, patting and embracing earlier arrivals as they looked for places to sit.

Everywhere were soft sounds of whispering and movement. The first of the tea was passed in shallow wooden bowls holding no more than a couple of swallows each.

Daya took a pouch from her belt and poured some shavings of tea into her own food bowl. Among such rough folk she felt it was only right for a civilized person to make the gracious gesture the occasion called for, even if it beggared her and was not properly appreciated. She passed the bowl.

The Mares looked curiously at this offering. Each one took a bit as long as the supply held out, though none chewed it as fems would have done.

Alldera had warned Daya that to soften bad feeling that might arise over the capture and ransom of a prisoner, it was the prisoner's right to tell the first version of her own downfall. She was entitled to make as much fun of her captor as she liked. Patarish Rois launched into a long preamble. It seemed to Daya that she was narrating all the raids she had ever been on, and acting them out complete with imitations of women involved—and, Daya thought at several points, of horses—to roars of appreciative laughter and comment. She would stick out her chunky rear and prance in a little circle, or stab her fingers through her wiry hair until it stood up on end. In one or two cases Daya could even see that she produced a creditable impression of someone present in the tent.

Women were elbowing each other in the ribs and grinning. Then Patarish told how Alldera had felled her from the saddle.

Silence and unbelieving stares. Alldera had said once that it was very unusual for a woman on foot to bring down a mounted one, let alone kick her down. The idea of a fem doing such a thing was plainly incomprehensible.

Then Alldera moistened her mouth with tea and took her turn. The women listened intently. At the end, when she said that she would gladly demonstrate the exact kick she had used except that she had nearly crippled herself doing it the first time, there were some smiles.

Someone got up and told a story about Alldera's past among the Mares, something about a hunt. Other stories were told, branching out to feats of her "family" members at Holdfaster Tent and their relations, and news of their doings since her departure from Stone Dancing. The women seemed a little anxious, possibly because they had never before been confronted with someone who stood in need of several years' news all at once.

They did their best: raids, races, hunts, horse swaps, quarrels sparked and put out, journeys made, gifts given, a death here and a birth there, good seasons and bad, people grown ill or well or staying the same. They did not speak of Alldera's cub, nor did she ask.

She told them about her capture of the wild horses, which seemed to impress them. They asked many questions. Daya felt proud of her.

At length food was brought, and Daya realized that at least some of her weariness was due to hunger. A brace of foals, roasted and cut into steaming joints and chunks, was served on trays of stiff leather. The stringy meat had a strong scent, but a sweet taste.

Daya thought Alldera looked extraordinarily natural in this setting. Indeed she could have been one of the women. Muscular and brown, greasy to the elbows from her meal, she gestured widely as they did and had swiftly fallen into their patterns of intonation and pronunciation. Her hair, trimmed by Fedeka to shoulder length, was bound back Marish-style with a rawhide thong to keep it from getting plastered to her cheeks with meat juices. She seemed to understand what would interest them most about the pasture and the wells she had passed on the way here.

Abashed by the Mares' frank stares, Daya withdrew into herself. Their yammering dinned in her ears. The odors of unwashed leather and horse sweat, added to the stink of burning dung, made her feel queasy. She sucked at one of her scars where it bulged inside her cheek. She felt very tired, disturbed and put upon. It was a great relief to her when they were told that a special sweat tent had been prepared so the two of them could bathe in privacy.

Much later, outside the sweat tent in the dusk, she and Alldera sluiced each other down with water from buckets left there for them. The sudden cool gush was remarkably pleasant and refreshing. The whole experience of the sweat tent had been unexpectedly agreeable. Watching Alldera drying off, Daya wondered idly what the Mares' bodies looked like under their leather clothing.

No one seemed to be around. The tents glowed faintly in the dusk by the light of small fires. The Bawn chiefs had provided fresh clothing for the two of them, laid out on a leather platter by the sweat tent. Daya had never put on a full Marish outfit before—trousers, boots, breast wrap, tunic, and the striped headcloth of wild cotton. Alldera dressed with obvious pleasure.

"These are wild people, remember," Daya said, unnerved by a feeling that Alldera was changing into one of them in front of her eyes. "They despise fems. Why did you leave them before, if it wasn't because they're savages?"

"The trouble wasn't with them, it was with me," Alldera said. "I demanded too much of them, I think." She chuckled ruefully. "A fault of mine. I'm older now, I think I know a little better." Then, somberly, she added, "I liked them even then, and I like them better now. I need to remember who my own people are when I'm here. That's why I asked you to come with me."

Daya whispered anxiously, "But also because you love me?" knowing it was only habit that made her worry.

Alldera's hands rested on her shoulders. "A lot of people have loved you, a lot more will," she said. "Perhaps some women of the camps will love you. We both know that you and I aren't much as lovers together. I need your friendship here."

"I don't know," Daya murmured, full of anxiety still—was she no longer desirable?

Alldera stood before her, solid, indistinctly outlined in the dusky light, not touching her; waiting.

Daya had never been a friend before.

V
Kindred

12

"Heartmother," Sheel murmured, rising on one elbow in the darkness. She knew the smell of the woman crouching by her bedding: Jesselee Morrowtrow, her own closest mother. She followed the limping woman quietly out of the tent.

There was a faint dawn pallor in the sky against which loomed the low, spreading shapes of the tents of Floating Moon Camp. The air was cold. Somewhere nearby a horse ruffled its breath loudly through its nostrils.

Sheel embraced her heartmother and leaned her head against the weathered cheek. "I'm glad to see you. Let me get you some tea and some food."

"Don't trouble yourself. I have food from my travels." Jesselee lowered herself awkwardly to the ground and laid out a pair of bulky saddlebags, which she set about unlacing.

Sheel crouched opposite her. "You're the only one with a thought for me. My other relatives have just barged right in and started haranguing me even if it was the middle of the night, regardless of who was with me."

"I may shout a little myself, Sheel Torrinor. Who else has come to see you?" Jesselee poured something into a bowl and handed it to Sheel.

"Who hasn't come? Women I haven't spent time with in years, Jesselee, women I'd almost forgotten."

She drank; cold tea, not bad. "Mates from my first raid, my other two living mothers—Derebayan wept buckets and made a spectacle of herself—several cousins and a Hont woman who familied with my Carrall mother two generations ago! The only person I really wanted to see was you."

"Tch, I'm not magic, you know," Jesselee said. "I'll only tell you what everybody else tells you." She turned her head from side to side. "This camp smells of fresh meat. Who slaughtered?"

"Sharavess Tent. They had a feast last night to return gifts they were holding for their tent child. The pack brought its body in yesterday morning—some quick illness, we think."

"Pity I'm too late," Jesselee said. "I know good stories about the Sharavess line that I could have told."

The sky was lighter, and Sheel could see her better now: a dumpy figure gnawing patiently and with effort on a strip of dried meat with the teeth on the good side of her mouth. She looked smaller than when Sheel had last seen her.

"What's the problem, Sheel? You are a mother of the child of Holdfaster Tent, and she's due to come out of the childpack soon. You should be at Stone Dancing Camp. Even I'm going, as a family member, though I should be taking my last comfort in my own home tent before dying; so what keeps you away?"

As long as Jesselee kept talking about her own death, she was unlikely to do anything about going to meet it. Sheel, loving her, had to smile. Yet she hesitated; daughter and mother of heart closeness were privileged to talk by themselves, but she did not enjoy the idea of being seen trotting out her troubles to her heartmother like a worried girl.

She said, "Let me do your hair for you while we talk." That would relax them both. She settled herself behind Jesselee and began to undo and do up again in a new pattern the small tight braids in which the old woman's gray hair was tied.

"There are fems in Holdfaster Tent." Word had

reached Sheel that Alldera had shown up at Stone Dancing Camp after the last Gather with Patarish Rois as her prisoner and another free fem companion. The Rois had been ransomed and released soon after. Now it was mid-Cool Season, two months later, and women said that Alldera and the other fem were still living in Holdfaster Tent.

"Alldera knew she should be home for the child's coming out," Jesselee said.

"With another of her kind?" Sheel turned her head and spat. "Alldera alone is bad enough. Because of her I haven't been allowed to go on a borderlands patrol in years. Because of her the Torrinors had to pay horses for the tent herd of Holdfaster Tent."

Jesselee moved her head from under Sheel's hands. "I love having my hair braided up but it always puts me to sleep. Come around here where I can see you, now that the sun's getting up. Good. Now, tell me more about how you feel."

"I don't want to."

"Aren't you curious?"

"No."

"Not about the visiting fems; about your child."

"No."

Jesselee sighed. With both hands she eased her leg into a slightly different angle of rest. It always hurt Sheel to see her do that. She could remember her heart-mother as an active young woman, lithe and strong. Now every time they met, Jesselee was a little stiffer, her limp more pronounced.

"Let me tell you what I've dreamed three nights since I left Stone Dancing," Sheel said. "I dream that I'm back on patrol. I go to the food cache in Long Valley by myself. There I find Alldera, swollen with her cub. I charge her and kill her and throw her body in the river. Then I ride to the others and say no one was there.

"Feeling—dreaming such anger—I don't want the child to sense that in one of its own mothers!"

"Let me tell you what's been worrying me for some time," said Jesselee. "I hear that you've been traveling around lately with one of those Omelly women. Now, I have nothing against the Omelly line; they are women like ourselves and worthy of companionship and affection. But it doesn't do to be careless with them, Sheel. They're dangerous.''

"Grays Omelly and I are thinking of raiding together when the Dusty Season comes," Sheel said. "Omellys make raid mates as good as anyone, if you don't let them provoke you and you watch your own behavior so you don't set them off. I can handle Grays.''

"Then you can handle Holdfaster Tent." Now Jesselee's lined face was fully visible: thick eyebrows arched as if in perpetual surprise, heavy mouth drooplipped, nose spread out on the face. She looked to Sheel like one of those leather dolls, features lined on with dye, that mothers sometimes made for their daughters. But Jesselee's eyes, drilled deep and small, glittered sharp as stars. Oh, those Morrowtrows were homely women! For as long as she could remember Sheel had connected that homeliness with warmth and enfolding support.

"Except for you, Sheel, there would be no Holdfaster Tent. You cared for that baby, you nursed it, just as the other sharemothers did. That child will look for you in Holdfaster Tent, and she won't find you in Nenisi or Shayeen or Barvaran or Alldera and her femmish friend. You are the only Sheel Torrinor there is. The child has a claim on your mothering right to the end of her childhood, whatever her background may be, whoever her other mothers are.''

"All right," Sheel sighed. "I'll go.''

However obscurely, a heartmother was always on your side.

Jesselee said, "I'll look for you there.''

Later, while cleaning her horse's feet, Sheel told Grays Omelly that she was returning to Holdfaster Tent. The Omelly breathed, "Sharu!" and gave her the flickering, nervous glance everyone watched for in women of her line. It meant the onset of the unpredictable anxiety which plagued the Omellys and could make them dangerous.

Sheel said, "I can't fight off my heartmother."

"No," the Omelly said. She had a length of rawhide in her hand and she twisted it first one way and then another. "I guess she decided you'd spent enough time with a crazy Omelly."

"Not exactly," Sheel said, bracing more firmly on her thigh the horsehoof she was picking clean. "Come with me to Stone Dancing."

"Ikk. You won't catch me hanging around a tent with fems in it. Fems smell."

"Everything that lives smells." The horse jerked its leg. Sheel said, "Ho, there!" The horse breathed in groans as if Sheel's careful extraction of packed dirt were torture.

"I'm going raiding as we planned," Grays said. "Maybe later I'll stop by and give you a horse for your sharechild. I'm curious to see a fem's child."

Sheel let go the hoof and it clumped back to earth. "You have seen her. You were at the last Gather. She's in the Stone Dancing pack. Didn't you go out viewing the packs at the Gather like everybody else?"

"You know Grays," Grays said, snapping the knotted end of the rawhide against the tent wall beside her. "They all look alike to Grays, she can't tell one from another till they come out and their families clean them up."

Someone inside the tent shouted, "Will you stop that tapping, whoever's doing that? You're driving us crazy in here."

Sheel said, "I have to go to my family. It's not any sort of insult to you."

"Nobody insults the crazy Omellys," Grays answered. "You never know what they might do in return."

When Sheel reached Stone Dancing Camp, the days were beginning to lose their cool bite and turn dry against the skin. She had taken her time, stopping to visit along the way. Jesselee was already in Holdfaster Tent. The tent child had not yet come out.

Alldera looked older, steadier, more muscular than Sheel remembered. They avoided each other.

Shortly after Sheel's arrival, two more fems came. They had deserted their wagon crew to join Alldera and Daya, and they arrived hunched wretchedly on the backs of spare horses belonging to women of Towering Camp. The women had been heading for Stone Dancing and the fems, claiming kinship with Alldera, had begged them to guide them there. Since the Towering Camp women were related to Barvaran and to Shayeen, they had felt bound to honor the kinship claim, and had assented.

The women had not enjoyed traveling with the fems. One of them reported to Sheel, "They made a fire of their own every night and cooked their own food as if our food were dirty."

Sheel saw that Alldera herself looked grim to see more fems come. Maybe she was selfish about losing her unique status here. But how could that be, since she had brought the first of them herself?

The new fems draped hides over the inner tent ropes, screening off one wing for themselves. This had never been done before in the camps and mortified Sheel. Alldera sometimes joined them behind this divider, though she seldom slept there at night; she was sleeping with Nenisi again. The scarred one, Daya, moved her own bedding behind the divider, however.

According to Nenisi, the new fems said they put up the curtain because they felt they were being watched —and judged—all the time by the women of Stone Dancing.

Sheel fervently wished they would make a tent of their own and live in that, because the curtain of hides did not shut out their femmish voices. They argued incessantly. At first women stopped to listen, but few could follow the rapid Holdfastish speech. One Calpaper woman said, "When they quarrel they sound like sharu in rut."

As tormenting for Sheel as their voices was the sweet smoke of the drug the fems called manna. Women occasionally brewed up a medicine from the plant for use in the treatment of certain conditions, but these fems put bits of the leaves on the fire and breathed the smoke. The fumes made Barvaran sleepy and silly, and Shayeen said she got dizzy from them. Sheel found the odor cloyingly sweet and heavy. The fems would not give up the drug or use it outside where, they claimed, the smoke would escape and be wasted.

One evening the fems came out from behind their curtain and joined Sheel and some other women who were gathered outside the tent. The pretty fem called Tua announced, "Daya is going to tell a story. We thought maybe you'd like to hear it too."

Everyone was polite and interested, and a few women drifted over from other tents to sit and listen as the little scar-cheeked fem began:

"Let me tell you all how it will be when we fems return to our own country, the Holdfast. We will find the men hiding in burrows in the ground like sharu, sharpening their teeth on the bones of the dead. At night they come out, scavenging for food in the burnt ruins of the City. We'll be able to smell them through the walls. They've let their hair grow to cover their bodies, because they have no clothing without fems there to weave and sew for them.

"One day I find a sick one creeping and hiding. I catch him with my rope, and I bring him back to feed and keep for my amusement. He trots after me for his handful of food, and I kick him or beat him as I like. He won't run away because where else would he get food and a warm place to sleep? He knows nothing of making food grow without slaves to do the work for him, so starvation has tamed him. I ride his shoulders when I choose not to walk, and everyone envies me and pays me to borrow the use of this creature that was a man. We'll have found another way to make cubs by then, so the man I own will keep his genitals only to piss through and for us to mock when we use him as our clown; as the horrible example that we show our children to teach them how debased a human being can be.

"I take my man pet into the City's ruins. I let him visit his former private quarters—he was a rich man —for the pleasure of seeing him weep and sniffle into his beard as he handles the fragments of the statues that once stood in his garden.

"On this day one of the statues leaps up to attack me! It's another man, a wild creature all hair and teeth. He charges me, a broken-bladed knife in one hand, the other brandishing his penis, for the wild men have stories that the fems in the old days worshipped the rod that beat them.

"I draw back my arm to hurl my hatchet at the wild creature, but my man pet throws himself on the attacker before I can do it. The two roll in the dirt, leaving spots of their blood where the splinters of brick and broken tile pierce their skins. My pet gets the other by the beard and smashes the back of his head against a fountain rim. Then he bites his throat out—after all, he was used to eating raw flesh. I whip him back from his prey.

"That's when my pet first sees clearly the bearded face of the dead man. He recognized his own lover of years before. He screams, he rushes away and hurls himself into the river.

"But I'm not unhappy to have lost my pet. Ask any master: a crazy pet is worse than no pet at all."

It was, Sheel thought, a very peculiar story. Women of other tents who had stopped to listen did not stay to comment and discuss it, but thanked Daya politely and wandered on to chat at other fires. Many women talked about the last remark afterward. No one claimed to understand it.

Sheel said to Jesselee, "They meant to provoke us. They know we'll never allow them to return to the Holdfast."

"Go and talk to Alldera about it, if it disturbs you," the old woman said.

"I don't want to talk to Alldera."

"Then don't let yourself be provoked."

The sky was full of tantalizing clouds that Dusty Season. Soft herds of them floated high over the gritty haze which hung above the ground and sifted into a rider's mouth, nostrils and eyes. There was, of course, no rain.

With some help from Alldera the scarred fem, Daya, had taught the two new fems to ride. Those three borrowed mounts and went away for a few weeks to catch wild horses. Alldera said she would wait in camp in case the child should come out; other youngsters of that generation were beginning to emerge from the childpack.

To Sheel's astonishment the fems brought back fourteen head of passable beasts which they set about breaking to the saddle under Daya's direction.

Sheel could not watch. It hurt her to see fems subduing horses.

Sheel sat in Periken Tent with her friend Tico Periken drinking shake milk together in bed. Grays Omelly, who had gone raiding and was now visiting as she had promised, was there with them. So was an older woman of the Caranaw line, a raid mate of Tico's.

The Caranaw sat by the milk cradle and punched and rocked the bag which hung there, mixing the dried milk and water inside. She rambled along meanwhile about horse breaking, and ended up saying that she did not like to see the new fems riding.

"These new 'cousins,' Daya and the rest—they don't act like women. Not at all. What woman stews greens with her meat, or wears a slave smock over her trousers and a blood rag under them, or kicks up dust everywhere she goes with those big, stiff sandals they wear? What woman keeps to herself and speaks like rocks clacking together, what woman steals?"

Sheel had more to say about the fems than any of them, but she was bound by the ties of kinship and hospitality not to speak against any person in her

family's tent. She tried to turn the conversation by
saying shortly, "Complaints about the free fems should
go to the chief tent."

"Why, Sheel?" Grays said, her blue eyes innocently
wide. "We don't run to the chief tent with every little
thing, like that fem Tua who went there because she
couldn't get Tacey Faller to pay up on a bet. As if
anybody can get a redhaired Faller to pay just by
asking! I don't know why these fems can't go and talk
with a person's relatives and let the lines and families
smooth out problems instead of blowing every spark up
into a grass fire."

"Hush now," Tico said, rolling onto her belly and
reaching for the shake milk skin. "You know Sheel
can't talk about the fems."

Grays thumped Sheel on the arm. "Put their stuff
outside the tent to let them know they should move on,
that's the way! Why are there fems in Stone Dancing
Camp anyway? Suppose all the fems come over from
the tea camp and move in with you?"

Patiently Tico said, "There are only forty or fifty of
them in the tea camp, and anyway I hear Alldera had
some kind of quarrel with them, so it's not likely they'll
come here. But those who do come are allowed to stay.
I've explained it twenty times to you, Grays. They're
blood kin of Alldera. Think of them as a sort of outland
Motherline made up of lots of cousins instead of
mothers and daughters. Each fem is a distant cousin of
each other fem, if you see what I mean. Now, let's leave
it at that."

Maralas Caranaw shifted her bottom on the pile of
hides under her. The Caranaws were afflicted with sore
joints in middle age. She said, frowning deeply, "It's
our weapons that bring them, our bows."

"They have their own weapons," Grays sneered.
"Those little hatchets and those clumsy spears."

"Never mind what brings them, then," the Caranaw
said morosely. "Look what's happening because they're
here. The trading crews of their wagons are angry
because we let the fems stay, so they want to get even.

Did you hear how some Hilliars over in Steep Cloud Camp were cheated over salt last month by a trading crew? Women at Steep Cloud are talking of going for salt themselves as we all used to do before the fems took over the trade. Nobody likes salting her food with sand.''

Tico gave Sheel a worried glance. ''We shouldn't bother Sheel with any more of this.''

Grays Omelly had been taking objects from her pockets and lining them up in concentric rings on the floor: bits of bone, scratched Ancient fragments, thread, a horse's molar, buttons, the rubbish with which she made what she called her ''spells.'' When she began to glance anxiously around, Tico contributed her own striking flint to complete the design.

Grays said, ''Sheel won't mind hearing that Alldera Holdfaster sleeps with Nenisi Conor. Or that Daya sleeps with me. Sleeping with Daya is like sleeping with a child, a child you hate. She makes you think she's helpless, as if you're somehow taking her by force. And you do, in a way. It's exciting, like hunting. You should try it, Sheel. She will come to your bed willingly, now that she's come to mine.''

Tico tried again: ''Let's drop it now. Look, you're getting Sheel angry with all this talk.''

''Magic of circles, tell me now,'' Grays continued, bowing over the floor, ''if I killed a fem, if she had a spirit, where would it go? It couldn't rise to the spirit country above the clouds and rejoin its Motherline because it has no real Motherline. It had no sharemothers to love it and no bloodmother and no horses and no sharu—''

''You're raving, Omelly,'' the Caranaw said sharply.

Grays flung herself headlong into Sheel's lap. ''Love!'' she said. ''Sheel's love is what all the fems need.'' She nuzzled Sheel's groin. ''I pinched Daya's nipples till she wept, but afterward she hugged me and said it was all right, it was because I am a wild woman and don't know how to control myself.''

Sheel pulled violently away, and her feelings burst

out. "You hug that filthy, man-used fem as if you were her master, you kiss her scars—they marked her like that, and she let them, and never fought back! You drink shame from her body, and now you come to me? Get away from me!"

The Omelly hugged Sheel's legs in both her arms, pleading, "It's a plot of the Conors. Nenisi and her line are corrupting me, making me play with these fems!"

"Get—off!" Sheel shouted, and kicked at her. Grays hit back at breasts and groin, sobbing as she fought. Sheel kept pulling her punches, trying not to hurt her.

Their struggles scattered Grays's design all over the floor.

One morning Sheel stopped Alldera in the tent when Alldera came in alone from running. She held out an iron bit she had missed two days previously.

"I went behind your friends' curtain, there, and I found this in the bedding of one of the new fems. I also found a dozen arrow shafts that belong to the Bawns and a lot of smaller things—leather lace, sharpening stones, ornaments—who knows how long the fem has had them? You tell her she'd better not take anything again."

"You know the culprit," Alldera replied. "Tell her yourself. She's a relative of yours."

"Not of mine! This stealing is a coward's kind of raiding—to live with us and take our belongings little by little! If I catch the thief, will you ransom her?"

Alldera said, "Let her alone, Sheel. Let them all alone. They're not what I'd have them be, but I share a long past with them. I'd speak for them in the chief tent."

Goaded by Alldera's cool refusal to apologize, Sheel burst out bitterly, "It's thanks to my own blundering that you came here! I had a feeling someone was at that food cache. Not a man; I can smell them miles off. One of your kind. So I said, Shayeen is sick, let's not take the time to stop. I was careless. I should have taken my lance and made sure, as I have in my dreams since. I didn't realize how dangerous you were.''

"Then you missed your chance, Sheel, because we are kindred now," Alldera said, and moved to pass around her.

Maddened, Sheel caught Alldera's shirt in both hands, as if to raise her up and dash her to the ground. But the fem said grimly, "Remember, Sheel—we're kindred. If you so much as bloody my nose, you'll be outlawed for it and have to run south."

Sheel released her. "Your lips are white, you're scared, fem!" she sneered, her own voice breathless with rage.

"Yes," Alldera said, pulling her shirt straight. "You're a formidable woman, Sheel, and your anger is frightening. But I think you know as well as I do that we're way past this kind of scuffling. What you and I started in the desert between women and fems is out of your hands and mine now."

Sheel sat soaping her saddle outside the tent where Grays Omelly was staying. Nenisi came and sat with her. Nenisi looked worn and tired. Like all women of the Conor line, she was outgrowing her painful teeth at last. But now she kept scratching at her sore, red-lined eyes. The inflammation showed bright as blood in her black face. She had been having eye trouble since the hot winds had begun to blow.

"Are you thinking of leaving?" Nenisi said.

"This camp is like living in a dust storm for me."

"Be patient, Sheel. The tent child is growing breasts, and there's hair between her legs. She's bound to come out soon. Then it won't be so difficult, you'll see."

Sheel heaved the saddle into a new angle in her lap and lifted the stirrup leather so that she could reach underneath. "I can hardly talk to my friends without getting into a fight. My own tent is full of strangers that I hate, my enemy speaks to me as if she were my mother—and it all goes back to my own mistake, Nenisi. How can I hold up my head here?"

Nenisi sat with her a long time, saying nothing,

looking as troubled and unhappy as Sheel felt.

On the way to the squats the following evening, Sheel saw that Grays had taken up one of her frozen stances on the dusty dancing ground outside the camp, arms outstretched, face blankly fixed. She could stand that way for hours, captive to the visions that were an Omelly trait.

The two new fems walked past, returning from practice with their bows. One of them shouted something at Grays, who did not answer.

Sheel hesitated, half expecting Grays to leap at them. Someone should have told them to keep away from the Omelly.

The fems called to Grays again. They walked on. Then one of them wheeled suddenly, stooped, and shied a stone at the motionless woman.

Shouting, Sheel took a step after them. A rock whizzed past her own head. She yelled for help.

Women swarmed out of the nearer tents and a brawl spread on the dancing ground. Sheel, barred from fighting against her own kindred, ran for the Shawden chiefs. Hard on her heels came a crowd of women dragging the two fems, so that the chief tent was soon filled with shouted accusations and insults.

Grays, unresisting, had been stoned by the two fems. They said they had done it because she had mocked them by refusing to speak to them, and that they had not recognized Sheel, their cousin, when they had thrown a stone at her. The Shawden chiefs set them stiff fines of skins and salt, and that was that.

Sheel avoided the discussions of the incident at other tents and even in Holdfaster Tent, which bore the brunt of the fines. She thought about what had happened through several sleepless nights. It outraged her that women did not seem to know how to deal with these upstart fems, and so fell back on treating them as if they were women.

The herds had been culled at the beginning of the Cool Season, before the fems came. Now the grass was too sparse, and it was agreed that a second culling would be necessary this year.

The night before the culling was scheduled Daya slipped away alone after dinner, heading out of camp quietly on foot. Sheel saw. Taking one of the night horses tethered outside the tent, she followed.

There was a bright moon. Out by the tent herd she found the tracks of Daya's favorite mount, a stripe-legged dun that Daya had brought with her to Stone Dancing Camp. The tracks led eastward, away from camp.

Riding through the moonlight like a real person in a ghost-white world, Sheel could feel the distress in her bones that meant cruelty from the past was accumulated here or nearby. The women called these feelings "ghosts." Not that anything tangible or even visible would arise here to startle her horse or raise her own hair; but in some places you could feel the lingering vibrations of long-ago cries of pain.

Her horse stopped and stood flicking its ears this way and that. The night hung still around her. Sheel turned in her saddle, seized with a sudden anxiety. Why had she left her tent to wander solitary by moonlight like a person without kindred? Had hatred for the fems done this to her?

Someone was moving over there, on foot, heading back toward camp: a fem, slender and small and very graceful. Sheel heard the faint chime of the little bells, love gifts that Daya had taken to wearing bound into her hair.

Sheel waited.

Daya did not alter her course but walked right past as if Sheel were invisible. She seemed to be following her own tracks back to Stone Dancing, singing some sorry femmish song under her breath.

Sheel turned her horse and followed, thinking, No one would know if I did it out here. I might smash Holdfaster Tent once and for all.

She said, "Stop singing. The sharu sleep lightly."

"My song is a prayer," Daya said, not looking up.

"A prayer won't save you."

"Not a prayer for me," the fem said in her soft, deceitful voice that never seemed angry. "A prayer for the safety of my dun mare. She was marked for the culling. Alldera gave her to me for my own, not to be your food."

Sheel stood in her stirrups and looked out, away from the camp. "You drove the dun off, did you? I suppose you think Moonwoman will take care of her?"

Daya said, still soft-voiced, always soft-voiced, "You have no right to speak of Moonwoman."

"Why not? The moon shines on my head too. I grew up beside water with tides that answered to the moon—the Great Salty River to the west. I would know if there were some single great moon-being controlling all movement in the world—the tides, the growth of plants and creatures, the weather. That's the sort of thing the Ancient men believed in. We women know better. We celebrate the pattern of movement and growth itself and our place in it, which is to affirm the pattern and renew it and preserve it. The horses help us. They are part of the pattern and remind us of our place in it. What can a horse do for you, a stranger?"

Daya raised her hand to touch the shoulder of Sheel's mount. Sheel reined the horse aside, out of her reach.

Daya said, "A horse can trust me."

"Trust you for what? Why? Because you think it's love if you save one horse from the culling? That's not love, it's silly and useless." She looked contemptuously at the fem's bent head. "There is no way you can make a place for yourself in the pattern." She knew what she was saying to herself: it would make no rent in the pattern if I killed you; it would be no crime. Carefully, she chose words Nenisi had spoken once.

"Our bond with our horses is old and true and the center of our lives. The horses lend us their strength, their speed, their substance for food, their own dim wisdom. We protect them from the sharu, we dance with them and look after them and put our bodies in their power, too, in our own way. Then when we die our corpses go to feed the sharu, and what do the sharu do in turn? They dig in the earth for roots and to make their burrows, which prepares the soil for the grasses the horses eat.''

''The dun mare was a wild horse,'' Daya said almost inaudibly. ''She belonged to me, not to you women. I had my own understanding with her.''

She looked up at last, and Sheel saw the glitter of tears, the vulnerable face, the delicate line of the cheek rutted with slave scars. She felt no pity. This was a creature who would throw stones at an Omelly.

A preliminary thrill of violence tightened the muscles of her hands and arms, and the mare pulled protestingly at the bit. Sheel slackened the reins, annoyed with herself for having needlessly hurt her horse's mouth.

She remembered who she was, and that was much more important than who or what this miserable fem was. Fems had no kindred to teach them how to behave. They were not women.

I am never alone, she said to herself. My line and my kindred and our ways are always with me. If I killed now, I would not be a woman. I would be responsible to no one, solitary, worthless. I would be like this fem.

''I'll show you the way back. You can't see any more,'' she said. ''Look, the moon has set.''

The fem trudged on, head at the level of Sheel's hip. ''I can find the camp myself.''

''You claim to be cousin to the bloodmother of my sharechild,'' Sheel said acidly. ''My sharechild wouldn't want me to ride on and leave you wandering here to be eaten by sharu.''

By morning the dun horse had drifted back to the tent herd, having nowhere else to go. It was butchered with the others.

''Don't be foolish—my horse has never mounted a woman,'' Sheel said impatiently. She hated being fussed over in the middle of a game of pillo. ''He's much too big to mate with. You're safe from him, Shayeen.'' She tightened the reins on the red stallion dancing under her.

At her side Shayeen said, "All the same, he's got his hanger out. I wish you'd ride a mare, like everyone else."

"Not in a pillo game," Sheel said. "Have you seen the rump on that Faller woman's horse?" She pointed disdainfully with her chin. "Imagine entering the game on a mare in season! That's why this stud is all excited."

Sheel was winner of the previous round in their game, so she was now the quarry. She crouched on the back of her sweating mount, the heavy braided rope supple in her hands. One end of the rope was tied to the pillo itself, a stuffed sharu skin; the other end was knotted. In the hands of a skilled rider the ten meters of rope were a strong weapon, the only weapon permitted on the pillo field. The red dye with which the stuffed skin was saturated left marks like blood on an opponent that took her out of the game, just as if she or her mount had been slashed by a real sharu.

Sheel craved the cleansing power of violence, the release. A good, rough game of pillo gave that. She could hardly wait for the coming clash, and part of the red horse's impatience he had picked up from her.

The twelve women who were Sheel's opponents lined up at the opposite end of the field. They held their lances points downward, aslant beside their horses' shoulders. Hidden behind these riders was the "burrow," a sheet of leather propped on sticks like a tent. Sheel's object was to ride through the opposition without losing the pillo, which she would try to sling into the mouth of the burrow and earn a goal. Each other rider would try to prevent her goal by pinning the pillo to earth with a well-placed lance thrust.

Around Sheel friends and rivals laughed, called bets and counterbets, commented on the states of the horses and riders in this second half of play. Shayeen moved around the red horse, checking its gear and its feet. She need not have bothered; nothing short of a broken leg would stop the stud, a five-year-old named Fire. Like other stallions, he was no use in a real race or a raid, either of which entailed a run of three days or so; only the wiry little mares had that kind of endurance. For a day's hunting or a pillo fight, he was superb.

"What are we waiting for?" Sheel groaned.

In the center of the field a dark woman of the Clarish line sat her horse, lance raised straight in the air. From its end drooped a white horse tail. When the horse tail dropped the play would resume. She was looking from one end of the field to the other.

The sky was overcast, presaging the end of the Dusty Season and the coming of rain. Over the distant mountains seams of sunlight opened in the dark, rich layers of cloud. Assured of new grass by a week of thunderous skies, the women had used the last of their precious grain to strengthen their fittest horses for the game.

Sheel shivered in the breath of a breeze. She was wet with the sweat of anticipation. If fems were permitted in the game, there might now be femmish blood spilled by a woman of the Torrinor line. But pillo was a clean game, not for slaves from the lands of men.

The red horse snorted and mouthed the bit. He had gone four rounds already and his coat was dark with sweat. He jigged and fretted for the start of his run, one eye on the Faller's high-tailed mare.

The Clarish's lance dipped.

"Go!" the women screamed.

Fire shot forward. Sheel lay along his neck, riding him with weight and legs. Her right arm yanked back the taut rope with the pillo bounding at the end of it, preparing a low, skimming whip-stroke to catch the legs of the oncoming horses.

The riders came like a dust storm, yelling and jostling, their lances cocked shoulder high to jab at the pillo. Sheel slung the pillo forward on its line, and the horses rushing toward her sprang aside.

The red stud ignored the gap they left. He veered toward the Faller woman on her foam-streaked bay mare, fifteen meters down the field on the left. Sheel hauled on the reins and beat him over the shoulders with the knotted end of the rope. He would not turn.

"I'll kill you!" she screamed into his back-laid ears.

"You're dead as you run, sharu-vomit!"

The Faller's mare, trying to stop and piss, swung broadside across other riders coming up along her flanks. Women on the sidelines shrieked warnings to their friends and curses at the Faller.

Then someone swept up alongside and punched the distracted Faller out of her saddle. This player lashed the mare across the rump with her rein ends and headed her back full tilt the way she had come, while the Faller skipped about on foot in a panic, trying to avoid being trampled. A friend caught the Faller up and carried her out of the melee.

Fire stopped trying to stand on his hind legs. He plunged after the Faller's mare at a dead run, and into a swarm of riders. Other horses cannoned against him; Sheel felt him stagger. Flying clods were hurled up by the hooves of the horses as they dug for purchase. Sheel shortened the rope swiftly with both hands so that it would not drop slack and foul her own mount's legs. She laid about her with the knotted end, beating the riders, whooping.

She was at a disadvantage. Everyone was too excited to feel much pain, force was all that mattered. They hooked at her with knees and elbows. To beat them back she used the rope with both hands. Women swung aside, dripping red where the pillo had struck. The press thinned about her. She brought Fire's blocky quarters over hard against the shoulder of a pursuing mare and had the satisfaction of hearing the rider curse as she was jarred from the saddle. At last Sheel was in the clear.

She clamped the shank of the rope hard between her leg and the saddle, leaned forward with both hands on the red horse's mane, and summoned breath to call to him. He groaned and stretched out over the ground in a flat run. If anyone caught the pillo now as it streaked and bounded along at the rope's end, it would tear free, unhorsing her, but she did not care, did not even look back. Fire ran on, laboring. The women roared.

Judging her moment, Sheel caught up the rope and with a triumphant sweep of her arm she slung the pillo

at the burrow. The frayed rope parted in midair, the
heavy leather bag flew wide. Groans came from the
sidelines.

"Sharu drink my blood!" Sheel swore. She turned
the red horse in a long, faltering curve off the field.
Dismounting, she stepped away to keep from hitting
him. Her eyes stung and her legs shook under her.

Women crowded around, patting her on the back,
hugging her, congratulating her on a game well played
despite the bad rope. Her bruises began to ache.

Close at her side Nenisi said, "I hate that lumpy red
horse of yours, but he is a pusher in a game—once you
get him to concentrate on the business at hand, that is."

Women laughed.

Limping back to Holdfaster Tent, Sheel leaned on
Nenisi. A flying stirrup iron had struck her in the calf;
she remembered the impact, now that she felt the pain.

Good pain; she was still well within reach of other
women's hands, their buffets as well as their caresses.
She still belonged despite Daya and Alldera and the
other fems.

She hugged Nenisi's shoulders more tightly and
flinging back her head shouted out a victory song that
pressed at her chest and throat like the onset of weeping.
There were no words to the song, there was only her
rough, glad voice.

13

Under a wet-season sky ripe with clouds the mothers and the child of Holdfaster Tent moved in procession around Stone Dancing Camp. Alldera found the slow pace maddening. Nenisi's descriptions of the coming-out ceremonies kept settling in her mind. This was the last stage of their child's absorption into the lives of the women, and she kept wondering if some unexpected intrusion might yet break it all up and leave the child unclaimed—or even back in her own hands. She did not know how she would take that.

The child walked close at Barvaran's side, a naked, dirty rain-streaked figure, its face half hidden by its mat of greasy hair. Looking at it, Alldera felt detached. She reminded herself many times as they wound their way among the tents, this is the child of my body. It was incredible! The child had matured rapidly into a young adolescent.

She seemed to Alldera rather stocky, certainly not tall. She had a wide, well-shaped mouth and her alert eyes looked everywhere, at everyone and everything. Sometimes she licked her lips, or clenched her hand on Barvaran's so that her dirty knuckles paled. Alldera saw she was afraid, but there was no whimpering or shrinking. Alldera approved in an abstract way.

This is the child of my body.

At every tent women came out smiling to embrace the

sharemothers, laughing, congratulating them, eyeing
but not touching the child. Each clasped Alldera's
hands or stroked her shoulders or straightened her hair.
Alldera was continually reminded of the day, years ago,
when she had given birth among them. To this child.

The sweat tent was not quite ready. The five
sharemothers waited outside wrapped in their leather
capes while other relatives—including free fems from
the wagons, four of them now besides Daya—finished
preparations for the ritual. Jesselee, as a grandmother,
directed all this.

Alldera could not stop yawning with nerves. Her belly
rumbled, and her left side, where she had been hurt once
in the tea camp, ached from the Rainy Season dampness. She looked at Nenisi standing close by, her face lit
with joy. The child had come out late, a month after the
pack mates of her generation, and she was small. She
would not mate at this year's Gather, or even next
year's. But she had come out, and Alldera could see the
women's relief and was glad of it. Now it was only
required that this go well, that the gift to the women—to
Nenisi, really, who wanted it so badly—be ac-
complished, whatever else might happen.

As they went inside the sweat tent, Nenisi's hand
brushed Alldera's and tightened briefly on her fingers.

Scrapers had been laid out on a leather mat, fresh
white slivers of soaproot gleamed, and the floor had
been strewn with aromatic grasses. The sharemothers
spread their leather capes on the floor and sat upon
them, nude.

The child crouched by Barvaran's side. Her instant
affinity for the red-faced woman meant that Barvaran
would be her heartmother. Alldera felt relieved. For the
moment there was no necessity of close contact between
herself and the youngster, contact for which she felt
totally unready in spite of all Nenisi's preparations.

Barvaran began to speak softly to the child in the
quick, fluid slang of the childpack. Alldera felt a
startling stab of jealousy. If she were to address the
child in Holdfastish, there would be no understanding

between them. Never mind, she thought; what would I
have to say to her?

She sat down near the stone pit, feeling the heat
tighten her skin. Nenisi, squatting next to her, began
pounding soaproot into paste. Cheerful Barvaran,
handsome Shayeen whose reserve Alldera had never
pierced, and Sheel, more wiry than ever and seeming
very deliberate today, the family was gathered again.
Naked, all but Nenisi and coppery Shayeen were pale-
skinned except on their hands and faces, which sun and
wind had weathered.

Alldera looked down at her own thighs—once brown
from exposure below the short working garment of the
fems, now pale from the protection of the pants she had
adopted from the women—and her own darkened
hands resting on them.

It amazed her to think that Sheel the raider, Sheel the
fierce who rode stallions, killed men and hated fems,
had once entered a tent like this as a child among her
own mothers. But so had all the women.

At the first hiss of steam from the stone pit the child
shrank back into the enclosure of Barvaran's arms.
Gently, still speaking in a low voice, Barvaran scooped
up a handful of lather and soaped the child's shoulder
while the others watched. The child glanced from one of
them to another and back down at the shining film of
soaproot that Barvaran spread with great tenderness on
her skin.

"She has clear hazel eyes," Shayeen commented,
"and her teeth look good and straight."

Sheel said, "I think a horse bit her there, on the
arm."

"Neat hands and feet," Nenisi said. "She isn't big,
but she's well shaped, with good proportions."

Barvaran held up one of the child's arms and gently
moved the hand in a circle with both of hers.
"Something happened here," she said with concern. "A
break, I can feel the knob where the bones knit. But the
wrist moves smoothly."

The tricky part of the ritual bath was coming; apparently all the youngsters fought against the discomforts of having their hair washed and untangled. Nenisi said that this was good: in her struggles to avoid her mothers a child learned that though they overpowered her, they did not harm her; she could trust them.

"I think she's going to give us a good fight," Shayeen predicted approvingly.

Barvaran began lathering the child's hair. In a moment the youngster let out a yell of outrage and tried to lunge away. The women rushed to help hold the slippery, thrashing limbs so that Barvaran could finish the hair wash.

Alldera hung back, reluctant to lay hands on this strange young body.

"Come on," Shayeen shouted to her, "get the feel of your child, and let her get the feel of you!"

Alldera thrust her own body among the bodies of the others. They were all dripping and lathered now. Helping to pinion the thin, flailing arms, Alldera kept her head pressed next to the child's head to avoid being smacked in the face by her hard skull. Stinging soap had gotten into her eyes and she could not see, but she could feel the muscles pull and thrust under her grip, and she smelled the first blood flow which had led the childpack to expel the child. She kept remembering with disbelief that these straining limbs belonged to her own offspring.

A douse of rinse water left them gasping and ready for the next stage.

Barvaran blotted the child's long, tangled hair in a blanket. The child still tried to pull away, abusing them all in pack slang. She yanked out her menstrual plug twice before Barvaran could get her to accept its presence in her body. Barvaran sat with her, grooming her sleek hair and talking quietly in her ear while the other sharemothers washed their own hair and scraped each other down. They showed off to one another the red marks where the child had hit them and ruefully compared bruises.

The entryway was tightly laced. Alldera saw how the

child's eyes kept flashing in that direction; she no longer fought back, but she had not given up.

Alldera thought, this child would never have lived to come out of the Holdfast kit pits. The older fems would have judged her too ready to fight. Before she could break some man's teeth for him and bring a flood of femmish blood in reprisal, we would have killed her ourselves. An ordinary idea, in my old life.

The child watched each of the adults warily. For an instant her eyes met Alldera's. There was no spark of special feeling. She seemed rather ordinary now, a draggled youngster, hair dark with moisture, skin dark with years of running naked, flickering eyes of an indeterminate color in the silvery light of the sweat tent; hazel, Shayeen had said.

Alldera looked away. What came next would exclude her because she was not a Riding Woman. Nenisi had prepared her. She withdrew to watch and sat with her back against one of the tent poles.

The others rose to their feet and stood in a group near the stone pit, leaving the child apart for a moment.

Something very small and simple happened. The child jumped up and glanced quickly at the entry; as she did so, the women turned their heads toward her. That was all, but there was something in the carriage of their heads, the wideness of their eyes. They seemed to Alldera to mimic with extraordinary power the way that horses lift their heads from grazing to look and listen.

Then Sheel squatted, and moving backward on her haunches she began to smooth the sand outward from the pit toward the sweat tent wall behind her. Time had touched her, Alldera saw; veins and tendons stood high under the skin of her forearms and hands. Nenisi and Shayeen did as Sheel did, palming the sand flat. Barvaran stood with a hand on the child's shoulder and still talked to her, pointing, smiling, as the smoothed sand was marked by the others with lines, dots, circles, zigzags, all oriented to the stone pit, which symbolized the present campsite of Stone Dancing.

This was how women gave a child the plains.

As heartmother, Barvaran took the first turn, leading the reluctant youngster about the tent by the hand. The other women walked in attendance as Barvaran named all the places that were special to her, places mapped by the markings on the floor. She walked the child over their world; all heads bent to follow Barvaran's stubby, pointing finger: "The Star Saddle," Alldera heard her murmur, "where we found water just in time coming back from a long, hard patrol, and here is the spring of the split-hoofed horse. . . ."

There could be no turn for Alldera in this, Nenisi had said; "The first place you show the child is where the bones of your own bloodmother were left for the sharu."

Nenisi came out of the group and sat by Alldera at the tent wall. With the back of her hand she pushed aside the hair plastered to her gleaming black forehead. Her eyes were on the other women. "It's going well. Is it making some sort of sense to you?" she said.

Alldera thought of that moment of magic when their heads had turned. "I think so."

"Good!" Nenisi hugged her. "A great day, finally, this coming out. Some say that on such a day all elements of the world are placed fresh: living and nonliving, past and future, the spirits of animals and of grass and wind and time passing and even the spirits of stars. Each time we make again the web that is the inner pattern of all things, all things are balanced, the world is made steady."

Alldera did not say aloud, Are not the men and fems beyond the mountains elements of the world? She did not want to disrupt the ceremony or the triumphant mood of Nenisi, whom she loved.

Then it was Nenisi's turn to take the child walking over the world. Alldera sat back, thinking.

She recalled Nenisi's joy at her return, months back now, and her own almost sensuous delight at what had taken on the color of a true homecoming, so familiar had everything seemed.

Coming from her years away with the free fems, she

had at once noticed the changes that only a woman of
Stone Dancing Camp would notice: this person gone,
these horses newly arrived or newborn, such and such a
family richer than before while another once prosperous
group used other women's cast-off tent leathers and
awaited its turn of luck. Rayoratan Tent had gone,
having packed up after a quarrel with the Shawden
chiefs and joined Waterwall Camp in the north. Shan
the bow-maker who had made Alldera's first bow was
dead, carried off by a bout of lung fever. When Alldera
expressed her shock and even a touch of real sorrow, the
women nodded and patted her just as if she were one of
them and had a right to mourn.

She was no longer trying to catch up to them. Their
distance from her—when she felt it—was now simply
part of their nature and their beauty. She found that she
did not need Daya to remind her of who she was.

From the first the little pet had been much more than
a shadowy companion. She had become a teacher of
other fems and lover of Grays Omelly, of all women!
Alldera knew she had underestimated the pet fem. She
had asked Daya to come as a companion of her own
kind, thinking it could make no difference to the
women. The effect that Daya made among them
delighted her. Despite the women's low opinion of free
fems, the little pet's grace, her elegant manners, her
beautiful marred face as serious and watchful as an
animal's, intrigued them. Also, they could not hide their
startled admiration of her skill with horses.

Alldera had never considered the free fems who admired Daya and who would be attracted and reassured
by tales of her presence here. Four had come, and
maybe there would be others. Their presence made
Alldera uneasy.

They brought friction. There was their inveterate
stealing, their pathetic arrogance, their clannishness.
And Daya's affair with Grays Omelly—how long before
other free fems moved into the beds of other women,
with what consequences? Fems were intense and jealous
lovers, totally opposite to the casual behavior of

women. They insisted on wearing sandals, chewed tea
instead of drinking it, spat everywhere in a way that the
women found offensive. . . .

So many irritating matters, so difficult to cope with
and to explain. Even Nenisi did not fully understand;
and there was an aspect of the fems' presence that
Alldera could not even try to explain at all. Perhaps
Sheel felt it too—the unpredictable influence of a number of free fems living in a women's camp.

Alldera had wanted to make changes, first in herself
and then in the free fems, but never in the lives of the
women. Now change had followed her to Stone Dancing
Camp, and she could not see where it would lead. It
frightened her.

Alldera felt that she and the black woman were closer
than ever. She no longer took lessons at Nenisi's knee.
Often they did not speak together at all, but clung close
in simple gratitude for each other's presence. They
shored each other up; maybe Nenisi was not as confident as she seemed. Don't think that. She's no more
perfect than anyone, but grant her her strengths. . . .

There were traces of gray in Nenisi's kinky hair now,
like curls of pale ash in charcoal. Nenisi was not afraid,
and she was wise. Didn't the women say, Those Conors
are always right? If Alldera said what she was thinking,
Nenisi would say, Why these gloomy, anxious
thoughts? This is a day of gladness for your child's
sake, our daughter's sake.

The women were sitting grouped around the stone pit
now, home from walking over the world. They hugged
the child and patted her, and she shyly accepted their
embraces.

Barvaran murmured something to the child, who rose
from among the women and came to stand in front of
Alldera. She put her hands on Alldera's jaw and tilted
her head back to study her face: warm hands, light and
steady, that Alldera did not resist.

"Is my nose flat in the middle like yours?" the girl
said, frowning over the unfamiliarity of the language of
adults or perhaps over the idea of having a flat nose.

"No." Alldera paused. She searched the bold young face before her. "You'll be better looking than I am."

The youngster laughed like metal chinking on metal. "But we're blood kin, how could one of us be prettier?"

Alldera found that she could not now remember the face of either of the two men who might have been this child's father.

Jesselee, in charge of the coming-out arrangements, did not alter the traditions in any way for this unique child. There was feasting, dancing on the dance ground, gift giving, and gift acceptance, all centered on the child and her introduction to the women of other tents. These ceremonies involved the rest of the family, but not the bloodmother. The bloodmother always tended the tent herd. The effect was to insulate the bloodmother and the child from each other.

The bloodmother looked at her child and saw her own image made young, her replacement in the world, Nenisi said. The child saw in her bloodmother the pattern for her own being. Women said it was best not to let this powerful connection unbalance all the other relationships that guided their two lives, and so it was appropriate that the bloodmother and child be separated for a time.

"Such a fuss," Daya said, riding with Alldera on the second morning after the coming out. Daya had brought a flask of blood broth from which Alldera drank gratefully. "Not that we ourselves hold back. Tua's given the cub a tooled leather belt. The other three made her sandals."

"She'll never wear them. What did you give?"

Eyes downcast and showing some enbarrassment, Daya said, "Fedeka's here, traveling a while with a trade wagon. I got the kit a jar of perfume in case she should ever want to smell like something besides horses, sweat, and old leather."

Alldera said soberly, "Couldn't you persuade the other fems with us to go back to the tea camp with the trade wagon?"

"They didn't come here just for me, Alldera, and

they won't leave just because I tell them to. Maybe if you said something to them—"

"I'd look pretty foolish, telling them to go home to Elnoa after what I used to say about her. Look, Daya, I have something on my mind.'' Although there was no one near them on the green and glistening plain, Alldera lowered her voice: "It's the naming. Nenisi told me how it's supposed to be—I smile and produce a name and use the formula: that the name came into my mouth with the food I ate or with the water I drank from the wells.

"Only no names come. Nothing."

"How about 'Tezera'?" Daya said hopefully. "That's a pretty name." She listed several others: "Fenessa, Maja, Leesha, Tamsana."

Alldera disapproved. "Those are all femmish names that a master would give a new-bought slave."

She saw Daya's eyes widen slightly. "She is a femmish cub, Alldera."

"Is that what they say at the trade wagon?"

"Yes," Daya admitted. "They think she should have a femmish name, ending in 'a.' We've all kept our slave names, in respect for our past. And she was conceived back there."

Alldera laughed. "A femmish name wouldn't make any difference. The women would just drop the 'a,' since to them she's a woman, not a fem—unlike ourselves, who wobble along somewhere in between." She kicked her horse into a brisker stride.

Daya kept pace alongside. "Some fems are saying that we should insist on taking the child and dedicating her to Moonwoman. They'd be furious if they knew I'd told you."

"Why do they care about her all of a sudden?"

"You know many fems in the tea camp thought from the beginning that you were wrong to leave the cub with the Mares," Daya replied. "They thought you should have brought her with you to the tea camp so she would grow up with her own people. These Mares are admirable in their way, but she doesn't belong with them."

"The fems talk as if I owe them something." Alldera thought angrily of her broken ribs. She pressed Daya: "What about you? Do you believe I owe you and Fedeka and the rest of the wagon fems?"

"No; but I think that we do need, for our own sakes, to make a claim on that cub."

"What's this 'for our own sakes,' Daya? Is this you?" Daya looked older, more beautiful and less mischievous—something of a stranger. "Go and tell them that I won't have them—or anyone—meddling with the child's life, not in any way. This cub has nothing to do with them. You had nothing to do with her. That's the men's disease, thinking they're so important that everything connects to them and their schemes and desires. How I hate that mixture of the worst in both men and fems—cowardice and conceit together! That's what they'd teach the child if they could get her."

"Alldera, don't turn on me," the pet fem said unhappily. "I'm not your enemy."

The rough words had not been meant for Daya, Alldera knew. She was sorry, and they rode on without speaking. Then she tapped Daya's knee. "I've got to find a name! Not a name from the old life, like those you've suggested. Think of a name that's not the property of the fems and not the property of the women either."

Daya smiled her scarred smile. "Call her 'Alldera.' "

The flaps of Holdfaster Tent's front wall were pinned back to make a wide entrance. The women of Stone Dancing Camp had assembled outside, all but the Holdfaster sharemothers, who sat expectantly within. Alldera, seated by the fire cage, could see the child coming flanked by Sheel and Shayeen. The two women were bringing the last of the child's presents. It was time for the naming.

All the femmish names from Alldera's memory seemed harsh and ugly. My mother, whoever she was, never named me, she thought as the child drew nearer. I chose no names for my other two cubs. The master did that. Why do they leave the naming to me? Her palms and her face began to sweat, and she sat there thinking over and over, the one who gives the name is the master.

Sheel and Shayeen brought the child into the tent, and she went right to Barvaran, her heartmother. Standing before the red-faced woman, the child said formally what she had been told to say: "Heartmother, I am not wild any more. Stone Dancing Camp has welcomed me among women. I need a woman's name."

Barvaran said, "Your bloodmother has a name for you."

The child turned to Alldera.

It was two days since the beginning of the coming out. Looking at her now, Alldera saw something new: the color of her hair, which hung dry and clean and fire-glossed. She saw very suddenly and strongly the color of the two men who had fucked her shortly before her flight from the Holdfast: one tawny, the other pale-skinned with thick black hair. She said the first thing that came into her head:

"You haven't got the color of either of them. Your hair is like the coat of Shayeen's sorrel mare."

She saw the consternation on the women's faces.

Then the child of the tent, oblivious, laughed her shining laugh and announced with her thin arms out-flung, "My name is Sorrel! I'll ride nothing but red horses all my life, so watch out for me, you who keep red horses in your herds!"

"A lucky beginning," old Jesselee muttered. She got up and closed the tent. The naming part was over.

Shayeen began her self-song:

> My blaze-faced bay carried me for seven days,
> From Red Sand Wells to the Great Salty River,
> And she was twelve years old then,
> The year I first raided for horses—

Each sharemother was to sing her self-song, and Alldera was to sing last. With Nenisi's help she had put together lines telling of her escape and her life among the women. She hoped she could remember them. She was still shaking inwardly with relief that the naming had gone off all right.

Something noisy was happening outside. Alldera stopped breathing. Shayeen turned, glaring as she sang.

There were furious voices, and someone fought loose the pins that closed the edges of the entry flaps. Fedeka strode inside, fierce-faced, a one-armed vision. Fems from the wagon crew peered in past her.

"Alldera! You forgot us!" Fedeka cried.

Sheel had her hand on the haft of her knife.

Alldera sprang up. "What are you doing here, Fedeka?"

"Why is she singing? Why the women's songs?" Fedeka demanded. Her eyes glittered hard as metal, and below the drooping line of her long nose her mouth was grim with anger. "You should be singing for the cub, Alldera."

"Get out of here," Shayeen commanded, outrage cracking her habitual calm. "You're not supposed to be at this ceremony."

Panic gripped Alldera, she could not think well. Who knew what the invaders from the trade wagon might do? Didn't Fedeka understand that Alldera's turn to sing would come later? Was she infuriated by the child's non-femmish name? With relief Alldera saw that Daya was sidling into the tent at Fedeka's back. She would appeal to Daya for support; but then Fedeka shouted, "We have our songs too!" and opened her mouth wide and wailed out a verse:

> The greedy whip scorches, the load burns me down,
> the eyes of my master are everywhere.
> My lover has fled, I will not pursue her.
> Shall I see her bloody footprints halted by a closed City door
> And the flames of the masters' eyes suck at her face and hair?
> The greedy whip scorches, the load burns me down. . . .

It made the women flinch. Sorrel stared open-mouthed.

When the singing stopped, Daya said in her soft manner, "Women of Holdfaster Tent, that is a song of Alldera's bloodline. Not a self-song—we fems had no self-songs—but we did sing our lives."

"We'll go back outside now," Fedeka said, "but not far. We know whose cub it is, so we came." She stared reproachfully at Alldera. "Even though the dam forgot us."

Daya put a hand on Alldera's arm. "I said they should come," she whispered under the sound of Shayeen's renewed singing.

"You want to tear me in two, you want to force me to choose," Alldera whispered back.

Daya replied, pleading, "You said I shouldn't let you forget who you are." She left. No one looked at Alldera except Sorrel with her wide, dazed eyes and Nenisi.

Sheel sang next, her voice breaking with fury. Barvaran sang, Nenisi sang, Jesselee sang. The tea bowl was handed to Alldera so she could moisten her throat. She sipped, hiding her face with the bowl. Into the silence came the singing of the wagon fems from outside. Muffled by the walls of the tent, their voices were to Alldera like the voices of generations of ghosts far away in the Holdfast.

Alldera said over the singing, "I resign my right to sing for my bloodchild. Let my femmish kindred sing in my place."

They listened in silence to the fems singing:

Wash all clean, black sea, roll stones,
Break walls, salt sand, spare none.
Men will moan, and fems will roar.
We breathed earth all our generations.
We can breathe an ocean of dead men and not care.

In the trading fems' wagon late that night the fire bowls were lit, and there was a scent of manna. Alldera

came because she could not stand the angry looks of the
women, and she did not want to be alone tonight. The
naming of the child had made her feel old and unim-
portant.

She needed to find out how the free fems would greet
her.

They made room for her without fuss, and she sat
down with weary relief amid the tea-scented bundles of
trade goods and the rolls of bedding of the crew. The atmosphere in the wagon was vibrant with victory. From
their triumphant glances at her she guessed they felt they
had repossessed not only the child but its mother.

Daya was telling an ugly Holdfast story about a man
who betrayed his lover and how his lover killed him with
a whip and ran his flayed skin up the flagpole of their
company hall next morning.

"Mother Moon," sighed Tua, leaning her head back
against the wagon wall, "I don't miss the men and their
mad, mean city, but how I miss the smell of the great
salt sea!"

A flood of reminiscence followed.

"The sea," they said. "The taste of fresh laver, when
we could steal it." "Remember the look of the beach at
Lammintown on a bright morning, with the town
coiling up the hills behind it?"

"Once we got hold of some prime manna that
belonged to the master of a friend of mine—"
"Remember how quiet the City got when the men went
dreaming on manna? You could sit in your quarters,
cool and waiting, and listening to how quiet it was. You
could think about how it would be if those quiet
buildings belonged to us, no masters there at all."
"Remember the sound of the sea, and the beaches
shining hot in the sun?" "The moon was better. A poor
fem could look straight at the moon and not be roasted
or blinded by it, and it spread the sea with a cool, silver
light."

"In my company's hall they had four different sets of
tableware and another dozen small sets for the Senior
men—all the colors you've ever seen, each set to go with

a different meal. The eating hall used to glow with the brightness of it. We never minded washing up, it was such a pleasure handling those glossy plates and platters." "I never handled anything but a weed hoe and a ditching shovel, but I remember how the land smelled. We used to stumble around half dreaming at manna harvest time."

"I used to polish my master's jewelry for him and pin it on my lover when the master was gone," Daya said. "We made ourselves splendid for each other! There was a brooch of silver in the form of a kneeling boy, with eyes of colored stones. . . ."

They spoke of greenness all year round, the smell of the river, fog in the morning, storms that shook the cliffs of Lammintown and threw the sea up against the sky; of good, strong beer from the City breweries, of the excitement of inter-company skirmishes fought in the big square, of the brutal, crazy arrogance of the men and the sly, perilous stratagems of fems.

Alldera listened with her head bowed, for she knew they did not see what she did: the vast rift between these cherished memories and the songs of pain they had sung for Sorrel. The fems' blindness made her feel dismal and exhausted.

For years they had sat around their fires here in the Grasslands and carefully picked over their Holdfast lives, extracting the few bearable bits, embroidering them for their own and others' comfort.

Pity for their need wrenched at her. Pity for herself, too; their cheering stories were just fantasies to her. She shared only the anguish of their bitter songs.

What are we, here? Alldera thought, looking around at the rapt, firelit faces. Outsiders, eking out a living at trading, which women must have handled perfectly well for themselves before free fems ever came here. The women don't need us, there is no next generation of fems that need us, we don't need ourselves. If we vanished tonight, whisked away like dream people, who would miss us?

Someone was absent from the gathering, the one fem

who had always seemed to her to belong to the
Grasslands. Leaning nearer to Tua, Alldera murmured,
"Where is Fedeka?"

"She left," came the answer. "She said that with the
rest of us staying in Stone Dancing Camp, she wouldn't
have to worry about leaving the child here among
women."

"The rest of you are staying?"

Other conversations ceased. Everyone was looking
this way. Several of them said yes, nodding, and a fem
back in the shadows called, "Daya says we're all your
cousins, that's the way the Mares think of us. Your
cousins can visit you, can't they? Your cousins can learn
from you what Daya has learned."

They came for the child and now they mean to stay
and have me teach them to ride and shoot and track. . . .
It was what Alldera had feared, or part of it. She felt
anger—would they never cease to complicate her
life?—and yet some pride. It did not do to un-
derestimate them, ever. They needed to show that they
mattered; they needed to make their marks on the
Grasslands.

Eagerly they told her of what had been suffered
already in her cause. They spoke of fights and bitterness
in the tea camp between fems wanting to join Alldera
and those remaining loyal to Elnoa. Many said they had
wished to come to Stone Dancing Camp sooner, but a
fading allegiance to Elnoa had held them back, till now;
till Sorrel's coming out. The Plan was just the Plan,
always in the future, but Alldera's child was real now,
and they kept hearing of real things happening now at
Holdfaster Tent—free fems on horseback, free fems
with bows.

So they came, newly bold, animated with the daring
of their decision. Telling her, they watched her face. She
blinked water from her eyes, shook her head without
speaking because she did not trust her voice.

Daya said, "Time for another story." She sat alert,
resourceful-looking since she had taken up riding;

grown-up, Alldera thought. As these others will soon be.

"This one is about Kobba. She's with a group of us that goes to Bayo to rescue some fems that are said to be trapped there by men. The free fems try to storm Bayo town, but the men have fire throwers and dart throwers and slings, and the fems run out of arrows. Kobba and her troop are driven back into the swamp, up to their thighs in water, struggling southward through the sucking mud among the reeds and the roots. In the night they hear the prisoner fems singing, calling for help as we all used to speak to each other in songs."

"I don't like this story," Kenoma said. Others shushed her.

"Deeper into the swamps, Kobba sees her companions cut their own throats rather than fall into the hands of the pursuing men. She refuses to die or be caught. She eats roots, she drinks marsh water and doesn't let sickness slow her down. She forces herself on even when the swamp is silent and she knows the men no longer follow. She thinks she has caught the smell of smoke. She finds a broken sandal strap.

"One day she stumbles onto the shore of a huge island in the marsh, where reeds give way to trees. Someone is watching there—a fem, scar-backed, solid, one of those who slipped away from Bayo and hid in the swamp. There are many others with her.

"They have houses of reeds and clothes of grass, and they've found live creatures to catch and eat in that warm southern water. Some creatures the fems have tamed and trained to attack men.

"The swamp fems welcome Kobba. They say they thought all the fems of the Holdfast were dead, for none have slipped out to join them in a long time. But Kobba tells them, Come and help me, the men still hold Bayo and twenty of our kind prisoners there, many of them pregnant with cubs we need. This time we will surely batter through the walls.

"We have a better way, say the free fems of the

south. They follow Kobba carrying not bows or even spears, but cages full of swift water creatures with poison in their mouths. Kobba and a few others go close to the walls of Bayo and from hiding shout taunts at the men. The men attack and chase them into the swamps as before—but the fems step onto solid ground that they have marked in their minds, and they release the water creatures.

"The creatures swim along the channels of the swamp and find the men and fasten onto their feet and legs, flooding their bodies with poison. The men die loudly. They have no discipline, they scream and cry and flounder in the water, they beg to be saved. The fems listen from hiding. They want to laugh, but they stay silent.

"Dead men drift in the water and lie on the banks where they have hauled themselves up to die. Then the swamp fems call their water creatures by slapping the water quickly and lightly, and the creatures feel this through the water and return.

"The fems still do not laugh. They hug Kobba, but silently. They will not laugh, they will not triumph, until the prisoners are rescued—and that's another story for tomorrow evening.

"We won't laugh either when we go back, armed with our new strengths and new weapons, until we've rescued all the fems still living there."

There were murmurs of approval. They were all looking at Alldera.

She left the wagon, descending into the dark. She walked among the tents, keeping to the dark places, sorting out her thoughts.

They want to go back to the Holdfast. They are sure of me now, and they want me to teach them fighting and riding so they can invade the Holdfast like women going to war—that's the fantasy Daya has woven for them with her stories!

Fems have always learned what they needed to survive. They could learn to ride and shoot, not like women who've done those things all their lives, but well enough. But what would they be once they learned? They'd still be no stronger than I am, no more skilled or brave, just people like me—not witches armed with killing spells. We'd be a pathetic little band, desperate fems trusting to tools only recently come into our hands, keeping each other's courage up with stories and lies. It's impossible.

But suppose we did it: went back, found the Holdfast in ruins but some men alive, took it all over, made it ours. How many of us are fit to bear a new generation? How many captured men would be young enough to father healthy cubs? Would we all want to bear cubs if we could?

They envision taking over the masters' luxuries but the Holdfast must be in ruins. We might have to kill our horses for food, assuming we could get them that far to begin with. What good is an archer if she can't move around quickly on horseback? In seconds a man can charge too close for an arrow shot and break her head with a rock.

No one has come across the borderlands since I came, ten years ago, or is it eleven now? The Holdfast people may all be dead. We could spend our last months wandering an empty land, turning on each other in our hunger before we finished.

If we ever got there to begin with. Free fems have already come to blows over joining me here. Elnoa has lost a whole wagon crew to me now; she'll defend her place as leader harder than ever. And the women will fight to keep us from going back. They have to protect themselves too. The men would only have to catch sight of us, armed and mounted, to know that over the mountains there's more than emptiness and the monsters of their foolish legends. They would come, they would invade the Grasslands looking for slaves. I would do anything rather than endanger the freedom of the Riding Women.

I once wanted to move the free fems to action. Now they move despite me, and they mean to sweep me with them. It doesn't matter to them that I am happy with the women. No wonder I've been afraid.

She walked in the darkness among tents murmurous with the voices of women still awake, or silent with sleep. It seemed to her that the surface of the plain stirred slowly, purposefully, inexorably beneath her feet, carrying her and all of them east toward the mountains like waves to the rocks.

When it was time for the Gather, the free fems of Holdfaster Tent—twenty-one of them now, with Alldera—went off to work on the Stone Dancing granaries. They labored hard, well, and without incident.

On the way back Daya rode with Alldera, fiddling with the string of small bells she wore in her hair, a gift from Grays Omelly. She said, "They're very attractive, these women. At best they have a crude sort of power. Sheel has it, all armed against you—against me, too. Haven't you felt it? She looks at you as if she'd like to bite the heart out of your body, but you're too strong for her, so she just glares and glares."

Daya's intrigues, Daya's sensitivity, Daya's fantasies—today they exasperated Alldera beyond measure. There was much else on her mind that she needed to speak to the pet fem about, but somehow whenever they managed to get a moment alone lately there were other matters in the way, or the time felt wrong. She saw now that Daya wanted to talk, not listen, and she held her tongue. She watched Daya twine the bells into her horse's mane.

"It bothers you, doesn't it—me and Grays? Well, you've never feared finding your bed empty, like me," Daya said. She pulled the bells out, looped them around her wrist.

Alldera tried to answer evenly. She knew by now the feelings of small worth that sometimes unreasonably afflicted the pet fem. "Grays Omelly wouldn't have been my choice."

"No, I know your choice, but it's different for me. I'm not strong Alldera the runner, proud Alldera who brought a cub over the mountains, tough Alldera whom women respect and fems learn from. Look at me: Daya that was a man's pet, a man's toy, good at games. So your Marish friends see me, though they know little enough what it means. I had to take those who'd take me, like Grays.'' She added in a voice turned half playful, ''Were you jealous, a little, of Grays and me?''

They rode quietly. Alldera thought again of bringing up the whole question of going back to the Holdfast; the other fems had dropped back a little. But the fact was, Alldera could not seem to get it straight enough in her own mind to discuss, even when an opportunity came.

Daya said, ''There'll be no more games with Grays, anyway. She came into the wagon nights and listened to us telling stories. She said she knew the stories were spells to get us home to the Holdfast, and she wanted to hear them. Then, a few mornings before we set out for the granaries, she came to me and said she couldn't be with me any more. She told me she felt like someone moving without sound or weight through our femmish dreams. She asked me to kiss her. 'Make me as real as you,' she said. I tasted tears when I kissed her.''

Alldera and Daya entered Holdfaster Tent, weary and dusty.

''You just missed your child,'' Jesselee said, as if this were Alldera's fault. ''She's out hunting. Why did you stay away so long?''

Shayeen, the only other woman in the tent, added, ''We were beginning to worry about you. It takes only a day or two to patch a leak in a granary roof and not much longer than that to put on a whole new layer of oiled hides.''

Alldera said, ''We stayed out to build a new granary building, out of stone. The sharu will never be able to get in and eat the grain again. We even paved the floor.''

''Paved—?'' Shayeen was clearly unfamiliar with the word.

Alldera explained.

No one commented at first. Shayeen sat frowning at the tangle of straps in her lap, a bridle she was mending.

At length Jesselee said, "Mud-walled, earth-floored granaries have served for years. Why change?"

Daya said, "The sharu have always raided your granaries. Now in the Dusty Season the horses can have the grain the sharu used to take."

Jesselee shrugged. "We steal stores from sharu burrows sometimes. It's a proper thing that the sharu should sometimes steal from us."

A low voice said, "This work of the fems is surely meant as a gift." It was Nenisi, lying unnoticed till now in her bedding, deeper in the recesses of the tent.

"What's the matter with Nenisi?" Alldera asked, full of alarm.

"Her eyes still, but worse today," Jesselee said. She turned her head and added solicitously, "If we're annoying you, Nenisi, we can go outside to talk."

"Stay," Nenisi said. "I want to hear you."

The old woman sighed. "You won't like it." To Alldera she said, "All you were to do was make the old granaries rainproof. Anything else should have been the decision of the whole camp."

Alldera drank from the shake milk bag hanging by the entry. She said, "My cousins have skills that you women lack. Can't you give them recognition for what they've done, instead of complaining?"

"What Alldera means," Daya said sweetly, "is that we aren't afraid of a job that lasts more than a few days or needs careful planning. We're not too proud to dig a foundation ditch or trim a stone."

Shayeen snorted. "You fems make no sense about what you call work. Women need time to talk and play and ride out hunting, not just to work. You work all the time, learning something, building something. We do what satisfies us."

"Yes," Daya said, "women are satisfied to do the same things over and over, year after year. It's a woman who is satisfied when every year her horses fall to the butcher knife to keep them from starving for lack of grain."

Jesselee's reply crackled with anger: "A person is in the world to live in it, not to make it over. Only a creature who belongs to nothing has to keep making things to belong to. A woman isn't like that."

Alldera saw the glittering tears of anger in Daya's eyes and swiftly said to her, "Our cousins are growing hungry while we stand here arguing. You'd better start setting up for a meal. I'll come later."

With Daya gone, Alldera felt free to go to Nenisi. There was a bowl of water by her. Alldera took the cloth from Nenisi's eyes, dipped it and wrung it. She saw that Nenisi's eyelids were swollen shut and crusted around the lashes. She replaced the cloth across the black woman's face.

Nenisi said, "I bet you wish you hadn't come back. Excuse our bad tempers—the Gather was out of balance this year. There were some fights, and two women got hurt in the mating."

"And more will be hurt," Jesselee said ominously.

They told Alldera about some quarrel that had sprung up at the Gather between the Conors and the Periken women. Insults, warnings, scuffles that ruined games and races—it was a messy affair of obscure roots, which Jesselee was trying to explain when Nenisi said finally,

"Oh, leave it, it's not worth talking about, I'm sick of it!" She groped for Alldera's hand and clasped it with her thin, dark fingers.

"This quarrel of yours isn't connected with my femmish cousins in some way, is it?" Alldera said.

"It's an old dispute come alive again, that's all," Nenisi said. "You don't really think that everything that happens among us involves you, do you?"

In some years vast numbers of sharu swarmed over the plain devouring everything. They could overrun a camp and consume food, grain, leather gear, even tethered horses or women immobilized by accident or illness. They ravaged the grazing land, gnawing the grass down to the subsoil and scattering the women's herds beyond retrieval for months after.

Sorrel, Barvaran and Sheel came back from their
hunting with reports of large bands of sharu traveling
roughly east to west toward the Great Salty River, on a
path which would bring them across the Stone Dancing
lands.

Stone Dancing Camp became a moving war center
against the sharu. Groups of women ranged in all directions, each rider armed with two bows and several
quivers of arrows, to destroy or deflect any sharu
hordes they could find a day's ride from camp.

The free fems wanted to join the hunt. Alldera explained that fems would be more useful taking over
camp duties so that more women could go after sharu.

There was no argument against her advice. Daya
simply came to her and said, "Tua and Lexa and a
couple of the others want you to know: they are going
out of camp to hunt sharu on their own."

"When?"

Eyes down, Daya said, "I can't tell you. We need to
go. We're not old women or children in the pack."

"So you're going too?" Alldera said. "Eager for
sharu blood yourself?"

"Oh, no," Daya said, looking very domestic. "I
don't like the bow, you know that—I'm not propor-
tioned for the thick arms that archery can give you. But
I'll find a way to be useful."

Alldera spat out the dregs of the milky tea she was
drinking. "What am I supposed to do?"

Daya waited silently.

Alldera said, "Tell Tua and the others to meet me out
by the herds in the morning."

They were changing. The quarreling and lying and
stealing were giving way to other things: pride in new
skills, ambition, some kind of group spirit. Standing
together openly against her mistrust of their old com-
petency, they forced her to look again and re-evaluate
them.

She assessed the abilities of each of the fems with
horse and bow, consulting with Daya in front of all of
them in the cold dawn. The fems stood eagerly soaking

it all in, their breaths misting before their faces. Alldera
assigned each fem to accompany one of the groups of
women going out that day. She had talked with the
women the night before, enlisting Nenisi to help over-
come the reluctance of some who feared they would be
distracted from their work against the sharu by having
to save the lives of incompetent fems. A schedule had
been made by which fems would take turns riding out
just as women did.

Since their arrival at Sorrel's coming out, the fems of
the wagon crew had been working furiously with horse
and bow. What they had not yet mastered they now
learned fast under pressure. There were no complaints
from women about the free fems' efforts, once it was
apparent that they really were able to handle their
mounts and weapons. Suddenly, Alldera's worrisome
"cousins" were transformed into useful allies.

Sorrel came clamoring to her mothers to be allowed a
part in the killing, saying that if even her bloodmother's
cousins were involved, she could surely be. It made
Alldera uncomfortable to think of this handsome
youngster, with her alert, quick-smiling face and
beautiful hair, at risk among the sharu.

There was risk. A woman of the Shawden tent fell
from her horse when her girth strap broke; she was torn
apart by sharu before she could be picked up. Another,
her arrows spent, met a sharu's charge with her lance.
The sharu took the point in its breast and kept coming,
impaling itself but ripping her knee with its teeth and
claws as it died.

Alldera did not have to speak against Sorrel's pleas.
The women in the tent said firmly that Sorrel might help
with weapons, childpack, horses, or with any work in
the camp, and perhaps in emergencies she might run
messages; but that was all.

"Just like your age mates from the pack," Jesselee said.

"Most of them are pregnant," Sorrel objected. "I'm
not."

"And you never will be, if some sharu claws your insides out."

To Alldera's surprise, Daya did not turn to making arrows or to some other protected, camp-bound task. She became a collector of arrows for the archers. Looking back, Alldera would see her riding in long sweeps back and forth behind a shooting party, leaning steeply out of her saddle to retrieve arrows from dead and dying sharu. Daya rode gauntleted and booted in boiled leather like that which shielded her horse's legs. Unwounded sharu sometimes turned from devouring their own injured to attack a passing rider, and even in dying the beasts could be lethally quick and strong. Daya's leather armor was soon black with blood. She looked like some dream warrior, the more terrible for her stained armor, her neat, small figure, her scarred beauty.

She worked closer to the sharu than anyone. Alldera noted with satisfaction that even Sheel received her arrows from Daya with a civility verging on respect.

Sorrel did get into the field, in a fashion, by racing out one morning to tell Alldera that Daya had been injured.

Dropping back from her group of archers, Alldera said, "Tell me, quickly."

"A big sharu jumped on her horse's rump and raked her down the back. She had an arrow in her hand, and she jabbed the point right into the sharu's eye and killed it. They say they found her bent down from her saddle, streaming blood, trying to work the arrow back out of the eye socket, but the barb had caught, and Tico says it was the coolest thing she ever saw, but Daya was weeping and screaming the whole time and kept throwing up all the way back."

Sorrel had come armed with a lance, not a bow, so there could be no excuse for her staying. The plain shifted and rippled with moving sharu only thirty meters off.

"Thanks for the message," Alldera said. "Now go back."

"Aren't you going to ride home and see how she is?" Sorrel cried. "I could relieve you here. Jesselee says—"

"I'll come like everyone else, when I'm out of arrows."

"But I want—"

"A good messenger takes back the answer as soon as she has it."

"I'll tell Daya you're all right, I'll tell her you'll come." Sorrel galloped away.

Later, Alldera found the pet fem sitting by Holdfaster Tent, her torso and one arm wound in a band of soft leather, a bloody shirt draped over her slim shoulders. She looked very white but composed, and she was stirring one of Jesselee's pots of medicine with her free hand.

"Poor Daya," Alldera said. "More scars."

"I got the arrow back." Daya invited her, with a graceful wave of the stirring spoon, to sit.

"I need to change horses," Alldera said.

"You need to rest," Jesselee said. "I can see the muscles in your arms jumping with fatigue. If you go right out again, you'll only shoot wildly and make more work for others." She got up stiffly, laying aside the leather she had been cutting into strips. "I'll go shift your saddle to a fresh horse, if I can find one."

She limped away, chirruping to Alldera's mount which plodded at her shoulder.

Alldera sat down with Daya in the sun outside the tent. "What horse were you riding?"

"Dark Tea. She was cut badly, but Jesselee has stitched her up. Poor beast, she'll have scars worse than mine."

"They could have given you something younger. I rode that horse when I was first here, years ago."

"That sharu jumped right up onto her. She staggered, but she didn't fall or bolt, so I had my balance and could put some thrust behind the arrow in my hand. She's a good, steady mount, Dark Tea. Though my dun would have been better."

Daya stirred the steaming brew erratically. Some of it slopped over the rim of the kettle now and then and made the fire underneath hiss.

The camp was unusually quiet. Most of its inhabitants were out shooting sharu, and the childpack was confined safely in the sweat tent. There was a faint smell of decay on the wind. Not enough sharu were swarming in this area any more to eat up their own dead.

"How long can this last?" Alldera muttered.

"We needed the practice," Daya said. "We need to be thoroughly blooded before going back. It's different, wearing armor, seeing the teeth of a ravening sharu snap shut only a hand's breadth from your face. I feel strong—the way I did when I first learned to ride."

Alldera leaned forward, elbows on knees, looking out past the tents at where wheeling groups of mounted archers drew gouts of dust from the plain. Her arms and chest and back ached. She felt as if she had had no rest for months. Wearily she surrendered to the inevitable subject: "You really mean it, don't you. Going back," she said.

"You've never talked about it with me," the pet fem said. "It's been on everyone's mind for so long. What do you think about it?"

"Daya, must the free fems go back to the Holdfast? Not the free fems of your stories, mind you. The real ones."

"I can only tell you about myself. Look at me, Alldera—a first-quality pet fem, marred certainly, but still—! Here I am, dressed in stinking leather, with dirt caked in the roots of my hair, living among beasts and very little above them in houses of their skins. I own my clothing, my saddle, a few ornaments, and the knife on my belt. Oh, and that gray horse the tent gave me to make up for butchering my dun. I spend my time tending animals or fixing things or talking—about old times, another life. I drift over the plains as aimlessly as the clouds, my direction dictated by weather, by grass. I love the horses, the women too; but my life is just floating past me here."

Angrily Alldera said, "Must the free fems go back because you are bored?"

Daya touched her lightly, pleadingly. "Don't you

ever think of the richness, the excitement and color of the old days in the Holdfast? It wasn't all horror and pain. Nenisi is certainly a splendid person in her way—even rather stylish; but what about the brilliance, the music—"

"I have only pain and anger from those times."

"Maybe that's what we have to go home to do, then," Daya said. "To give the pain and anger to our masters, if there are any of them left, and take the brightness for ourselves. It was all built on our backs. Can you blame us now for wanting to claim it?"

"And if we find nothing but bones?"

"Then we'll make something beautiful out of bones," Daya replied, her eyes lustrous with excitement. "Here, everything is already made and it all belongs to the women. We can only borrow. At home, what we find and what we make will be ours."

"Ours. All twenty-two of us?"

"The others will come too. Except Fedeka, probably, and Elnoa."

"Elnoa! She's led them for years. They won't all desert her, she won't let them."

"She's a leader only as long as we follow her," Daya pointed out.

Women's reasoning, Alldera noted with grim amusement, and in the women's country, true.

She laughed ruefully. "Recently a woman came to me and asked me to interfere in the private affairs of one of us. I said no, and she said in a sneering way, 'Why not, you're their chief.' I told her I hadn't spent all that time alone here in Stone Dancing without learning a few things—like how not to be a master. I thought that was a pretty smart answer at the time."

"Left to yourself you'd stay here forever, wouldn't you," Daya said. "I'm sorry. It's a pity that we should require you after you've made peace with this place, but you're part of what draws the free fems. It isn't me, you know. I'm like the others, I make my peace with the people around me, moment by moment.

"Don't look so astonished. I know you expect to hear

such clever things only from Nenisi. The Conors are wise, the Conors are always right, and besides you love Nenisi and you still don't think much of me.''

It was still so shamefully easy to forget that Daya's feelings could be hurt. Alldera shook off the pain of having caused pain and capitulated. ''You win, Daya. I can't see fems come galloping in, red with the blood of sharu and grabbing for more arrows, and pretend not to know that the free fems are spoiling for war. It's my doing, some of it. I'm even proud of how strong they've grown, but that doesn't make going back any less wretched for me.''

''I told them you understood, I told them I knew you!'' Daya exclaimed. ''Some fems said you'd been bewitched by Nenisi, but I knew better. Alldera, if word gets to the tea camp that we'll take in anyone else who wants to learn to ride and shoot, they'll come—they'll all come. Say you want them and I'll get them for you. We can be more than forty strong when we ride home!''

''Go ahead,'' Alldera said, kicking savagely at the edge of the fire with her booted foot. ''It's the best story you've had for them so far. They'll trample each other finding places for themselves in it. Put it all down to the will of Moonwoman, that's what Fedeka would say. Only I wish you'd told some stories about fems staying with the Riding Woman, living good lives here, instead of about going home.''

''I tell the stories that come to me to tell; don't be bitter,'' Daya begged. ''Even you say 'home' now when you mean the Holdfast. It's your triumph too, that we turn homeward at last.

''Listen, here's a story for you: we are a small, grim army drawn up on some high path on the far side of the mountains, looking out in silence—except for the stamp of an impatient pony's hoof, the creak of leather as someone rises in her stirrups to see better—over our own country, green to the horizon line of the sea. . . .''

VI
Epilogue

14

Sheel was making a new boot patterned on the leathers of an old one. Outside the air was crisp. The tent was closed and the fire glowed under the draft of the smoke hole.

Sorrel lay on the bare floor of the tent, kept in on account of various abrasions and one furiously multi-colored eye. She had put on muscle and weight since coming out, but she was no match for a crowd of her pack mates.

The tent was quiet. Guests had come, a daughter of Barvaran's traveling with a couple of cousins. They and the fems and the rest of the family were all out gossiping and borrowing extra bedding and supplies for tonight. Jesselee was home doing nothing, Shayeen was in charge of the food, and Sheel was in charge of Sorrel.

Sorrel said, "I don't like Saylim Stayner."

"You still shouldn't have tripped her with the dung rake," Shayeen scolded. She was pounding dried meat for the evening meal. "You made gossip for the whole camp. If the others hadn't given you a licking for what you did, you'd probably come up in the chief tent for a fine."

Her words were barely audible over the pounding. Sorrel was making faces at Sheel, trying to convey the joke of not being able to hear the rebuke.

Sheel said, "Shayeen's right about the dung rake."

"Oh, Saylim didn't get hurt or anything. Just insulted."

"Don't sound so satisfied."

"She insulted me first!"

"How?" This was Jesselee, listening from her bedding.

Uncharacteristically, Sorrel paused. Sheel watched her push the floor sand around with her fingers, making ridges and valleys. Then Sorrel said, "Saylim said the self-song I was making left out the most important part: about my bloodmother being from over the mountains, and how she had a master there. She said it sly and droopy-eyed, as if it meant something rotten."

Shayeen whacked the meat one last time, scraped it into a bowl, and marched off.

The youngster brushed the hair back from her face, showing the bruised eye in all its splendor. "I don't much like my mother Shayeen Bawn either," she muttered.

"Why not?" Sheel began punching holes around the edges of a leather piece with an awl.

"She's always telling me what to do."

"Let's talk about the Stayners for a minute," Sheel said. "Myself, I don't like that line. The Stayners pick their noses."

"Rosamar says—"

"I know, they always say they have some kind of funny crookedness inside their noses that bothers them. I don't care. They could still blow their noses as other women do.

"And I don't like the Ohayars because they're sneaky. The Fowersaths are quick-tempered, the Mellers borrow things and don't return them, the Churrs have ice cold hands, the Hayscalls mumble till you think you're going deaf."

Jesselee joined in zestfully, "The Clarishes are vain, the Perikens exaggerate everything, the Farls are lazy and their fingers turn back in a sickening way and make a horrible wet cracking noise doing it besides. As for the

Morrowtrows''—she was one herself, of course, gappy-toothed and wide in the jaw—''they like to stick their noses into everything that happens, especially to children of their own families.''

''However,'' Sheel said, ''there isn't one of those lines that we don't both have kindred in. I forgot to add the Bawns. I don't love the Bawns, but here I am, sharemothering you with Shayeen Bawn.''

She wished she had not said that. After all, it was not a matter of choice that she was familying with Shayeen.

''You don't know, though, what it's like to have Shayeen as one of your mothers,'' Sorrel said, doodling a frowning face in the sand with her finger.

Sheel set her foot into the curve of the boot sole. She had cut the thin sole wet and set it days earlier to dry in a sand mold of her footprint. It was a comfortable fit. ''No, but I do have mothers I don't love.''

Jesselee interrupted. ''Sorrel, you'll be related to women all your life whom you don't love or even like—raid mates, pack mates, relatives of your mothers, captives—you may even find that you don't care for your own bloodchildren. Liking women has nothing to do with being related to them, and you might as well work that out and get used to it right here in your own family.

''Have you slept with anybody yet? Since the pack, I mean.''

Her face burning, Sorrel nodded.

''A pack mate who came out ahead of you? Yes. Well, when you start yearning after a grown woman see that you go and lie with Shayeen. Then you'll like her better.''

''You shouldn't talk that way about things like that,'' the youngster whispered hoarsely.

''Save me from foal love,'' Jesselee groaned. ''Who are you sleeping with—that young Bay that lost a finger roping a sharu instead of lancing it like a woman?''

Sorrel's blush deepened. ''Not everybody would be so brave.''

"Not everybody would be so stupid. Archen Bay risked herself and her tent's best hunting horse just to show off."

"My leg hurts," Sorrel said disconsolately. "One of those piss faces kicked me." When no sympathy was forthcoming she tried a new subject. "I don't know why you bother making yourself a pair of boots, Sheel. I have three pair. You're not much bigger than I am in the hands and feet. One of my pair would fit you."

"Then the woman who gave that pair to you would be unhappy with both of us."

Sorrel brushed the sand flat. "Do you like my blood-mother?"

"No," Sheel said.

"Why don't you like the fems?" Sorrel had spent more time with them since the sharu swarming.

"Why do you like them?"

"Oh . . . ." Sorrel made a ludicrously long and dreamy face. "I think they're very strong and sad because of their terrible lives."

"They're from the Holdfast," Sheel said. "I don't like things from the Holdfast."

"Am I from the Holdfast too?"

"You're one of us."

"I am a little Holdfastish in my blood, and special."

Irritably Jesselee said, "Don't get stuck on yourself. Everyone's flawed, everyone is still a woman."

"I know my faults," Sorrel said, sulky again. "I ought to. Everybody's always telling me."

"So they should," Sheel answered. She refrained from adding, They should because you have no real Motherline to look at and see your faults mirrored in it. There were always the oddest gaps in her conversations with Sorrel.

"What's it like, beyond the borderlands?" Sorrel asked.

"No one's been there."

"My bloodmother and her cousins have."

"Then ask them."

"I don't always understand what they say," Sorrel admitted, "and if I say they don't make any sense, they get angry or shrug and change the subject. Is it true that a man has a hanger-and-bag, just like a stallion, and hair on his face like the Chowmers?"

"More hair than the Chowmers," Jesselee said absently, mouthing a bit of food or the memory of a bit of food, "less hanger than a stallion."

Sorrel snorted. "It sounds silly and clumsy, like carrying a lance around with you all the time." She sighed. "I wish my bloodmother liked me. Maybe she will after I make a good raid." She rolled over and sat up, wincing slightly. "Why can't I go raiding with Shelmeth's band?"

"No. Shelmeth Sanforath is not experienced enough to lead a raid," Jesselee said.

"But nobody will be expecting us, it's so early in the season! It's going to be a triumph!" Sorrel blazed with enthusiasm.

Sheel began to stitch the uppers to the sole. "Early raids have been tried before. It takes good judgment to pull them off successfully."

"I want to go!"

"No," Sheel said. "You've asked about this before. Jesselee says no, Shayeen says no, Barvaran says no, I say no, and Nenisi says no."

"You all treat me like a baby, but I'm too big to ride in a hip sling, you know. I have to go on my maiden raid sometime. How am I supposed to find women to sharemother my first child with me if I don't start now to get a good reputation?"

"Try avoiding the reputation of the sort of person who attacks other women with a dung rake," Jesselee suggested.

Ignoring this, Sorrel went on, "I want to have a dozen wild raider daughters and then go wandering with you, Sheel, and the bravest of my pack mates. I'll be the scourge of the plains and make my daughters rich with gifts of the finest horses in the camps."

"A dozen daughters?" Jesselee said. "After a dozen daughters you'll be lucky if you can still get your legs together around a horse's ribs."

"Really?"

"No, not really, silly. Worry about real dangers, like having your arm broken in a fight."

Sorrel laughed. "I'll get Alldera to teach me kick fighting so I can kick Saylim's eye out if she comes after me again."

"I don't like that kind of bloodthirsty talk," Jesselee began in a tone that promised a lecture; but then some youngster put her head into the tent and shouted,

"Pillo fight starting!"

"I'm coming," Sorrel said, jumping up.

Sheel said, "Youngsters' rules—no rough stuff."

"It's no fun then," Sorrel objected.

"We'll be careful," said the girl at the entry, having learned more than Sorrel about placating her elders. "Come on, Sorrel. I bet you my old gray horse can—"

They were gone, their voices already locked in argument.

Jesselee lifted one knee and began kneading her calf. "Cramp," she groaned. "Hits me even in the middle of lovemaking, no respect for an old woman's last few pleasures. . . ." She sighed. "The child is right, Sheel. She should get one good raid behind her so that women will start to think of familying with her for her own children. I'd like to see her show everyone her quality myself, before I die."

"You want me to organize her maiden raid for her?"

"Which of her mothers would do it better than you?"

Why am I hesitating? Sheel thought, frowning over her work. Sorrel has courage and intelligence, there's no sign yet of her femmish heritage. But after her first raid—the next step is preparing her for her mating. That's where it could come out.

"Heartmother, what's going to happen to that child if she turns out not to be fertile to a stud horse but only to a man, like her femmish bloodmother?"

"You, daughter of my heart, know better than I do

that a woman's worth doesn't lie only in the children of her body—though sometimes women do lose sight of that truth.''

"It would make a difference,'' Sheel said. "Sorrel has no blood relations to keep her line among us. If she has no children of her own body, after her death she'll just—disappear.''

"Would you forget her?''

"Never.''

"The self-songs of many lines have words in them about women who 'disappeared' that way when whole chains of descent ended. Those women are not completely lost.''

Sheel said, "I don't want Sorrel to be lost at all.''

Sheel asked Sorrel to come with her to choose horses for the raid they were planning. Delighted, Sorrel dug out her favorite gift, a light leather shirt covered with big flakes cut from the hooves of dead horses and sewn into a sort of armor of overlapping scales.

"I want to see how it feels,'' she said as they rode out toward the grazing grounds. "Maybe I'll take it with me when we go raiding. I like to hear the little pieces all click and rub together.''

"A fancy shirt like yours is only a gift thing, something to make bets with. Women don't wear them.''

Sorrel promptly wrestled the shirt off over her head and tied it behind the cantle of her saddle.

A little distance from the grazing horses most of the new fems had gathered, sitting like Riding Women in the shadows of their mounts. One of them walked a spotted mare back and forth before the others. Their voices carried clearly. They were agreeing, more and more confidently, that the horse was lame.

Alldera, sitting chin on fist among them, demanded, "Which leg?''

"Off fore,'' said a blond fem. What a pale people they were under their sunburn, not a black skin among them, Sheel thought.

"How can you tell?"

"By the way she walks."

Alldera directed that the horse be led away and then toward the group again, head on. "Which leg?"

"Near foreleg," Sorrel whispered to Sheel. "See how she drops her head?"

"I know," Sheel said dryly.

Alldera spoke to the fems with the faintest trace of weariness. "The leg she drops her head over is the leg all her weight is going on, to spare the sore one."

"Near foreleg," someone volunteered.

"Good. Now, leg or foot?"

Some of the fems had noticed the two onlookers and a few called to the child to join them. She had become immensely popular with them after a period of shyness on both sides.

"Go on, then, if you want to," Sheel said. She settled to watch and listen herself a while, one leg crooked across her saddle bow.

Sorrel hobbled her horse and sat down next to Daya, who seemed to be her favorite among the fems; not so terrible a choice as Sheel would once have thought. The little fem with the scars had done all right during the sharu swarming.

Alldera continued her instruction with only a glance at her child: "If she takes a short step, the foot is sore. Soreness in the shoulder would make her swing her leg out stiffly to keep from using those muscles. See? Maybe it isn't the kick she took that's bothering her at all. Lora, go ahead and find out what the trouble is."

"Can somebody hold her for me?" the blond fem said nervously.

Sorrel whispered, Daya whispered back, knotted cheek close by smooth one. Sheel could see that the slow method of instruction was not for Sorrel, who had grown up with these horses while in the childpack.

Alldera said, "You have to be able to handle your own horse, Lora. There may not be anybody with you when trouble comes up. If she were skittish—which she isn't, but suppose she were—how would you control her while you looked her over?''

Visibly unhappy, Lora untied a strip of soft leather from her belt and bent to hobble the horse's front feet.

"But you'll have to lift her forefoot to look at it,'' Sorrel pointed out politely to her. "Better hobble the back feet instead.'' She flung Sheel one bright, amused glance over her shoulder.

"She won't kick me?'' Lora inquired, looking anxiously at the mare's shining eye.

Alldera said tartly, "Not if you do as our expert there suggests.''

It had all been gone over before, and would be again. How could they bear it? Sheel supposed that by femmish standards they were quick learners, or they would never have survived their deadly crossing from the Holdfast. Yet all these lessons seemed so excruciatingly repetitious. Alldera worked away session after session, as if she were polishing hard stones.

Hard stone heads, Sheel thought, looking over at the big one, Kobba, a relatively new arrival, fierce and melancholy. All of the free fems were living at Stone Dancing these days except for the one said to be so huge that it would take two horses to carry her, and one or two who had stayed behind with her. Women of Royo Camp, returning from cutting tea in the hills for themselves, reported the tea camp deserted and its great central wagon shut up tight. Hearing this, Daya had said that the fat one, the free fems' former leader, must have withdrawn to the caves where she kept her books, to stay with them until they were found. No one understood what she meant by this but the fems, who seemed subdued by the idea. A few even wept.

The one-armed one, Fedeka the wanderer, still wandered. She stopped at Stone Dancing often, however, and always took time to talk privately with Sorrel before leaving again. Sorrel said she told even stranger stories than Daya did. Daya had assured the women of Holdfaster Tent that the dyer meant no ill, and had appointed herself a sort of special guardian to Sorrel for some vague time in the future when the girl would need her.

The newly arrived fems studied horses and the bow so hard with Alldera and Daya that women joked about how they must be meaning to make Riding Women of themselves. They had given up their ungainly wagons and now had their own fem tent pitched next to Hold-faster Tent.

Even Sheel, unwilling as she was, had to admit to herself that the longer they lived here in the camp the more their slavish ways fell away from them. Everyone noticed that they all quarreled and intrigued far less among themselves than they had when they had been only a handful. With women, their manner was no longer brashly alien, but guarded and self-contained. Except for Alldera, they chose their lovers only among their own ranks now; even Daya did.

"I don't sleep with Daya any more," Grays Omelly had told Sheel. "When she looks at me, I feel like a ghost. They see us and hear us, but they're all gone away."

These days Grays's circular spell designs were turning up everywhere, and Grays was found crying among the tents that everything was losing its place. Sheel had brought her back twice from outside the camp where she had been sitting, beating on a drum at the full moon "to make it stay where it belongs."

Here was Alldera surrounded by her own kind, obviously in her place. Yet to Sheel she did not look happy, only intent and serious.

Lora edged closer to the spotted mare again, her face tight with fear and determination.

"Help, if you're going to, Sorrel," Alldera commanded suddenly. "I don't want this horse to think it can frighten us."

Covertly Sheel studied Alldera's face. No humor there; hardness and hostility showed in the set of the wide mouth. No wonder; Sorrel knew in her blood and bones from her earliest life so much that these clumsy,

thick-headed outlanders were laboring to grasp. The
youngster would make a better teacher than her bloodmother, if she were patient enough to command the
fems' attention for long.

Sorrel went to the mare's head and took hold of the
reins, patting its nose and scolding it in a cheerful voice.
Her cheeks were flushed; she knew when she was the
center of attention and enjoyed it. She looked down at
Lora, who had bent to lift the horse's hoof in her hands.

"You tap the foot lightly all around with a stone,"
Sorrel explained, "to find the sore place."

She looked over the ground for a stone. The horse,
taking advantage of Lora, leaned more and more of its
weight on her. Lora did not realize that the horse was
using her as support, but Sorrel saw, called it a sharu's
foal, and gave it a punch in the shoulder with advice to
mend its manners.

Sheel and the watching fems grinned, and even
Alldera smiled. Sorrel was clearly playing to her bloodmother. She turned toward Alldera her most appealing
glances to make sure Alldera would miss nothing that
she did.

Sheel thought of other bloodmothers she had seen
with their daughters. There was always a period of
assessment; then each began to think about taking the
first tentative steps toward the other. The coming
together always took time. Without the pull of iden-
tically patterned minds and bodies to help, it might take
unusually long for Alldera and Sorrel to meet. But Sheel
recognized the beginning—on one side that cautious attention to the child, a touch perhaps of wary pride, and,
on the other, curiosity and eagerness to please. A
strange thing, the start of such closeness between a femmish bloodmother and a woman-child.

Yet Sheel had to admit to herself that Alldera was no
longer the anxious, touchy, self-absorbed young fem
who, thanks to Sheel's own error, had come to Stone
Dancing years ago and lived as a woman. Now she had
no time for the women, only time for her own. Sheel
hardly saw her in Holdfaster Tent. Alldera was like a

hard, scarred stud nursing a wild band along through a dry, dry season toward water. Her face bore what the women called "chief lines," marks of unremitting concern.

Startled, Sheel thought, Why, she came to us still in her youth, and her youth has been long gone.

Moved in some way that she did not wish to be moved, Sheel pulled her mount's head up from its browsing and rode slowly toward the tent's horses. Sorrel would soon tire of the instructor's role and catch up with her. As she rode, her practiced eye noting the condition of each mare and of the grass they grazed, Sheel became more and more convinced that Grays was right: if things were not exactly out of place, they were at least in a new alignment, moved by some deep, slow, powerful shift of events, long in the making and still only dimly perceptible.

Sheel could remember now how it had been once: thinking about correcting her original mistake and killing Alldera; rejecting that course because she would not stoop to be outlawed on account of a dirty little fem. The thoughts came back and even some of the fierce feeling, but none of it seemed to apply in the least to Alldera Holdfaster sitting over there teaching her followers about horses.

Which was strange, because plainly the thing Sheel had always feared—that the free fems would truly determine to return to the Holdfast, with unforeseeable consequences for all women—was clearly happening. As a nightmare, the idea had maddened her. Now, with the phantoms of angry imagination vanished in the face of reality, it became simply a fact of the future to be dealt with in its time.

She felt saddened by the loss of her hatred. There would be no brilliant, satisfyingly violent clash between herself and Alldera. The fems, and Alldera among them, belonged to whatever current had drawn them to Stone Dancing Camp, where now they toughened themselves to be drawn elsewhere on that current.

Sheel looked back again. The wide plain, the deep sky glowing blue overhead, the curves of the leather tents, even the drifting horses, were like a picture painted on a tent wall, against which were thrown the free fems' coarse shadows.

15

Alldera would not have believed that a woman's death could affect her so strongly. Everyone was stunned: who could have imagined Barvaran, red-faced and crude and good-hearted, caught up somehow in Nenisi's quarrel with the Perikens and rushing into a duel on the dancing ground?

Returning from a ride to check the location of the next campsite, Alldera found the Holdfaster women assembled by Barvaran's bedding. Barvaran lay gasping, her mouth frothing blood. There was a wound in her chest that opened with every breath she drew. The woman who had struck her had fled to seek refuge with relatives in another camp.

Barvaran was dead by morning. They took her body, lashed limply over the back of a horse, to abandon it in the grass far from camp. They laid the body down, washed clean and clothed, and they left it for the sharu. That was all. Women did not speak over corpses. Their farewells had been taken during the night, while Barvaran's spirit still lived and struggled.

Shayeen said, "Later we will think of who should die for this, which well-loved woman of the guilty line."

Sorrel argued furiously with Jesselee all the way back to the camp and wept and insisted she was going to find the killer and cut her throat. She lashed her horse into erratic bursts of speed and bloodied its mouth with her wrenching on the reins until Sheel rode up, yanked her from the saddle, and set her on her feet on the ground.

"The horse has done no harm," Sheel said. "If you can't ride like a woman, walk like a fem."

The youngster hugged her mare around the neck, remounted, and on a slack rein let herself be carried homeward, crying bitterly.

Alldera trailed behind them, wondering what would be good to say to comfort Sorrel; thinking that it was better the fems had stayed behind rather than coming along to criticize the women's death customs; thinking most of all of Barvaran's red face looming above her in a gully in the desert years ago before Sorrel was born, the way Barvaran's breast had yielded under her hand, that first touch of a Riding Woman, that first amazement. . . .

Who would have thought that Barvaran and I would live together as members of a family? My family, the family of my child that I brought to them, gave to them.

Shared, she thought suddenly; I shared her with my sharemothers. One part of Sorrel isn't given and can't be—my share.

I really did it. I was no mother, I didn't know how to become one—I was just a Holdfast dam. But I got her away from the men and I found her a whole family of mothers, and saw her into her free life as a young woman. Not that I set out to do it, and it's not all I've done on this side of the mountains, but it's done.

She looked at the dejected figure of Sorrel up ahead. Will she ever realize, and thank me for it? Not that a family is forever, your mothers leave you—Barvaran, maybe Jesselee, myself, soon. Still, it's something.

What's she going to be like, I wonder? I'll come back and find out, if I can.

Nenisi rode up alongside Alldera. Strapped to the bridge of her nose she wore a wooden mask with a slit across the center, used for protecting the sight from flying stone slivers when chipping flint. Now it protected her swollen eyes from the sun and the wind.

Along the hard ground flickers of light seemed to dance: leaves from a brush bank, curled and dry, were

being driven in skipping circles by cool eddies of air.
The sky was half skinned over with high white clouds,
against which there floated smaller cloud puffs of
exquisitely modulated grays and silvers. To the south
the sky was clear, a blue of burning intensity in which
these same subtly shaped and tinted clouds hung with a
melting softness, sweet to Alldera's eye.

Nenisi said abruptly, "You will leave us."

"No!" That was a lie. "I don't want to." The truth.

Nenisi went on as if Alldera had not spoken: "For
generations women have watched so that no free fems
would go back to the Holdfast and turn the men's attention toward the plains. That was right to do as long
as we were few and the men were many, and as long as
the free fems were strangers to whom we owed nothing.

"Now that relationship has changed. The free fems
are kindred of the camps and free to go where they
like—and I'll say so, as a Conor, when the question
arises whether we should let you all return across the
borderlands. But women like Sheel may charge that I
can no longer speak as a Conor in this matter because of
my feelings.

"Let me warn you, my friend. What others say on the
question will matter. Some may even say to kill, and
take no chances on these fems, or on you."

Alldera fixed her eyes on the steadying sight of her
own hands clasped one over the other on the peak of her
saddle, as she groped for a response.

Nenisi turned toward her, her smooth black face
masked, red-lipped where the wind had bitten her
mouth. "You've lain in my bed, you've bathed my eyes
as tenderly as a woman; yet you've told me nothing
about your feelings. It's as if we were back when you
first lived in Stone Dancing Camp and you were not yet
yourself and didn't dare speak. Well, I know you better
now; you lie in the dark in the distress of your thoughts
and breathe harshly, like a woman toiling over the plain
on foot. Your hands wind together sometimes like
struggling enemies. But never a word, no speech to knit
us together.

"Making love is much the same for all, but each person speaks only her own words. I have few of your words from days past to keep with me."

Words, Alldera thought blankly. I was a messenger, and a messenger should know the importance of words without being told. I haven't paid enough attention.

She said, "I thought you had so much trouble already—your eyes, and this cursed Periken feud —look, Nenisi, nothing is certain yet." She stopped. Nothing was more certain, nothing more strange—she had been sent from the Holdfast to find allies, and not finding them she had somehow helped to make them; now she must return with them, years late. She recoiled. "Nenisi, you're a Conor! Find a way to make it right for me to stay here!"

Nenisi shook her head. "It's right to go with your close kindred. All Conors may not agree with me, but there are other women who will—perhaps enough of them to insure safe travel back for you. These last years our borderland patrols have found no signs of men venturing near the plains. No fems have come to us from your country since you came. Many women now think that the Holdfast is a dead place and men no danger.

"And as you know, there are women of Stone Dancing Camp who would cheer to see you and your people leave our tents, no matter what the long-range risk. Women of my Motherline want you gone for my sake—they see that your otherness, your singleness, has captured me, and they worry that I have become a stranger to my own. It frightens them that we are so close for so long.

"Don't worry about Sorrel. We'll look after her. She has a future with us: tent mates, raid mates, lovers, perhaps even a Motherline to found—everything that matters."

Everything that matters! Alldera drew her headcloth closer around her shoulders, too dismal to speak.

Nenisi glanced back the way they had come.

"Tonight we'll sit in the tent and tell stories about Barvaran," she said. "Tonight you are with family.

Tomorrow and the days after, you'll be busy with your
cousins Daya and the others, talking about returning to
the Holdfast. That will take a lot of planning. Later, on
the other side of the mountains, maybe you'll tell some
stories of us and this place. We'll tell about you and
how the fems lived among us and left us their child.
Most of that will be mine to tell; we Conors remember
well, that's why we're always right.

"You and I, Alldera, had better talk now, while we
have the chance."

Alldera stared ahead where Sorrel rode, bowed and
weeping, among Shayeen, Jesselee and Sheel. Suddenly
she felt the downward drag of her own shoulders, the
sting in her own eyes. She turned toward Nenisi and
spoke.

Riding slowly toward Stone Dancing Camp, leaning
in her saddle toward the dark figure beside her, she
stumbled and struggled to say what she needed to say:
that she, like her child up there, both grieved and was
comforted; that Sorrel was not the only one whose
world had been gladdened with kindred, nor the only
one to find and lose the mother of her heart.